LANA WALKED
ON THE SHORE

A NOVEL

First Published in Great Britain 2021 by Mirador Publishing

First edition: 2021

Any reference to real names and places are purely fictional and are constructs of the author. Any offence the references produce is unintentional and in no way reflects the reality of any locations or people involved.

A copy of this work is available through the British Library.

ISBN: 978-1-914965-25-8

Mirador Publishing
10 Greenbrook Terrace
Taunton
Somerset
TA1 1UT
UK

LANA WALKED
ON THE SHORE

A NOVEL

WILLIAM ECHOLS

Chapter 1

LITTLE LEGS CUTTING THROUGH GRASS. Little wings falling like leaves, spattering red against waves of green.

A monster in her wake. A shadow without sun. All the darkness from down below had found its way above. It forced flying things to run and running things to fly. Nothing of light, life or color could escape the dark tide.

And then she recognized the terror was all in her mind. Flight was the fuel that kept the nightmare alive. There was no choice but to stop and shake the bad dream with a blood-curdling scream.

So little legs came to a trembling halt. The shadow eclipsed her. The shadow eclipsed everything. One final spark of the heart and the dark wave crashed. A surge of adrenaline carried her up to the surface of self. Eyes opened wide to muted morning light.

Little did she know the nightmare was just beginning.

— — —

She sat on the edge of her bed, feet dangling, head held in a halo of grief. Her fingers barely touched the threadbare arm of her teddy bear. A small wisp of hair spiraling and golden tickled her to irritation.

Through a closed door, muffled shouts seeped into her room. They were fighting again. Always fighting.

The sky filled the frame of the window. Late winter clouds the color of coal-soaked cotton balls sucked up the sunlight. Branches slithered and forked upwards, lightning-strike veins on an outstretched patagium.

Everything was still. She waited, little feet swollen with a cold tingling.

Shouting erupted again. Wounding words resounded in Siberian wood. She flung herself back onto the bed. Puffy-eyed and pouty-lipped, tears formed warm and wet tidal pools in her pillow. She lay motionless, only to jolt, flailing fish out of water, pausing to gasp for life to fill her gills, thrashing around again when none came.

It was a bellyflop of frustration, not having the words to paint a picture of why, just the pressure building tea kettle crying under the flame. Then the emptiness …

Red, cried-out eyes, a damp pillow and the concrete sky just hanging there dull and lifeless beyond the pane. The grey natural light seemed to hum in her synesthete ears. Silence. A door slams. Silence.

— — —

Father's heavy feet went to and fro. A door shut, a stool scraped, a big body took a seat. She crept out of her room, catching his head held in hands through the glass of the kitchen door.

She put on her puffy, sky-blue jacket, matching gloves and the crocheted pompom-topped beanie her grandmother had made when she was even younger than she is today. She shuffled to the stool by the front door and sat down to put on her faded pink boots. Through the shut door to her left, Mom didn't let out a peep. Standing up with the squeaky-free joints of youth, she tip-toed two paces, gently slid the deadbolt out of the lock, and opened the front door.

Every movement was a half-hearted attempt at silence, but just loud enough to hear if one cared enough to listen. Her parents only wanted to listen to the sound of their own self-igniting hot air. That was their choice.

— — —

Heading down the stairwell, the stinky man who crouched like a bullfrog on the third-floor landing was smoking 1000-year-old cigarettes and spitting through the spaces where full teeth had once been. Those that remained were even darker than the gaps. He stared at her with his cold, amphibian eyes. She looked at him with a feeling of hate that was too young to come up with reasons.

"Ribbit," she croaked at him.

He muttered back at her, pond-scum dripping down his chin.

"Ribbit ribbit ribbit!"

The bull in the frog bellowed and seemed ready to leap off its ashen lily pad as she let out a scream and tumbled on top of feet down the stairs. She had never dreamed a frog could gobble up a rabbit.

Outside it felt like the world had wanted to cry but decided to take a nap instead. The sky looked like syrup-less snow cone peppered with the devil's cigar.

The mud and slush had nearly routed what was left of white snow. The first shades of green had yet to appear as brushstrokes on bark. She walked across the narrow, pock-marked streets, which angry little cars flung themselves down with no regard for the children darting or drunks crawling across. The static silence of the dense air buzzed in her ears.

She slid between parked cars to get to the small playground with its red and yellow contraptions rusting under the 10th application of cheap paint. The benches in each corner were flanked by black trash cans vomiting up beer bottles. The wind blew low and deep, a tantric chant from a far-away Himalayan kingdom. The puddles fell over themselves in ripples. She eyed the swings, but they too were sprinkled by the cold, March precipitation.

She dragged her feet against the wet sand, unearthing cigarette butt cenotaphs lit up and extinguished in memory of forgetting.

The clock hands weighed heavily on her. On a wet, chilly and friendless afternoon, time moved so slowly for a little girl trying to steer clear of home.

Without a dry place to sit or a warm place to go, she felt she could run circles around a puddle for half an eternity only to realize less than a quarter of an hour had passed. Nothing was more oppressive than not wanting to go home. Everyone wants to go home.

Plodding forward, she headed toward the bench on the other side. The sky persisted in its stone-faced, soporific silence. Beyond the shin-high, chipped-green enclosure, a small cluster of trees stood bare, forming a line above the large gas pipes slithering around her district. A rustling could be heard in the tangle of stems growing between the elongated toes of the ash trees. Hopping over the metal barrier, the little girl walked over ground that squished like old oranges until she reached the twisting stems of the large shrub, which looked like a giant spider sleeping on its side.

Through the crisscrossing branches, she saw something slightly smaller than an egg but fluffy like a cotton ball shivering on a damp little island formed by snow-melt rivulets. She edged forward ever so slightly, eyes locked on this strange creature stranded in the spaces formed by the murky circulatory system of late winter.

It peered up at her with two sparkling onyx eyes, cutting through the chalcedonic blanket above.

The little girl couldn't believe it. It had seemingly hopped out of last night's dream, a dream itself forged in the crucible of memory. Years ago, in a faraway land down by the sea, she had stumbled upon a nest of baby birds. A nightmare man had taken it by the wings and ripped out its way back to Heaven. That darkest of days had long been locked away in the basement of her heart. Now that door had been opened. Forgetting in the shape of a strange little creature was staring her right in the face.

"How can it be you? How did you get here?"

Apart from the shine in those big, black eyes, there were no answers.

Mystified, the little girl crouched down onto her haunches and extended her hand. The little ball of fluff shrank back.

"Don't be afraid. Don't you remember me? My name is Lana. We met down by the sea."

But then Lana remembered what the nightmare man had done, and knew it had every reason to be afraid. Maybe she did too.

"It's okay, he's gone now. No one will hurt you."

Two pairs of shining eyes locked on a lightless day. Lana slipped off her gloves and slipped them into her pocket. Her hands felt cold. The refuge they offered was warmth.

Standing shakily on little black dinosaur legs, it cravenly took a tiny step toward her and stopped.

The wind blew cold through the spindly tree fingers. A squadron of samaras spiraled down from above. Looking up, it seemed as if they had cut a thousand slits in the charcoal-stroked clouds, turning them into colanders pouring out blue streams of sky. Rows of crows sentineled the streets below. Lana looked back down at the wobbly cotton ball on legs. It began to shiver.

"Oh, you're so cold," she said with a sniffle. It apparently agreed, planting rubbery legs on Lana's warm palm.

A caw resounded in the distance; barren crow-topped trees exploded into monochrome piñata flight.

The little white something nuzzled into the soft, delicate pads on her palm, causing her to let out a girlish giggle.

"That tickles," she squealed.

It stopped and peered up at her with glimmering eyes. With a melting heart, Lana delicately caressed it with the faintest of fingertip strokes. Deep down, she felt the slightest tinge of apprehension. She wanted to hug it so tightly, but it was just too small for anything but the softest touch.

The wind blew and the small ball of down squeezed its tiny eyes shut. And then the memory of the nightmare man returned with a shudder. What if he came crawling out from the weeds as he had done once before? Unease set it. It was time to leave.

Lana carefully put her new-old friend into the breast pocket of her puffy jacket. It sailed down her hand like it was on the evacuation slide of a plane.

Securely nestled into the inlay, it looked up at her with those big black eyes. Lana let out a tiny sigh. Secretly, she wished they could switch places.

Lana headed back toward her building. But rather than returning home, she rounded the far side of her low-rise. Tracing an invisible line as a faint shadow moved alongside her in the segmented spaces between balconies, she hummed a song whose words she did not know. All sorts of filth floated in the snow-melt pits spilling over with dark water not far from her concrete shore.

Turning the corner of the apartment block to block out the mud-pit catchment basin that emptied out into a child's sinking heart most quickly of all, she was surprised to see that the door at the bottom of the small staircase leading to the maintenance room had been replaced with a smaller red hatchway barely a hair higher than her.

As a gust of wind rattled the tree branches, she timidly descended the steps, a tender hand feeling its way down the cold, cement wall.

Reaching the door, she noticed it was faded and chipped, with small strips of cinnamon-colored wood laid out like rows of corn amid the currant-red soil.

An old, lacquered knocker hung motionless in the middle. She reached out to touch it. Fingers gripping the ring, she slowly lifted it up, then dropped it with a heavy thud against the wood.

The door creaked open. The shadow of an inverted triangle fell into a deeper pit of darkness. Something howled from within. She took a step back.

The wind blew — the branches clacked together like skeletal knees in a clumsy otherworld waltz. Then it came, faintly at first, then louder and louder. The laughter of a madman. Lana turned around. The shadow from her nightmare was walking over the black water. Her eyes grew wide enough to suck in whatever light the clouds hadn't already swallowed.

Lana was frozen in place. Darkness was slowly creeping up behind her — darkness was ahead. Another crackup as the shadow loomed.

Her jacket pocket started to rustle. The little ball of white hopped out and scaled the black pyramid past its summit and into Aphosis' din.

Wingless flight snapped Lana out of her spell.

Her heart exploded fireworks in an electric storm. A million ants spit fire in her blood.

The shadow eclipsed her. Madness filled her ears. She followed a speck of light into the pitch black. A roar madder than a March hare tore through the sky.

The door blew shut behind her. A solitary glove was left outside, its match still tucked in a pocket, going deeper, deeper into the unknown.

Chapter 2

THE COLD, DIRT WALLS WERE round and smooth like the prison escape tunnel of a patient engineer who'd had a lifetime to dig. Something about the burrow reminded her of a story her grandmother used to tell her about a man in the belly of a really big fish.

It was from the Bible. Her grandmother was the only person she knew who read it. And whenever they were together, she would tell her incredible tales about what appeared to be a wild world and an angry, angry God.

Her other grandmother — her mother's mother — would laugh at the little girl's hurried attempts at ingenuous exegesis.

"It's a book full of fairy tales, that's it! And if one is going to read legends, there are much better ones than that!"

Despite Granny's disdain, Lana loved the stories all the same. Animals on boats, a man in the belly of fish, two mamma bears mauling 42 boys — the tales were tall but stirring.

And now, stealing away from shadows in the darkness, searching out a little bird with no wings, Lana felt like she had been plunged into one such fairytale.

Tracing tracks on the wall in the shape of fingerprints, she felt something stir in the unseeable distance. It moved invisibly — a large bubble floating on the surface of the darkness — a contact lens bringing focus to a black hole pupil sucking in fear. The undulating mass gave depth to the void and filled her little rabbit heart with terror. Her baryonic being feared being swallowed by the darkness that did not move forward, but sucked forward into it.

A thin canvas of skin stretched over her eyes, creating a doubly exposed Rothko. She had stepped into his chapel in the dead of night. His sermon was a lunatic's laughter under a blood moon.

Her heart continued to pound, ultrasound coloring the world in sonic palpitations. Each beat was seemingly sucked from her chest, shifting red across the event horizon.

And then her thin membrane flashed vermillion as the black mass found voice in Scriabin's Sonata 9, exploding into a million dots floating on blood and light.

The sixth seal cracked. The black mass surged forward. Lana kicked out the freeze and ran. Her mind stumbled on circles run under a southern sun from cousins with legs too long. It was they who first taught her the giddy thrill of inevitable capture. But this was no game. This was the end chasing down the beginning.

The surge swallowed the darkness making it darker still. It was gaining on her. Ichor dripped down the walls. Lana gulped down beets in panicked breaths. The smell of rain imbrued the blackwater rush.

Nothing she could do could grow the gap between life and death. Croaks filled her throat when she tried to cry. Closer. Closer.

She kicked out her own footing in death drive frustration, half praying for the darkness to swallow her so she could once again wake up on the other side of what felt like a terrible, terrible dream.

Further down the tunnel, a pinprick glimmer pierced the darkness. Lana chased down the beacon bright. The far-away sparkle sailed at the speed of light, outpacing the ink jet onslaught.

Flying forward, a stain glass star in the bottom of a well pulsed a warp speed pendulum in a disembodied hand.

The lantern glow lit up the walls in the amber shades of Tsarskoye Selo.

With the rush of blackness set to crash, the light reached her just in time. The darkness washed over the gilded cupola. The little girl quaked under shimmering shelter as the Earth stood still. The deluge raged a mile then drained down a hell-bound abîme in subterraneous steam.

In the ensuing silence, Lana shivered despite the warm glow of light. She finally rose on dizzy doe legs, with the last drips of near-disaster echoing long after ebb.

Her heart beat impossibly. Not waiting for a resting rate of still, the disembodied hand spun around like a samara and floated forward. The little girl had no choice but to chase down the dying of the light.

After countless meters of skirting the edges of a free-floating spotlight, the hand abruptly stopped before a barrel-bottomed shaped door. It lowered the lantern, spilling the honey-colored halo all over the ground.

Floating back up, it rapped its knuckles against the wood and waited.

"Who is it?" a sonorous voice bellowed from within.

The hand let loose with another volley of knocks.

"All right, all right, hold your horses, I'm coming!"

She heard a shuffling inside.

Then came the bolt slide and drop with a thud. The door swung inwards. A warm light from within washed the honey off the floor.

Standing before her, a short, portly old man in horn-rimmed spectacles and a green plaid vest peered at the row of knuckles floating before his eyes. Unafraid those knuckles would rap upon his bulbous nose, he rested his eyes on Lana.

"Well, well, well," he said. "It looks like he got to you just in time. Good. Very good. Come in, quick! What ebbs will flow. Those waters are bound to come back around!"

The hand dipped down and rose with the light, placing it on an old Singer sewing machine next to the door.

Lana hurried after it as the big door slammed shut behind her into a hermetic-seal.

The room, framed underneath a vaulted ceiling, glowed every shade of orange.

Scanning her eyes from candles to shadows to hearth, the floor flowed a marmalade sea. The space smelled of orange, cloves and dead leaves.

A giant, round oak table occupying the center of the room was backlit by the fireplace, stretching shadows onto the dark, corner shores being gently lapped by the citrus waters.

It was already set with placemats, tea cups and cutlery.

A rocking chair by the hearth remained unrocked. Books and bric-a-brac filled the shelf-lined walls. Ushak carpets with cloud band borders lined the walls.

It all felt like an autumnal hug from Mom.

"Mister! It's incredible! That hand, it saved me!"

"I do believe it did!"

"But it's just a hand! Where did the rest of him go?"

"That's a good question indeed, and one I wish I had an answer to! He found me, and I him, just as he is! But one day, I am going to thank the man who lent me that helping hand!"

Coming down from the incredible chase, Lana momentarily gathered herself. And then the strangeness of it all caught up to her.

"Mister. Where are we?"

"I am the watcher of the underworld light. And this is my home. Even in the darkest depths, I am a lodestar to all, even lost little girls like you. And this is perhaps the one place in all places where dark water cannot so easily flow.

"Now please, take off your shoes and coat. We don't need to be dragging muck across my groove."

Lana obliged, hanging her coat on a hook that looked like an upturned talon before crouching down and pulling on rabbit ears until they unraveled. She then slid on a fluffy pair of tapochki that were just her size. It was almost as if he had been expecting her all along.

"There, isn't that better? You must be hungry. Please have a seat," the old man said, motioning her over to the table.

Lana walked across the warm, hardwood floor and hopped up into the Afghan-draped chair, sinking into a cinnamon-colored cushion.

The old man disappeared into the kitchen, the hand sailing close behind. Minutes later, the hand floated back, effortlessly balancing a tray stacked with cookies, varenyky and jam, which it set down in the center of the table without rattling a piece of silver.

The hand moved toward the teapot and stopped. Lana nodded her head, at which point it poured a cup of black tea three-fourths to the top before pulling back without spilling a drop.

Lana dipped a teaspoon into the raspberry jam and pulled out a whole patch, which she promptly dropped into her steaming cup. The seeds spun around her spoon and anticipated settling between her teeth.

Ambling back with a grandfather's labored but patient step, the old man sat down across from her and let out a hearty sigh.

After the hand served him a cup of tea and put a few cookies onto Lana's plate, his steady eyes settled on her from behind his glasses.

"My oh my, that was a close call. In all of my years I've never seen such a flood. I do wonder: Where did all of that dark water come from?"

"It came from above."

"Well of course it did," the old man laughed. "But all of above is above me. So, which above do you mean?"

With crumbs now clinging to her fingers like damp clumps of sand and raspberry seeds building nests in her teeth, Lana put a half-eaten cookie down on the side of her saucer. She didn't have the slightest clue what he meant but tried to answer all the same.

"I think it followed me."

"From where?"

"Through the red door."

"Which red door would that be?"

"There is more than one red door?"

"Why of course! I myself have been through a million red doors. And a million more who have come here have entered through a million doors more. Was your red door on Pluke, Mars, perhaps Teegarden b?"

"Moscow!"

"Oh, Moscow. That's in Russia, isn't it? There are many monsters there indeed."

Despite all of the warmth, Lana's blood suddenly ran cold. She lowered her cup with a clink against the saucer and looked up at his face. The tangerine aureole pouring shadows down the ravine-like furrows that ran across his brow and 'round his crow-stepped eyes.

His cheeks almost glowed a blood-orange red, but his eyes, a color consumed by the backlight, radiated kind and calm all the same. It seemed like a place where no darkness could reside.

"I saw a monster," she said sheepishly. "The nightmare man, he found us. He was a big shadow walking on muddy water. My little bird ran. And I did too. And now I cannot find him."

The old man bristled.

"That sounds serious indeed."

"Mister, what should I do? The nightmare man already took his wings. I don't know what will happen if he finds him again."

"Well, to find a wingless bird, you have to go to a place where others soar between sea and sky."

"Soar?"

"Yes, to fly very high."

"So if a bird doesn't have wings, it goes where other birds fly very high? I, I don't understand. Why would they do that?"

"Because when a little bird has lost its wings, it goes to the one place where it has no other choice but to fly. Just as when there is nothing but darkness, you head to the slightest hint of light."

— — —

One could never tell how much time had passed with the rise and fall of the sun obscured by all that earth, so bedtime came when one was ready to sleep, and morning came when one was ready to wake.

Having had her fill of tea, cookies, cake and steaming Siberian dumplings, Lana's stomach was puffed up like the pipe's bag sans skirl.

The old man insisted she rest before setting off on her perilous voyage.

He didn't have to ask twice. The soporific spell cast through the floating hand's culinary alchemy had worked its magic. Seeing she was on the verge of making a pillow of now cold pelmeni, the old man led her back to a sleeping chamber. So much care had been taken to ensure the quarters' comfort, even the walls were stuffed with goose feathers, the floor fashioned from Chinchilla fur.

The bed was so big and tall the hand had to scoot a stool up to the side so she could get in. Rows of eyes from a stuffed jungle lined the walls, casting slanted-savannah-at-sunset silhouettes her way.

Lana reached up to the twin pillow peaks and upended the grassland, sending the zebras and lions scattering alike. Pushing her feet underneath continents and seas, she pulled the lithosphere up to her chest and felt the mantle glowing beneath.

Back down to scale the little girl molded perfectly into the Kingdom of Blankets like a larva in a cocoon.

Standing in the doorway, the old man told her goodnight.

"Good night," Lana replied, her breath already filling the duvet up like a balloon.

He lingered in place, a pensive look on his face.

"There's one thing I should tell you."

"Yes?"

This room is the key to a million rooms inside of you. It can take you to every you that has and ever will be."

Eyes already a third quarter to waning crescent, she lightly smacked her lips before replying, "What do you mean?"

"If only there were an easier way to put it. Let's just say that wherever your dreams take you, try not to be afraid. Why, you might even find a path to your little bird."

"My little bird ..." she murmured, consciousness receding like the tide as the moon skates down the meridian after culmination.

"Your little bird," he whispered as he soundlessly shut the door behind him.

— — —

Sleep came to her in waves, ego a sandcastle on the shore, swell pushing forward and stretching until slowly lapping away at her ramparts; flowing, dissolving back into self.

At first there was the void, all the colors of the dark blended into blackness. Then the surge crashed into prism palisades perched on the edge of eternity.

Iridescent arc crowned the circle — colors dripped down and subdivided into shades. Birdseye view revealed a perfect portrait of soul reflecting spirit; from those lofty heights nothing seemed too small, alone or afraid.

Sailing down a trail of violet, she awoke in the Kingdom of Blankets. A great still cradled the darkness. A slanted picket fence painted with Titian's brush pushed its way under the door. On the other side, a fire crackled in the night.

She turned her head toward the wall — peanut gallery of the savannah — perched on the threshold between the waking world and dreams.

Something moved through her, a montage of everyday life, sliced and diced into pieces each as sharp as a knife. And in that reel to reel click-a-clack clatter of the mind's projector, in a flash came her mother, in a flash came her father. The splice cut the words from meaning — only the feeling remained.

The peanut gallery remained silent when the tear formed in her eye's corner and fell; another, then another.

The entire room suddenly twirled down that tidal pool swirl on her pillow. She and everything fell and fell and fell, until the stain-glass star hit the bottom of the well. Click-a-clack-shatter-shatter-shatter! Where all the pieces went was of no consequence. This was a realm where what mattered was not a matter of matter.

Somewhere beyond, Hell found voice in a worn-down lover's turn to rage. Words slung serrated blades down vocal cords until all those sharp syllables coalesced into a wrecking ball of post-semantic havoc.

Silence was splintered and water taken in as that black mass blasted mast crumbling beneath a headwind. Adrenaline narrowed pupils into tunnels where no light shone at the end. Heart beat a war drum's tempo across a pirate's sea soaked in blood.

Shriek pierced a roar until stampede echoed thunder through the floor. Her door swung open, and a hawk swooped right into bed. A bear bounded after. The rabbit ran circles around her own throbbing heart. A hawk which could fly should never take shelter in a rabbit's hole.

"He's crazy," she cried, "he's crazy!"

A hawk could see everything but be so blind; a bear could scare away demons and then dine on its own young.

Roar echoed between brick-feet stomping. Hawk whimpered through its beak; eyes which could pierce horizons clouded in tears. Rabbit heart turned snare drum keeping time for a machine gun dead zone run.

Twilight slowly dyed the daylight to darkness.

Night light formed a seashell on a bedroom wall. Ear pressed to hear the low-voltage lapping. A whisper rippled on a distant wave: This isn't the first time their wicked waltz had threatened to rip her ship asunder.

Soviet parquet turned to driftwood, floating on a black, black sea.

Silence settled like dust. The air was electric. Dank breath blew hot waves under blankets. Talons dug into the mattress. Claws etched a low-relief rage into the floor. Talons fish-hooked the bedsprings in the eye of the storm. Rabbit's heart beat so fast blood-black strobe-lights flashed in eyes shut tight. Tension turned the coal-black loathing of a man's heart into a blood diamond.

Through the reverberations of rabbit heart, the endless stream of rapid rhythm erased the spaces between beats until she silently fell away from the red horizon traced on eyelids.

Lana fell farther and farther from her own windows onto the world, until the two frames of her outward became tiny red ovals floating atop the surface of her inward. Deeper and deeper she went, a disembodied spirit sinking and not soaring. The darkness expanded; the red dots receded until gone.

Rabbit could run, hawk could soar, bear could roar. Even if the war reignited above, you couldn't tear through enough fur muscle, tendon and bone to find your way to her.

No, if bear swallowed her up she wouldn't feel a thing.

He could keep chomping away but he'd just be chasing each layer of the nesting doll through the fractally forever and infinitely small.

Hawk could always find safety in heights. But rabbits, rabbits had their depths. Chase her down and you'll never get to the bottom of it.

And so the bear pushed on, looking to turn one patch of that white sheet of starvation red. The two twin ovals continued to float up, up, up into the black.

She floated through darkness until she found herself staring face down through a glass-bottom cloud with a perfect panoramic of Siberian weald.

High up above the endless white expanse, skopki protruding scales popped up across the land like the back of an ancient albino alligator.

On top of that Taiga beast cursed by the Ob, black coniferous stakes sprouted green filament fingers to snatch and stack floating crystal castles.

Down, down, down below, a big black dot chased a little one, leaving snaking trails of even smaller spots in their wake. As the glass bottom cloud floated over predator and prey, a hawk cut concentric circles in the sky.

From those impossible heights, life and death folded the third dimension into shifting lines and motes on a page. Oh, what a perfect view — one without depth! Rabbit rolled over onto her back and stared up into the infinite expanse where two tiny red ovals floated 10,000 light years away.

Stuck in a liminal space, she was dislodged by a thunder rumble rolling her down a cumulus tear duct. Breaking the membrane, the little spirit froze into a rabbit-shaped snowflake, refracting rainbow arcs as she spiraled through a sunbeam.

From a hawk's eye view to frozen rabbit dew, those lines on the page became language. Falling faster, a gust of wind was a breath of life; imago flipped the pages 'til animation turned black-ink Sumerian nail scratches into bear claw snow-slashed death dashes.

The bottom of a glass-boat cloud turned into a lens. Two tiny eyes from a rabbit in the sky magnified its terrestrially-bound snowdrift scaling dart — swerve and shift, swerve and shift — as one of nature's true murderers missed.

The macro-zoom fell at a parachutist's pace until the rabbit eyes in the sky lined up with the grounded eyes in flight. Spray of snow powder kicked up a crystal castle spiral galaxy evading the gravity of a black hole.

She couldn't even see death pounding paws into powder, couldn't feel his hot breath blowing steam through the still. It was just this force like an earthquake seeking to overtake, pop a horizontal line crack vertical and swallow you up by the scruff, world closing behind those fault lines realigned.

BEAT BEAT BEAT BEAT BEAT BEAT BEAT BEAT BEAT BEAT BEAT BEAT BEAT BEAT BEAT BEAT BEAT BEAT BEAT BEAT BEAT BEAT BEAT BEAT BEAT BEAT BEAT BEAT BEAT BEAT BEAT BEAT BEAT BEAT BEAT BEAT BEAT BEAT BEAT BEAT BEAT BEAT BEAT BEAT BEAT BEAT BEAT BEAT BEAT BEAT BEAT BEAT BEAT BEAT BEAT BEAT BEAT BEAT BEAT BEAT

BEAT BEAT BEAT BEAT BEAT BEAT BEAT BEAT BEAT BEAT BEAT BEAT BEAT BEAT BEAT BEAT BEAT BEAT BEAT BEAT BEAT BEAT BEAT BEAT BEAT BEAT BEAT BEAT BEAT BEAT BEAT BEAT BEAT BEAT BEAT BEAT BEAT BEAT BEAT BEAT BEAT BEAT BEAT BEAT BEAT BEAT BEAT BEAT BEAT BEAT BEAT BEAT BEAT BEAT BEAT BEAT BEAT BEAT BEAT BEAT

BEAT BEAT BEAT BEAT BEAT BEAT BEAT BEAT BEAT BEAT BEAT BEAT BEAT BEAT BEAT BEAT BEAT BEAT BEAT BEAT BEAT BEAT BEAT BEAT BEAT BEAT BEAT BEAT BEAT BEAT BEAT BEAT BEAT BEAT BEAT BEAT BEAT BEAT BEAT BEAT BEAT BEAT BEAT BEAT BEAT BEAT BEAT BEAT BEAT BEAT BEAT BEAT BEAT BEAT BEAT BEAT BEAT BEAT BEAT BEAT

BEAT BEAT BEAT BEAT BEAT BEAT BEAT BEAT BEAT BEAT BEAT BEAT BEAT BEAT BEAT BEAT BEAT BEAT BEAT BEAT BEAT BEAT BEAT BEAT BEAT BEAT BEAT BEAT BEAT BEAT BEAT BEAT BEAT BEAT BEAT BEAT BEAT BEAT BEAT BEAT BEAT BEAT BEAT BEAT BEAT BEAT BEAT BEAT BEAT BEAT BEAT BEAT BEAT BEAT BEAT BEAT BEAT BEAT BEAT BEAT BEAT

She dreamed of hawk swooping in to save her; a refugee up in the sky and not down in a hole. But rabbits were made to burrow and hide, not soar and glide.

The drums of death kept time, then skipped a beat, upped the tempo, felt its prey would soon be caught slipping.

Steam cracks the cold from wet, panting growls.

'I can't go on, I can't go on, I can't go on...'

The sky sped up to a time-elapsed clip; cloud car-wreck pile up broke spaces in sky. As grey turned to blue, the clouds purpled as grapefruit pulp and raspberry seeds swirled in sunset.

Underneath the bleeding sky, the terror of living grew greater than the fear of death. All she has to do is stop running and it'll all be over.

Just ... stop ... running...

Chapter 3

IT WAS NOT YET VIKTOR who ran down the stairs, exiting the building with torn hands and a blood-steeped gun. He stuck his paws into a man-made snowdrift shoveled behind the broke-down bench, turning the last whites of winter red.

Minutes later, the lights of the Moscow night froze around his speeding car in amber trails, the world a series of long-exposure photographs racing by in 24 frames. At the center were shaking hands gripping a steering wheel — somewhere behind them a man.

He raced down narrow back streets drifting on sludge, through the lattice work of pipes and the walking dead sleeping under them, past the dog packs chasing his mechanical horse in the open-air gas chamber. He turned onto Kapotnaya Street, absconding under the cover of bare Linden and Chestnut trees lining the road, without another headlight in sight.

Finally, he reached the Ring Road; finally, the distancing began.

His chest heaved up and down, up and down, up and down. The adrenaline flight in the pre-dawn hours turned his pupils as big as holes with downward-darted rabbits beating at the speed of narrowly-avoided death.

His face was awash in blood and sweat.

Memory played at gestural abstractionism, turning his mind a ruby red circus. His hands gripped the wheel, vibrating with the road, vibrating without the road. How could those hands ever hold his little girl again?

The nausea hit him like a wave, forcing him to pull over to the shoulder of the highway. He nearly fell out of his car, hopped over the knee-high divider into the mud and snow, and began vomiting.

A cold breeze blew, and the larches swayed with the pines. Doubled over, hands resting on his knees, he gazed at the dark outline of trees ahead. One car, then another, cut through the silence and rumbled off into the night. The crisp air touched his wet lips and eyes, cold comfort as the bile burn settled in the back of his throat.

On the other side of the boreal divide sat the Moscow Higher Military Command School. He straightened his spine and wiped the spittle from his mouth. His hands shook an alcoholic's goodbye.

His entire body ached from battery. He placed a hand to his boot-marked cheek, hematoma swelling a bee's suicide. His back was on fire; his legs, his shoulders smoldered.

Nerves reported back seismic activity from fractures in his right hand. In better light his knuckles would be the same color as the overripe plum sky soaking up street lights from across the city.

"'What have I done? My God, what have I done?'"

The night offered no reply. There was no going back. So he got back in his car and drove on.

In a near-fugue state he reached Savyolovskaya Train Station, a yellow and white neoclassical break in a neighborhood of otherwise grey Soviet dimensions.

He continued prowling the streets until he found a kiosk that was still open. He bought a small bottle of Ararat brandy from a wide-eyed woman who was far too old to be selling spirits to ghosts who had left arms and legs in Ichkeria.

He took a circuitous route through Marina Rosha, past the newly rebuilt "Second Moscow Synagogue," which had burned down several years ago.

He followed the tram line onto Obraztsova Street, past Melnikov's abandoned avant-garde garage and the massive Moscow State University of Railway Engineering.

He traced the tram line, beyond Battle Square and onto Dostoevsky Street.

Sipping from his bottle of brandy, his car slowed to a crawl as he reached the Mariinsky Hospital where the literary giant had lived as a child, forever to be haunted by the neighboring asylum and morgue.

He circled the roundabout by the Soviet Army Theater, which was no longer called that, though no one knew it by any other name.

Turning toward Ekaterina Park, his heart began to flutter. This is where he and Galya had gone on their first date. The hopeful young man of that day was no more.

Dawn was now breaking on the city. He stopped by the main entrance, shut off the ignition and got out, half-empty bottle in hand. Viktor faltered toward the big black gate, with the padlock still shutting out all that went bump in the night.

He steadied himself with one hand against the gate, putting lips to his only warmth, drinking until the last drop. The bottle slowly slid from his fingers and to the ground, clanking against the pavement.

He gripped the bars, pressing his face to the cold metal.

Memories of mayhem flashed again. The nausea washed over him. Viktor fell to his knees, hands still gripping all that was wrought, and began to sob.

Somewhere down the cobblestones once bathed in diaphanous light, past the trees and down to the pond where the Ruddy Shelducks would soon mate for life, Viktor had first placed Galya's delicate hand in his, gently grasping it like a filigree flower.

Eyes closed, the algid wind kissing his tears, the bars a cold compress against the pulsing throb in his head, he felt Raskolnikov's splinters dig in.

"What now? What now?"

The silence was interrupted by the sound of approaching footsteps.

Startled, Viktor opened his eyes.

On the other side of the gate, a large, shadowy figure moved down the boulevard.

Viktor released the bars and rose to his knees. Was it a guard coming to open up? At this hour, before sunrise?

Getting closer, the gaunt, towering figure looked like the silhouette of a down-and-out clown.

So close to madness already, Viktor turned his back on the lunatic heading his way.

The shadow man picked up his clip, hard soles echoing on the street. Viktor hurried to his car. Fishing his keys out of his pockets, his shaking hands struggled to unlock the door. He looked up. The man was fast approaching, having already passed through the gate. But how? Even under the street light, he remained a shadow casting shadows.

Jitters turned to terror. Viktor finally managed to open the door and jumped inside, immediately locking the door. He looked in the rearview. The shadow loomed.

Viktor fumbled to get the keys into the ignition. One, two drawn out cranks but the engine wouldn't start. The mad shadow sprinted toward his car. Viktor turned the key again.

"Come on, come on!"

Finally, a spark as the engine ignited. Viktor threw it into gear and sped off.

He looked into the rearview. The maniac was chasing him. Viktor couldn't believe his eyes. He made a hard turn onto Dostoevsky Street. The shadow was holding his pace.

"This is impossible. This is impossible. This is impossible."

Viktor floored it past the old-time asylum and morgue. Spectral cackling filled the air. He nearly crashed hanging a right onto Obratsoza Street. The mad dasher was gaining ground, running down the middle of the tram tracks.

Viktor broke into a cold sweat, booze seeping out of his pores.

He thought of his mother and all of her Bible tales. He had always told his mother the devil wasn't real. Now the devil was here, ready to take him. Viktor looked in his rearview. The glass was a cloud of black. His jaw was clenched so hard he feared his teeth would crack. He remembered the gun in his pocket. What, are you going to fill the devil with lead? And then the darkness eclipsed him. And then a thunderclap. He fishtailed as he struggled to steer his car from crash. More mad laughter. And darkness. Nothing but darkness.

Reaching the end of the street, Viktor drifted hard onto Third Ring Road, upshifting and flooring it.

Right behind him, the shadow flew out into the center lane. That shadow was swallowed by speeding headlights.

Wham!

A hightailing Kamaz cabover bashed Beelzebub on the beltway. Viktor watched in shock as the truck came to a stop, long limbs of the shadow man mangled under burning rubber. He looked ahead as the sun began to rise over the metropolis.

A mad cackle roiled down the road and followed Viktor all the way home.

Chapter 4

HE SAT IN THE KITCHEN bathed in half-light. The madman's laughter continued rattling in his head before falling down the empty echo well to his heart, a heart that remembered the night before, a night that a mere fifth of brandy had no hope of erasing.

When he awoke from that strange dream, his mouth was the Thar Desert. When he swallowed — the bitter taste of almonds and rancid camel spit. A small halo of 'peregar 'hung around his head.

The topography of his body was dotted with the shadows cast from storm heads. Bumps and bruises created a highland range from head to toe. Ferruginous soil formed the banks of the now dried red rivers that once flowed through the barrial.

His pupils swam like goldfish in bowls filled with sand.

He squeezed his eyes and gripped the bed with big, battered hands. All of those tense muscles and taut skin squeezing pain against the grain of black, burl-knotted knuckles. His whole seizure of a body seemingly fought to form a hermetic seal to block out the flow of consciousness serving as a force multiplier on the misery down below. And then the laughter. That horrible laughter, dripping with blood and a young man turned to mush.

He could close his eyes, he could open them, but that ceaseless cachinnation rang out the same, portending a path to sure madness. He had given himself over to a devil he didn't believe in. And then the devil came looking to stake his claim.

Galya came in when he failed to wake. Boy did he give her hell. Better than letting her see the hell he'd gotten them into.

He just about bit her head off to keep from losing his. As she stood there in shock, he dragged himself to the kitchen to marinate in shame and fear.

Just sitting there in a creaky wooden chair on the slick orange floor, cheap red fabric starting to shred; the wall a color of nicotine-stained fingers, all the decay of his life closed in on him.

The fridge hummed like a transmission tower. A great grey depression hung outside the window. Then he remembered. His hands bashing in cheekbones. Nausea. Sockets pop. Crunch. Crunch. Crunch.

His jaw cinched up again. His whole head was a toothache. Red flashes of lightning cracked the whites of his eyes, body buzzing like a generator in the night. Every muscle in his back tightened like the crisscross lacing of a corset being pulled 'til the boning threatened to turn his own skeleton into dust. A picket fence of light was cast through the curtains and crucified his shadow in sections. And like the flick of a switch, unseen clouds swallowed the light and the square spaces between them on the floor.

'No man can run like that. No man, no man…'

'No man can do what I did. No man, no man…'

His mantra of disbelief was stuck on repeat.

His eyes defocused. Shapes floated in the coal dust and milk spilling through the window and filling up the floor. He focused on the throbbing in his head until his inner ear itched with the metronome pulse. All of his insides felt like a ship lost at sea in storm.

"How will I go on? How? How?"

Just then, Galya called out to him, sending sparks through his generator, yanking on corset cords, triggering a tsunami in the charcoal-milk ocean.

He gingerly stood up, joint pops and pain flare ups accompanying every last movement.

"God take me! What is it now?" he shouted before shuffling out of the kitchen.

He moved through the foyer, into the living room, approaching the back bedroom where Lana slept.

He limped past the red couch, carpet hanging overhead, with East German 'wall furniture' on the other side, which housed all of her parents' books and knick-knacks, as well as a few artifacts to Viktor's own lost time.

Another couch was below the window looking out on the balcony. An empty, wobbly table was set in front.

There once was a time when her father had pulled this foreign-made furniture with a lot of pride. Now it was just more creaky junk that reminded them of better times.

Galya came rushing out of the bedroom.

"Did you see Lana leave?"

Viktor's eyes grew wide.

"What do you mean?"

"She's gone, Viktor, she's gone!"

Without a word, Viktor set off, a madman chasing his last shred of sanity down the drain.

Chapter 5

VIKTOR THREW ON A LIGHT jacket and raced down the stairs, foot-stomps echoing wall-to-wall. He ignored his body's pleas for mercy, but they did not ignore him.

He reached the third-floor landing and saw Murat perched there, a perfect picture of death. Hard to believe, but Murat had been a cop in Soviet times. Then drinking took its toll, and having already paid such a high price, he resigned himself to taking that road to the end.

To the bemusement of everyone, when some issue arose that required the swift intervention of Officer Nabiev, he'd put on his old police jacket and shuffle to their door in slippers and stained tracksuit pants, mumbling some barely audible command. Often it was him telling Viktor not to open the windows in the stairwell, even during late spring, because the chill would make him sick.

To tell him that chain-smoking in an unventilated stairwell while drinking medical-grade ethanol was likely the cause of his poor health was of no use. What's worse, Murat stank so bad the very essence of his wretched body was lifted on wisps of smoke and delivered straight through one's keyhole.

Smoking was one thing; Murat's weaponized funk was another. Forget about the cold. Viktor couldn't care less if a snowstorm was raging during the winter solstice. He'd still open the stairwell windows to keep the stench of that Tatar filth wizard out of his house.

Which was to say, Viktor and Murat were not the best of friends. And like all the rest, this interaction was anything but welcome.

"Murat, did you see Lana come down?" Viktor beseeched with slightly labored breathing, his head still beating the pulse of pounding fists set by the cadence of his boots.

"Seeeeeee wha…?" Murat muttered through dripstone speleothems housing a near-dead tongue in its musty sepulcher.

"Lana, have you seen Lana?"

Murat craned his neck. Without moving his head, he peered up over his brow, locking eyes with Viktor. Head hanging ajar, he languidly reached into his pocket, pulled out a papirosa and then a book of matches, lighting up with deliberate slowness.

The strong smoke hovering over his head, his eyes settled on the big, bruised man.

"Window."

"What?" Viktor scoffed. "My daughter, have you seen my daughter?"

"You … you opened the window," he mumbled before taking another drag. "I'll get sick if you … open … the … window."

Viktor flew into a rage, dragging Murat up by his shirt and slamming him against the rail.

"Have you seen my daughter?" he screamed, shaking Murat violently.

Murat just hung there, limp, dead eyes fixed on Viktor. It was hard to admit, but beneath the filth and ravine-like wrinkles, broken-beer-bottle teeth and oily road kill matted to his head, this degenerate had once-upon-a-time been a ladies' man. His saggy, sallow skin hung off a skull even his debauchery could not steal symmetry from. He could black and tan his teeth and kill the hope in his eyes, but this could not suck out their navy-blue brilliance. Once this had been a man who kept order in a place that is no more. Then, he too was no more.

"I see you, Viktor … I see you."

Murat started convulsing in a space between seizure and laughter. The tickle in his gut traveled up through his gullet and opened up the gates to the crypt. Chuckles, spit and bats flew out.

The stench nearly knocked Viktor over. Bile rose up in his throat.

"The rabbit," Murat said.

"What?"

He laughed even harder, his body hanging like a shirt on a clothes line in the breeze.

"The rabbit, the rabbit ran. From wolf or from bear? Where did the rabbit go? The shadow is coming. Run ... run rabbit ... run!"

The madness sapped Viktor of his vigor. Panic flashed in his eyes. Without thinking, he dropped Murat to the ground like a sack of potatoes. Murat landed with a thud and a grunt. He remained still until that wave of vibration caught him again. Cigarette still in hand, he took a drag before erupting a laughing-cough paroxysm.

"Run ...(cough) (cough) (cough) ... run rabbit ... (cough) (cough) (cough) ... run rabbit run."

Viktor's soul shook like a body submerged in Epiphany. Shadows' hands reached for him from the wall. He shook his head in disbelief, turned his back on Murat and ran down the stairs.

Howls followed him down. The bullfrog's tongue flicked at the bear's heavy paws.

Chapter 6

GALYA REMAINED PERCHED ON THE edge of Lana's bed. The stool in the foyer smacked hard against the floor, trailed by a string of curses before the front door slammed shut and a cold silence settled like dust.

She couldn't even begin to understand what devil had gotten into him. She wondered if it was the same one who had beaten him black and blue.

Viktor lost it when she pressed him on what had happened to his face. It was not like him to be so cagey and full of hate. Then again, he had been less and less him with each passing day. Soon enough, you wake up and realize the man you married is gone. And Galya was starting to ask herself: Is that day today?

Her eyes scanned the sheets before falling on Lana's threadbare teddy bear, a few seams splitting underneath the left arm. The sight of it was so pathetic she nearly burst into tears. A proxy for love unraveling, just like the real thing.

"So, this is it. This is when it finally falls apart."

She'd never thought the strains of these troubled times would saddle her family with a load they couldn't bear. In no avenue of life had she encountered a ridge so treacherous it didn't hold forth the promise of a pass.

And then she caught a glimpse of Cimmerian shade cast across Viktor's face, his eyes black with rage. It augured troubled waters neither kith nor kin could ever cross.

There were times in her life when Galya had been fearful, but never really, truly afraid. Now an undercurrent of dread lapped at her heart.

It had not always been this way. Before Lana was born, a strange spirit of hope had gripped the country. The Germans had torn down their own wall, while the iron curtain had become so rusty those little metal rings practically popped into dust when squeezed. And squeeze people did, first tentatively, then in ecstasy.

As that merry carousel of time went 'round and round', the satellites reached escape velocity, Soviet souls following ad astra per aspera. But then no one was left behind the lever to stop the ride, and everything spun out of control. Many overshot the stars and were left adrift. The endless black followed.

When Galya was in hospital giving birth, Viktor was quarantined in a haze of cigars as tanks rolled through the streets. Swan Lake was playing on TV, trying to drown out the swan song of an empire being sung in circles around the White House.

And just like that, Borya stood on the tank and Russia was free! Free, it turns out, from itself. And then, as the days of bubblegum and jeans took hold, Homo Soviectus was left a stateless man. Monuments to an imagined future cast across one-sixth of the world were left to rust away. Galya could not help but think: What could be sadder than watching the past's dream of the future disintegrate, especially when the present promised no future?

Soon enough, men took to TV preaching the virtues of mass psychosis. Grandmothers chattered about 9 o'clock miracles while stadiums filled up with suckers susceptible to cheap tricks imported from southern snake handling country.

In rudderless times, people need something to believe in. And when they don't have that something, myriad somethings spring up like mushrooms after the rain.

Then Kuroyokhin comes along trying to prove that Lenin was one such mushroom, and after the stir settled, it became apparent to half the country that the other half had lost its mind.

So Lana was birthed into chaos, a snowflake falling in a storm, a coruscant cracking through thunderheads. In those dark times, the light she gave was everything. And in that everything Galya still believed there was a future after all.

It was this belief that kept her keeping on as a math teacher at School 1189, even as her pay had long been in arrears. It was why she taught kids how to dance in her spare time. Despite the perpetual days of gloom, she would continue to seed her own corner of tomorrow as she saw fit. If only others saw things the same way.

Having lost his job as an engineer, Viktor for a time remained hopeful as well. Then one day the shine started to fade from his eyes, before nightly bouts of drinking covered them in a near permanent glaze. And then life was no longer about making the future, but forgetting today. So he joined the swelling ranks of the great escape.

Sitting on the bed grappling with those thoughts, Galya realized she'd already spooled a dozen hairs around her index finger and snapped them off. That was her dark secret, a self-harming prayer for control. The silence — the endless thoughts it engendered — was maddening.

She should have gone out to look for Lana instead, leaving Viktor to do what he does best. She got up and began pacing in the other room. She needed something to fill the still.

She pulled a record from the shelf and placed it on the turntable. The needle dropped. Shostakovich's Waltz No. 2 came with a crackle. Without a partner or a ballroom, all she could do was sway in a living room barely big enough for life.

A gifted ballerina in her youth, she had spun many a pirouette in a Pioneer's circle with envious eyes watching her grow too tall. And while dreams of the Bolshoi were long gone, movement remained the sole refuge from the vagaries of her mind.

What she loved most was the paradox. Flow came through the obsession with total control. Every muscle, ligament and jolt of pain was enslaved to the execution of an ideal — finesse through brutality.

Her toenails could split like the tops of weather-worn tomato stakes, but she held her suffering behind the mask like any other pose. Most of all, she saw that life was a dance all its own. Grace came through embracing suffering, not denying it. And yet those around her had embraced the great lie of denial, perhaps none more than Viktor.

She moved to the window, taking in the cold, grey day. The waltz came to an end.

The silence between songs was interrupted by parquet pops. A few brick feet were pounding next door. A muffled gust of wind was accompanied by static on the spin. Galya traced her fingers along the warm radiator. Then came the next melody.

Out on the street, the wooden bench in front of the entrance was empty — no passers passing by. Fogging up the pane, she traced pictographs in her own breath, then watched the diaphonous shapes shrink into smudges. Beauty was always in retreat. The darkness always creeped. And people were too quick to let themselves become too small.

Out there, wolves stalked the ruins of fallen sky touchers, casting enormous shadows, making chicken liver of sheep dogs.

And under their shadows, a once-soaring hawk found herself feeling far, far too small. Her thoughts brought her to a halt. Try as she might, she couldn't shake her jitters.

'Just what are you hiding Viktor?'

Chapter 7

HE ALMOST TOOK A DIVE running out the front door, hitting a thin patch of ice which hadn't quite decided whether it wanted to melt. Viktor slipped, shimmied, swore, stabilized, and swore some more, fighting off the shock absorber jolt down his spine; the pained pickled-brain rattle in his head.

He paused, taking a deep breath, beset by throbbing in bruises too deep to blanch. Murat's mad laughter echoed in the stairwell, evoking the horrors of the previous night.

The street was quiet, the sky dull, the air thick with a slight sting of cold. The wind blew — branches rattled. The pulse of his post-war hangover headache intensified.

The ceaseless throb through every part of his rocked-and-socked soma continued to ramp up.

The creeping emptiness crawled up his heart like ivy covered in hoarfrost. It was half the blood-sugar drop of the previous night's damage, half the sinking feeling of a soul swallowing itself, and the full knowledge that something superstitious folks called evil had somehow pushed its way into this world.

And Lana was somewhere out there in that world, alone.

'Where are you? Where are you?'

He crossed the narrow road and squeezed between parked cars to get to the small playground in the yard, all trash, mud and rust. Dripping water hit the tops of metal shells covering metal horses.

There was a certain shamelessness in the adults' inability to not spread their filth to the one space set aside for the kids. But drunks don't care for deontology.

Even a mud-covered bench in freezing cold and cigarette-ash snow could lose its sting a few pulls in. Swig away enough, and it all blends into the same great-big blank. A happy, heady nothing when the morning pain was part of some impossible future. It was the only way to be in the moment when the moment would otherwise suffocate you.

'So. This is it?'

(Throw the bottle back.)

'YES! THIS IS IT!'

Viktor had always wanted to draw a line between himself and the anti-natalist yardbirds. He'd never believed he too could one day be a bullfrog in a stairwell croaking up sorrows with spit and smoke. He never knew he could become everything good people revile.

But as the days passed, the lines blurred, collapsed and amassed into some great big black mass. And now he could see how quickly the score could switch from Tchaikovsky to Scriabin in the span of a few years. How the bad choices made in summer-wait could usher in winter eternal.

Viktor felt like he couldn't breathe. Months of cold and the walls of his tiny apartment, his tiny car, his tiny life had slowly been closing in on him. And then last night, he chucked dynamite at it all. And now here he was, dumbfounded by the damage, a madman's cackle resounding in his bones.

Running from the blood he felt his mask slip and his shadow step out, standing akimbo before raising its arms to eclipse the light. And that shadow met him at the cemetery gates of his now lost life.

Viktor had been white knuckling the red line for so long he felt the wheels would never come off. But off they came.

He was suddenly hit with a dizzy spell. He awkwardly plodded through the slush until finding a dry patch of bench where he could sit. His mind returned to the night before, retracing his steps, trying to see exactly when it all broke down. And like every collapsed bridge, the cracks had been forming long before the fall.

Chapter 8

THE PREVIOUS EVENING BEGAN JUST like the thousand before, sitting in the front seat of his car, waiting until the sunrise to call it a night. Same drained, dry feeling in the eyes. Same struggle between being too chilly and then too muggy once the blower motor finally started hotting up through the heater core. One second — muggy and claustrophobic. Crack open a window. Microscopic ice lice from the Moskva chew proceed to chew on his ear.

Viktor just couldn't win.

From one corner of the city to the next, the regularly irregular mix of passengers waved him down. All were in search of some iteration of consumption — champagne, caviar, cocaine and each other.

Leaving Moscow State University, in the rearview smoke swirled around a thoughtful young man's head. Cold air crept in through the crack and sucked out the stench with it. He had a lot to say about love and life. He didn't know much about either. But Viktor forgave him his youth. By the time he knew better, he would inevitably be worse for wear. Such was the cruel irony of fate.

Afterwards, he hopscotched across the center of town until being hailed by a pretty drunk provincial who had failed to get picked up by a smartly-dressed German or dim-witted American inside Night Flight on Tverskaya Street. She'd missed the last train home to Korolyov, an industrial city just north of Moscow.

The girl stared through the glaze and mumbled slurred syllables, breath leaving a fleeting impression of her profile against the frosted window. Smudges of lip gloss and blush stuck around a while longer. She seemed too young, too beautiful to be so cynical. Perhaps it was her youth and beauty from which that cynicism sprung.

Speeding down pock-marked roads cratered like a spring-thawing lake, each bump and dip added to the ache. Pin and needle pistons pumped in squeaky heel hinges as his feet danced between clutch, gas and brake. Packs of stray dogs regularly snapped at his tires, barking bellicose foam as he slid down ice sheets.

Finally arriving, she offered him payment in something other than rubles. He demurred. She huffed and puffed before handing the money over, cursing his manhood with the slam of a door.

He couldn't help but chuckle, ready to be done with it all. And then the three young men came knocking on his window. They wanted a ride to Kapotnya, a hole of a district all the way down in southeast Moscow.

At first Viktor refused. His warm bed was calling. Then again, it wasn't warmer than the burning hole in his pocket.

Still, they looked so strange, with high-rolled trousers, black boots and bomber jackets that were far too thin for this time of year. They didn't dress like criminals, but there was something criminal in them. Or maybe Viktor was just getting old and had missed the latest trend pouring in from the West.

Ignoring his instincts, Viktor finally relented. He would soon regret it in the raucous 50-minute ride that followed. Vodka shots, screams and enough cigarettes to fumigate a mental ward filled his car. Every time he looked in the rearview mirror, grey eyes locked on him. Menace flashed in a Cheshire smile. Even when he looked away, he felt the back of his neck smoldering.

They eventually reached what Viktor could only describe as the worst segment of the worst block of flats in that absolute pit of a neighborhood.

Held in a chock hold by the MKAD, this brick, low-rise block was not far from the Moscow Oil Refinery, where candy cane colored smokestacks were belching above the Moskva. There was no metro station. Without a car one was practically cut off from the world. It was home to those most cut off of all, the homeless heating themselves under the sunburst scatter of pipes, emanating miles out from the plant, carrying superheated oil and gas. Amidst the necrosis-affected denizens of the damp and death air heat huddlers, the wild dogs roamed.

This was the exact kind of neighborhood not to take dodgy young men to at this hour. And here Viktor was on the side of the curb, having taken just such a fare.

A big hand smacked him on the shoulder, over and over, sending an electric surge through Viktor's body.

"Really sorry there, looks like I'm skinned. Maxim, you got any money?"

"You got me, Losh!" the smaller one laughed.

"What 'bout you, Anton, you got anything for the driver?"

Anton preceded to incoherently mumble, having polished off the bottle of vodka which was now resting beneath the passenger seat.

"Well, buddy," Losh, the one with the grey eyes said, "looks like you're just gonna have to take this one on the chin."

The sting of condescension was amplified through several more buddy-buddy shoulder slaps.

Viktor was speechless as they piled out of the car, exchanging punches and curses as Anton struggled, and failed, to remain upright.

Viktor sat there for a spell as the anger ate away at him. It was the fourth time he had been stiffed in two weeks. His first instinct was to tuck tail and run, just as he had done before. And then something snapped.

'Not this time. Not this time…'

He popped open the glove box, reached in and pulled out a gun.

He ran his fingers over the cold metal. It was a relic, a Tokarev TT-33. The Georgian — his regular drinking buddy under the Savelovskaya pass — swore that it worked. And just like a samovar, it had been made in Tula.

Viktor ran his thumb over the small, indented star on the side. He racked the slide to chamber the round.

He stared at the gun, then looked at himself in the rearview. He saw a glint of fear in his eyes that only served to fuel his rage.

'When did you become so weak?'

Half his youth spent on the wrestling mat and here he was turning yellow with age. Viktor put the gun in his jacket pocket and shut off the ignition. He took a deep breath before getting out of the car. The temperature was hovering around zero, the road a mix of sludge and ice. The fenced in grounds were grassless mud pits blotched with retreating snow. The cold air smelled of stale popcorn and chestnuts from the nearby factory belch. Viktor began to feel lightheaded from the stench.

He stared up, searching the windows for a light. Like a haphazardly opened-Advent calendar, a few illuminated squares were shown on the first, fifth and third floors.

The bench out front was half broken down into firewood by falling drunks and stomping teens.

Viktor approached the entrance. Strange graffiti that resembled hieroglyphs was arranged around an Endekagram on the wooden door. The diagram seemed to have been painted in red phosphorescent pigment. It sent a chill down his spine.

"Just kids," he told himself. "Just kids."

He grabbed the handle and opened the door with a long, drawn out creak. Steeling himself, he entered the constructivist charnel house. The symbols on the door pulsed.

It was musty inside the stairwell, light flickering above the rows of battered grey mailboxes. The walls were painted russet, the checkered floor tiles, some missing, chestnut and canary yellow. Childish graffiti, often scrawled in big, looping magic marker strikes, abounded. Most of the barely-legible letters cried out a four-letter response to teen-aged boredom. They were nothing like what he had seen outside.

It was completely silent. With measured steps, he slowly headed up the stairs, each step echoing and expanding. The slight feeling of grit was faintly perceptible each time his soles crushed the grime back down into the tiles.

The long fluorescent tube had gone out on the second floor, although radiant rhombuses were visible through the handrail above, providing a cresting on the ceiling alternating between merlons of shadow and crenels of faint light.

He placed his hand on the wall and slowed his already tiptoe pace.

Viktor reached the landing between the second and third floor, feeling a distinct crunch underneath his left boot. Lifting his foot, he saw that he'd stepped on a used syringe. He walked over to the window and stared out onto the street.

Through the glass, scratched and splattered with muck like Pollack's Greyed Rainbow in inverted colors, he spotted his car by the curb, beckoning him to turn back on this fool's errand and return home.

A cold draft sent a shudder down his spine. A muddled gust of wind was audible outside. A tree branch tapped morse code on a window above.

'What the hell are you doing?'

The wind blew again. The tree's message was lost without a translator. The darkness, inside and out, seemed to grow.

Shaken by the sense that something beyond himself had temporarily taken hold, he turned back and stared down the stairs, toward the still shining light on the landing below. Galya was in bed waiting for him. He'd lost a fare for today but there'd be more tomorrow. He imagined Lana lying all warm and still in sleep.

He had never seen anything as beautiful as that little girl smile and squeal as he carried her across the world's shallowest sea; phytoplantkon painting the water surface a whirlpool of blue and green. Maybe this June he'd take her back to Berdyansk. Galya had always loved it there. Even her own overseeing eyes let go of their pain and had shown azure against the Azov.

Things had been hard, but life was not over. There was still time, still a chance to…

Laughter erupted from on high. It was definitely them.

The colors of the Azov faded to black. A serpentine slither from some subcortical substrate latched onto reins shaped like its own tail. Venom coursed through Viktor's veins. He followed it where it led. A growing shadow shed its skin.

Chapter 9

"I SHOULD KNOCK YOUR TEETH down your throat!"

'Something has clearly gone wrong,' Viktor thought as the grey-eyed punk held him by the lapels, nearly foaming at the mouth. He felt the gun sagging in his jacket pocket.

The little fire hydrant named Maxim shot up from his stool, kicking over several empty Zhigulevskoe bottles encircling the table leg. More bottles lined the table top, littered with cups, bowls, shot glasses and a jar of pickles. A half-full vodka bottle was planted in the middle. On a couch under the window, Anton was planted in the dreamless grave of drunks. The entire place smelled like smoke and old cabbage.

Viktor turned sky blue eyes to the tempest. Lermatov's words were dislodged by a gust moving from one iris to the other: 'He in his madness prays for storms, and dreams that storms will bring him peace.'

Viktor had found the storm he was looking for. All the while, the hot sweat stench of metabolizing poison emanated from the wolf's jowls.

"You made a big mistake coming up here," he growled, reaching for Viktor's pocket. As his fingers neared the gun, the switch in Viktor flipped. From out of the shadows came the animal in man.

Viktor slid off the counter, seizing up Losh in a bear trap grip. A number of shots to the head couldn't stop the whip crack spin that sent him sailing over Viktor's shoulder and crashing through the table.

A cacophony of broken bottles and snapping wood erupted.

Pain pulsed in Viktor's temple as shards of glass and other broken bric-a-brac flew like shrapnel.

The smaller one stared at his downed comrade in shock. Losh groaned on the floor, hand looking to stop more than one leak. The zombie on the couch seemed to stir before returning to oblivion.

Viktor stumbled back a few steps toward the counter adjacent to the door.

"About the fare. Let's call it even."

Maxim let out a guttural roar, charging him with his left foot forward. The adrenaline had clearly sobered him a bit, though he was telegraphing the smashing overhand right that he hurled Viktor's way like a discus.

Viktor slipped the punch from the far shorter man, which grazed his shoulder and smacked hard into the cupboard overhead. His assailant howled in pain.

Viktor clinched Maxim's neck and tried to plant a knee in his face. But the little tank managed to square his hips up and get an over-hook on Viktor's left arm.

The kid was a lot stronger than he looked.

The two strained in the clinch as Maxim kept trying to ram the top of his head into Viktor's chin. Viktor's back groaned as it grated against the cabinet's edge.

One hard thrust from the bonehead smacked Viktor's jaw shut with a sickening clatter. Bits of sand-ground teeth rolled on his tongue.

He turned his head to take the glancing blows on the jaw. Viktor did his best to avoid that relentless piston of rage, managing an inside trip that sent Maxim down hard.

Viktor mounted him, repeatedly finding a place for his heavy hand on Maxim's face.

But just as his arm arched upward to deliver a final blow, a forearm from behind dug deep into his throat.

Viktor struggled for dear life as the squeeze tightened. Spots began floating across his field of vision from the onset of asphyxia.

In the crush, darkness seeped into the corner of his eyes. Blood trickled down his face. The kitchen shrank to a dimly lit square at the end of a tunnel. Red dripped down that corridor. And in black-seeped blooming and the square of light floating on the surface, his soul fell and fell.

He surged the liminal of sentry realms. He saw rabbits run and wolves snap gums. He saw tiny-mouthed ghosts sucking blood from Hell beings. He saw devas caress beasts of burden.

Sinking deeper still, his lungs filled with the black death of drowning. And beyond the pain, the ecstasy of release beckoned as a lodestar in the night.

'Let Go. Just Let Go.'

He felt a slackening of soul. But below Orion's belt, Saiph burned brighter to match Rigel's light, forming blue white eyes that pierced the abyss. Lana. Lana. Knives were out for the cottontail waif.

Feet kicked against the bottom of hell.

He sailed up, up, up, finally smashing through water that had frozen to a snow-packed path of flight. The wolves were closing in.

Lana. Lana.

He hurled himself at death and life. With a whack, crack, and spray of blood on snow, the rabbit hunters died. A tower of coal-and-ice rose 84,000 Yojana high. A hawk carried a bear to the peak. Staring from up on high, two tiny windows opened onto a kitchen murder fight. And Viktor crashed through those windows a thief in the night. Little did he know the black sea beast in his lungs had crossed over to the other side of the bardo.

Back on Earth, Viktor tucked his chin into the crook of Losh's elbow and found a flow of oxygen. His feet fought for traction, soles squeaking against the debris-littered floor. He placed one hand on Losh's elbow, the other on top of it, pulling down with all of his might. They battled for the fate of Viktor's neck. Viktor twisted his body toward Losh's right side, breaking the choke and ending up on all fours.

Losh wildly began battering his head.

Viktor did his best to hold himself up on one hand and block the shots with the other, but again and again sharp knuckles cracked his face. Losh stepped back but failed to plant his feet before letting loose a sloppy kick. Viktor turned his head and took the awkward blow on the cheek. Sloppy or not, it stung like an angry hornet in heat.

Losh tried to kick him again, but Viktor got a hold of the frenzied pendulum and snapped it down.

The pair fell into the foyer. Losh squirmed to get to his feet, but Viktor got his back and drove him into the floor.

Just as he started slamming his fist into Losh's head, Maxim tackled him from behind, ramming Viktor into the wall. The two stumbled for footing on a pile of boots.

Maxim went to work on Viktor's kidneys. Wincing in pain, Viktor swung around and smashed an elbow into his face. A fang went flying in the air, striking the frozen clock. In this kind of hell, time didn't stand still as much as it destroyed any thought that there was ever anything on either side of this suffocating moment.

The defanged wolf fell to the floor, holding his face. Blood gushed out like an unscrewed fire hydrant from some Hollywood summer scene, in a place none of them had ever, nor would ever see.

Losh had crawled back toward the kitchen on all fours. He breathed heavily, bringing himself to his knees in a lion's pose. He remained stationary, sans the rise and fall of his chest.

Viktor huffed and puffed, finding it strange that he had just blown the wolf's house down. His lungs burned like a hair dryer seconds from blowing a fuse.

A countervailing cold wind blew in from under the door. The entire apartment block must have shuddered at the sound of late-night war.

Viktor cursed the thieves in a spray of spittle, the taste of blood filling his mouth.

Still panting, he silenced Maxim's whimpering with a well-placed kick. Losh remained silent, slowing standing with his back turned, heaving audibly.

"You asked for this!" Viktor screamed. "I'm just trying to make an honest living for my family. I'm trying to survive!"

Losh finally turned toward him with a gun tightly gripped in his hand. Hatred revealed the embers still burning in his grey eyes.

He raised the pistol in the direction of Viktor's chest. A small trail of blood trickled from his ear, a tributary flowing from the huge gash above his right eye.

He flashed claret-stained teeth, gritting them with rage.

Viktor's eyes widened. It must have fallen out of his pocket during the melee. Blood and sweat poured down his face.

"You don't want to do this! It's just a misunderstanding. You can't just shoot someone in the middle of Moscow, you..."

Click.

Viktor thought it was the end.

Click. Click. Click.

It was not his end.

Losh started frantically pulling the trigger, but the safety was engaged.

Viktor's fear of death was sent down a basket on the Phlegethon, circling the Earth in smoke before arriving an ash storm in Tartarus.

He forgot his red-lined lungs, the whines of the small wolf, Lana's laughter, Galya's skin, Azovian shores, Soviet fraternity, right, wrong, love, hope, death and himself.

The shadow engulfed him. And in the depths of blackness, all he saw was red. Viktor impassively walked down Losh until the gun touched his chest.

"I, I..."

Viktor threw a right down the pipe, followed by a left hook and another right. Losh hit the floor.

Viktor got on top of him, grabbed the barrel, and twisted it toward Losh's body until first a claw snapped, and then his cinch. The wolf began to howl as the bear paw with a pistol grip crashed down on his snout, again, and again and again...

Chekhov was wrong. If a gun is hanging on the wall in the first act, it doesn't necessarily have to be fired in the second. For there are far, far worse things you can do to a man with a gun.

Chapter 10

HEART BEATS AWAY FROM BURSTING. Eyes shut tight to keep out the leaking face-to-icicle freeze. If the coal-cloud sky of another world were squeezed between her tightly-shut eyes, diamond-shaped tears would stack snowdrift high.

Kicking legs burning under the fur, skin wind-whipped to numb. Pounding. Pounding. Pounding. Closer. Closer. Spittle spray from beneath the snout leaving shotgun-spread melt patterns in the beast's wake.

A warm hole called home cut through the iced earth and safe from harm far, far away. Small creatures from up on high shake and rattle needles from firs and pines.

Not us today, they say, not us today. Higher still, a White Goshawk perched on a branch lays pale eyes on a hawk of an entirely different kind circling the sky. From her bird's eye view, snow-tracked paws of vastly different size narrow in meter until they risk melding into one. Back down below, in that tiny vehicle of flight, there were no thoughts of what came next. A life had become a bringer of death, destroyer of the world, a new-found eleventh avatar of the dashavatara, or perhaps just Narasimha in a different guise, mistaking the powerless flight of fur for Hiranyakashipu.

Would his error come to be known only in extispicy strewn across the snow? Would a haruspex crawl down from a hemlock and read the will of gods in entrails? Or would not a drop of blood be left to divine, from a beast with jaws so big one gulp would call it closing time? And then the call of sweet surrender sounded deep inside. That occasion when the pace slows to expedite the inevitable and lift the unbearable weight of fear. The last step was ready to be counted. The snowball was resolved to being gobbled up. Some 1,600 pounds per square inch would melt her in an instant. It was time.

But just as she was certain the end had arrived, when the pain of her flight eclipsed the fear that she would die, when her pace had slowed and she could no longer go on, certain the curtains on yet another life would be drawn, 1,000 pounds of murder ran right on by, showering her in powder and leaving her alive.

The massive backside of the beast was framed in a tiny blink. And then, out of the corner of her now expanding tunnel-visioned eye, she saw that three wolves had plotted a diagonal course to intercept the no-longer-running rabbit. But the bear cut across her brow and made a mad dash for the timber terion of death. Seeing a predator beyond their match coming head on, the trio stiffened into static shocked balls of spiky hair and snapping teeth.

Bear breath blew steam in the cold before letting out a pulsing bellow. Rabbit breaths kept the same pace despite her now firmly planted feet. Wolves sized up the wall between them and their first course of dinner.

The one with the grey eyes snarled, a flash of pink gums and white fangs framed beneath snout skin bunched up into itself. They grey eyed alpha gave a signal. The wolves fanned out, slowly moving in orbit around the giant, seeking to get behind his revolving flank, or merely seize the morsel behind it. The bear pivoted around the heart-attack rabbit, the lightning flash of snapping jaws cracking the air to test their range. One gets too close, and a bear paw flies, a glancing blow that still sends tufts of hair airborne.

The wolf yelps in retreat before the circle dance of death briefly fans out.

Up in air teased by raptor feathers, the grapefruit sky turned a shade of sanguinello.

The circle in the snow tightened. One set of fangs flew into the bear's backside, biting down to break through armor of fur and fat. Another set lunged and struck blood on his front-right leg, a spray of slobber covered his retreat.

Despite the pain, the bear kept its eye on the rabbit. Sensing the whip-like thrust of the grey-eyed killer's jowls a split-second before the attack, five six-inch claws attached to a hammer were thrown out as the wolf leaped in, smashing him square on the spine. A snap resounded like a lightning-shot branch pop. A tortured howl erupted so loudly the skin of every living thing crawled with goosebumps. The would-be killer collapsed into itself and through the powder.

The other two were too taken to murder to watch shallow breaths taper off in a shallow grave. Hunger, unlike grief, is irreducible. Spines still intact, they snapped at the bear's flank before windmill paws swung back to break bones and snatch lives.

Another shower of fur, puncture marks of pain and narrow retreat. But despite their fury, their dying brother finally started to suck out their resolve through labored breaths.

Before the fright-frozen rabbit, clouds formed over the would-be killer's grey eyes. Gasps for air sucked blood into punctured lungs. Eyeing the one it had given its life for, calm came over the hunter who would hunt no more. Hunger dissipated. Darkness came. Desire, and then self, were gone. The saturation shifted grey-eyed windows to snow-reflecting mirrors. Creatures of flight were poised to pick still warm flesh from bone.

Already out of range, the bear half-charged and threw out a heavy paw, feeling the wolves' will to fight had been lost.

The new-found pair who'd lost their third had no shot at taking out the terrestrial tank. Much had been lost for an already too-small bounty to snatch. And then, as quickly as it had all begun, their offense came to an end. The bear let out a snort. The rabbit remained still. But the bear's bounty had not been secured.

With the four-legged bandits slowly retreating into dusk, the bear turned its eyes on something small and shaking below. The ever-enlarging shadow of a horizontally-held bow drew a clockwise circle from midday to midnight, eclipsing the big dot which itself was eclipsing the small one.

As big snout inched in on that small, shivering thing, a shriek pierced the short-lived silence as hawk fell out of the sky.

The bear barely had a chance to look up before a bolt out of the darkening blue scooped up the rabbit in its talons. Bear lunged in vain as the bushy tail sailed above the tree line.

The big brown beast huffed hot air that melted hoarfrost from the lattice array of branches and warmed up lichen clinging to Siberian firs. Moss cut horizontal lines across the northern side of a bewitching white birch with bark peeled back revealing black in slits and slashes. Another bear, far, far away, which would've gobbled a rabbit in a heartbeat, was instead snatching cookies and candles off of an Amurian grave.

Though the rabbit may have wished the bear had snatched it up in his mighty jowls instead.

For salvation in such great heights was even more terrifying for a creature that burrowed until it found peace underground.

As hawk and rabbit rose, the sun met them on the way down. The turn of the Earth shook off the red and violet flowers from the indigo ink splash of empyreal blue. But then thunderheads rolled in shapes like a kraken, shooting black ink across the sky. The hawk cut through the growing darkness, a star sailor in space.

And somewhere high up in the infinite black, two red dots signaled like beacons from outer space. The hawk shot up like an arrow until the blue faded to black and the red ovals grew larger.

THUMP! THUMP! THUMP! went the rabbit heart.

The ovals grew larger and larger, until they cut out an increasingly bigger share of the all–encompassing dark. The hawk in flight lost form and merely became an expression of speed. The rabbit dissolved into an increasingly rapid heartbeat. Toward the red ovals they raced as she braced for impact.

10...9...8...7...6...5...4...3...2...1...

With an earth shattering smash a plunger sucked the heart right out of her lungs. The little girl awoke with a cry and a gasp. The red ovals opened to reveal the sleeping chamber of the kind old man.

Chapter 11

BACK IN THE KINGDOM OF Blankets, Lana waited for her heart to still. She quickly placed hand on hand to be certain she'd still feel the skin of a girl. Those hands then raised, forming a cup on her face. Her quick breaths tapered off in a wet tickle against her palms. Moisture settled in river beds that psychics read to plot courses of life.

But whose story would a master of divination be telling? In now clammy palms she could still feel the snow compacted between pads, cold air on her face, bear breath on her back — the all-enveloping cloud of fear beginning to suffocate her burning lungs.

She wriggled her toes under the heavy blankets, creating a slow-moving wave of warmth. What a contrast to that flight in frozen dreamscape that seemed as real as real could be. As her eyes adjusted, the marmalade light from the fireplace continued to dance beneath her door. The faint outline of a doll-stacked credenza protruded as darkness out of the darkness.

The stuffed savannah to her side looked on.

She struggled to make sense of it all. Why did that bad dream feel so real?

With the last speck of sleeping dust rubbed from her eyes, Lana felt it was time to go, whatever time it was, wherever going went. So she shimmied down the double-stacked marshmallow mattress until tiny feet touched the smooth, warm wood.

Lana walked over to the door and pulled it open until the marmalade spread covered up the blankets. Tiptoeing halfway across the living room, she stopped to take it all in. The kitchen table remained clear. The rocking chair stood unrocked. The crackle of the hearth played like the oldest record in the catalogue of human warmth, its light painting every wall the color of Arcadia at sunset. Beyond the round front door was the cold black tunnel burrowed beneath a frozen world.

Doubt crept in like a draft. Something was calling her back.

Then a voice cut through the fireplace canticle.

"Sleep well?"

She turned around to see the kind old man standing in his bedroom doorway.

"I had a nightmare," she replied.

"Oh my. Tell me, what did you see?"

"There was all of this darkness and then I fell through the clouds. And then I was a rabbit in the snow and a bear was chasing me! And then there were wolves, and they had a terrible fight and then whoosh! A big bird grabbed me and took me back to the sky. It was incredible! But then this big monster came and turned the sky black. We went up, up, up to get away. And then I woke up."

The old man exhaled sharply.

"That was no dream."

"Of course it was a dream!"

"No. I'm afraid it wasn't. Remember how I told you that room was a key to all the rooms in you?"

"Yes."

"Well, that was you, in a different place and time!"

"But how? I was a rabbit!"

"That's right. You were, you are! And you have been so much more than that!"

"I, I don't understand."

"No one does, not really. But we have all lived different lives. And all of those lives are a part of us. It is easy to think that some are past, some future, and just one present. But in truth, they are all here, all of the time."

Lana shot him a quizzical look. He read her face and replied.

"You don't have to make sense of it. Most never do. People tend to live their lives trying not to even ask the question. Who am I? Why am I really here? Because trying to see what we really are can be a very scary thing indeed. Especially when you are married to one ripple on the sea."

Lana remained stupefied by his string of seemingly non-sensical words.

The old man rubbed his chin for a minute before his eyes lit up.

"Do you like music?"

"Sure!"

"Great. Maybe you can think about it like this. Right now, you are a note. Let's say concert C," he said, humming a sound. "Now, is that a song?"

"No."

"You're right. That isn't a song. A song is made up of many notes. For example, I'm sure you know this one," he continued, humming the melody to Blue Wagon.

"Yes! Yes! Crocodile Ghena sings that song!"

"That's right. And you see, there's an AM, and then a DM, G7, C and E7," he said, slowly voicing each note. "Now that song is not any one of those notes. It is all of the notes, and the spaces between the notes. The song cannot be any one moment in time. For any moment in time is just one note. It has to be all the moments, one flowing to the next, from beginning to end. And it gets even more complicated than that!"

"It does?" Lana asked in disbelief, already lost in the first part of the lesson.

"Let's say instead of a children's song, you have a symphony. A big one! And in a symphony, you have many people playing many parts. There are lots of different instruments. Even the same instruments don't always play the same thing. Sometimes some instruments are silent while others carry on. Sometimes they all play together. Sometimes one part gets to shine in a solo. And sometimes a musician does nothing more than hit a triangle or crash cymbals at the very end.

"Even those modest parts have their place in the whole. And you are the same. Right now, you are a clarinet playing a concert C. Yesterday you were playing a D — tomorrow an A. And that rabbit you saw was you playing not a clarinet, but a violin. And there are so many yous playing their own parts across all of space and time. And alongside you is every other person playing their part, in every version of themselves. And when you get to hear it all at the same time, that is when you meet God."

Lana screwed up her eyes, all sixes and sevens.

"You talk so funny," she said, summating 13 out from his ominous musings.

"I certainly do," he said with a laugh. "Just remember this one thing. We are all music. Can you remember that?"

"I can."

"Good. As for your little bird, he is a very key part of this song, and the nightmare man doesn't like it at all. He wants to take ink and pour it on the sheet music, so all of the notes become one big black nothing. He knows that if he gets your little bird, the world will fall out of pitch. And if he has his way, the music will die."

"So, I really do have to save my little bird?"

"You do!"

Lana tried to take another step forward, but her feet felt frozen in place. She lowered her eyes in shame.

"Mister, I want to save my little bird. I really do. But I don't wanna go back out there. I'm afraid! Does that make me bad?"

"No, no, no, that is perfectly natural. Why, I wouldn't want to go out into that dark tunnel either, not when I can stay right here in all this warmth. And I'm a big old man who knows those catacombs fairly well, and not a little girl with no sense of direction in a darkened world."

"What ... what should I do?"

The kind old man reflexively rubbed his chin.

"Well, you could always stay here. We have everything we need! The fire always burns, the kettle is always set to boil, the dumplings always filled, the cookies always warm, the jam always fresh – all and sundry in abundance. Why, there isn't a whit of darkness here not licked by flames, not a hint of must not doused in citrus and cinnamon spice. Even the spiders make webs of rainbow fiber. And at least for now, the dark water cannot come this way."

"But if I stay here, I cannot save my little bird from the nightmare."

"That is also true. So…"

"So I'm going to go find him!"

"Even if it's dark out there?"

"Even if it's dark!"

"So you tell me, little girl. Why will you go out there in the cold, dark world to find a little bird rather than stay down here where it's warm?"

Lana pensively bit her lip. And then a light came to her eyes.

"I know why!"

"You do? Then tell me: Why?"

"Because you can't be warm if someone you love is cold! Like when Mama hugs me. She always says I warm her heart. And if my little bird is out there in the dark, I want to warm his heart too! Because if the nightmare man finds him, then it doesn't matter where I am. I will feel so bad! But…"

"Yes?"

"I … I'm still scared."

"I know you're scared. But let me ask you, are you still going to go, even if you're scared?"

"Well … yes, I will still go."

"But why?"

"I … I think I will lose something bigger than my little bird if I stay down here because I'm afraid."

The kind old man gave her a solemn nod.

"See. It turns out you understand everything after all."

Chapter 12

BEFORE SETTING OFF, THE FLOATING hand brought Lana a kerosene lantern, which the kind old man claimed burned like an eternal flame as long as it wasn't tipped over. He said most spirits one might encounter would not be able to penetrate the halo of light, though they might try to scare Lana into whipping up a storm and knocking over her hurricane lamp.

The talk of spirits gave Lana a start. Was the dark not scary enough without having banshees and bugaboos to contend with? And what about her little bird? How would it survive its journey through the deep without a light to guide it, and ghosts looking to gobble it up?

As the door opened before her and the cold, musty air came in, Lana hesitantly stepped out on Bambi legs. Turning around and seeing that circle of light and warmth cut from the darkness, what with the marmalade sea, tea and cookies on offer, she had to fight every instinct not to go bounding back between the old man's legs.

"Are you sure you're ready?"

Lana sighed as deeply as her little lungs would allow.

"I'm ready."

She was lying.

"Okay then. And just remember: As dark as it gets, just like your little bird, the light is within you too. You find that, and you'll be okay. Good luck!"

The two shared their last goodbyes before he moved to seal up his barrel-bottomed abode.

And just as the space between door and frame became a waning crescent of light cut against the darkness like Sagittarius 'bow, Lana had to beat down the panic in her double-time heart.

Once the overlap of ecliptic longitude was complete, all the world turned black, sans the lamp-cut citrine circle shining for a shaky-handed sojourner. Lana breathed out mist into the yellow light and set off into all of that darkness.

Pushing ahead, the diameter of the tunnel dilated. What had once been a hole big enough for a rabbit would easily accommodate creatures of far greater dimensions. Lana raised the lamp to the earthen wall.

Under the light, she saw perfectly symmetrical helical grooves running down the tunnel. Tiny tallies and sketches traced the fluting in infinite repetition. It looked like the atavistic language of cannibals whose world-view was a violent expression of murder.

Lana extended a tiny digit to touch the etchings. Fingertip oils leaked into strokes and incisions, taking on a brief red luminescent glow. Lana's eyes grew wide as the red light rode the length of the helical line before fading out. At first a muffled rumbling could be heard down the passage. The sound grew to a whooshing rapids' swell. Lana's heart looked to jump right out of her chest. On little legs she ran from the still unseen surge.

The hurricane lamp swung in her hand as if caught in a storm. Sweat began to form on her tiny palm, dripping down the handle. Lana clinched her tiny fist as the thin metal handle hook looked to slip and slide from circle of light to crash-darkness egress. Squeezing somehow seemed to further lubricate the metal. Fatigue was working its way in.

Lana felt her fingers peeled from the hilt by a maleficent force. The lamp fell like a Chinese lantern shot out of the sky. Inches form hitting the ground, Lana reflexively lunged and caught the handle midair.

The flame danced to and fro against the glass globe.

"Whoo!" Lana exclaimed, wiping the sweat from her brow and saying a wordless prayer of grace to the solitary flame. A maniacal cackle resonated in the darkness, turning rabbit skin to goose flesh. And then the swell behind her only grew in intensity. Lana went running to catch a rabbit heart that jumped right out of her chest.

The tiny halo of light swung to the ebb and flow of sightless terror. But without prying phantasmal fingers, her grip remained sure.

The rumble and rush of unseen cataclysm grew. Lana felt herself again a rabbit running from a bear. She could almost hear the crunch of packed powder under her feet.

'I don't want to die, I don't want to die, I don't want to die!' her mind chanted to the blood organ dirge. It was a funeral song of rhythm without melody serenading a soul too young to have such hymn in her liturgy.

But pray as she might, she couldn't stop the onslaught of the unknown. There had to be some way out. The torrent was gaining fast as Lana's legs sighed for slow. She let out a cry that echoed until hitting the bottom of a bottomless well. She felt spray on her neck, just like the hot spittle of a bear bearing down on its prey. The rush was so loud Lana felt the world of sound drowned out, foreshadowing the inundation of her lungs. Beads of dark water flecked the swinging lantern. The tunnel narrowed. The air thinned. Darkness and infinite tons of dirt and death closed in.

So, it was possible for someone to both drown and be buried alive. The nausea pushed the butterflies in her belly to escape. Lana felt herself choking on thousands of frantically flapping wings. A dizzy spell looked to send her for a final spill. Lana fell forward. She instinctually winced as her body was set to crush burning glass into the dust, only to be extinguished by blackening rush.

A sharp tug at her hood. Her body plucked against gravity's pull. Somehow the lamp stays held upright. Hands slid and wrenched themselves beneath her armpits.

Lana winced at the pinch. Back pulled to the wall, she was yanked right off her feet. A whirling under sole as spray commenced. She was pulled right through a hidden passage. The flame in the globe feverishly danced, but not its last dance.

Chapter 13

" HOLD ON!" A GRUFF ADOLESCENT voice shouted, firmly planting Lana's feet on the ground.

The young lad struggled to pull a round stone into place as water streamed into the crypt.

"Don't just stand there, help me!"

The boulder the young man was bearing against easily weighed a ton.

Lana hurriedly looked around, spotting a small ledge where she could set the lamp down. She took several steps forward but then froze in place, not knowing how her soft touch could help move an unmovable mass.

"Well," the boy said, grunting as he drove his shoulder into the burden with all of his might, water gushing forth and lapping at their feet.

Certain she had more to offer than an unavailing gesture, Lana nonetheless placed her soft hands on all that hardness. And to her great surprise, like magic, the stone rolled into the slot with a resounding thump. Seemingly air tight, neither water nor the deafening rush on the other side of the stone seeped in. What had flowed in was carried away by drainage grooves until there was not a drop left of the barely averted inundation.

The young man excitedly slapped his knee and rejoiced.

Boy, that was close! I thought you was gonna get carried off by all that blackness," he said, pulling out a cigarette and lighting up with a satisfied "aah".

Lana stepped back and picked up the lamp, holding it between them. With a skeptical eye, she surveyed the adolescent who stood on the edge of her hurricane light.

In the gloom it was hard to tell if the furrow in his brow was cut by shadows or frowns. His dark track jacket had a torn sleeve. A hood was pulled down over a beanie, which was pulled down even lower. The circles were so dark under his eyes, you'd think they were bruises, if it were not for the fact that on the left side he had a black eye too. The tips of his fingers were so dirty one could barely tell he was wearing fingerless gloves. He looked like he was 13 going on 40.

Lana breathed in his lethal relief and coughed.

"Smoking is bad for you."

"Drownin 'is worse. Ain't ya gonna thank me? I just saved yer life ya know. And yer gonna lecture me 'bout smokin'? Where'd ya get yer manners?"

Even in the dark, Tima could almost see Lana's cheeks go red.

"Thank you," she said, still somewhat reluctantly, as deep down she was struggling to fit the image of a smoking hoodlum of the kind her parents had so often warned her about into the shape of a hero. But a hero he had been.

Lana stood there, trying to find words she just didn't have.

"Didn't yer mama teach ya not to stare?" Tima chimed in to break the tension, taking a paper-cracking drag before exhaling.

"I wasn't staring!"

"Why yes ya were. Just 'bout needed a spatula to pry 'dem peepers offa ' me! So, what's yer name anyways ya peepin' lil' thing?"

"Lana," she said meekly.

"Lana like Svetlana?"

"No. Just Lana like Lana."

"Well I'll be damned, that's the strangest thing," he said, lips puckering in a whistle of surprise. "I don't know no parents who ever just upped and named their kid a lil' name!"

"But I am small!" Lana protested.

"That you are, Lana like Lana," he said, taking another lazy drag and filling the space with stink.

"It's just Lana!"

"Like I said! So what? You ain't gonna ask me my name?"

She pursed her lips.

"Well...?"

"What's your name?" she diffidently complied.

"Me? Why I'm Timofey, but my friends call me Tima!"

"Nice to meet you, Tima."

"Likewise," Tima nonchalantly replied, blowing a smoke ring above his head. "So what in the devil are ya doing down here, Lana? Tryin' to get ya'self killed?"

"No!" she said in a low voice." I'm trying to find my little bird."

"Lil' bird?" Tima said quizzically, arching his head back to spit through re-puckered lips. "You ain't gonna find no damn bird down here!"

"You're wrong!" she said with unexpected vigor. "I know he's down here."

"How da' hell a bird get down here?"

Lana became crestfallen.

Tima shot her a mischievous glance through lantern-lit wisps. A barely perceptible glint came to his adumbrated eyes, which were well-trained on finding chinks in children's armor.

"Don't tell me: YOU took him down here?"

"No, I didn't! The nightmare man, he chased us!"

"Nightmare man? Which one would that be? Where I come from, there's an awful lotta nightmare men."

"Where do you come from?"

"Well, down here, sorta'," he said, taking one last drag and flicking a red-tailed comet across the room. "Really I live down in the metro tunnels. Sometimes above ground, at Leningradsky Station. But mostly down below."

Lana looked at him with astonishment.

"Why do you live down here?"

To stay warm stupid!," Tima said, arching his head back to expectorate into the dark. "You ever slept on the streets when it's 40 below? Ya damn near freeze to death. In fact, I know ya freeze to death. Happens to da' bums all the time. Then those snowdrops melt and their spirits drip on down!"

"They do?"

"Hell, yeah they do! I reckon' they get stuck here forever once spring comes. Never found no way in life, never find no way out in death. And I'll tell ya what! You can tell how they died by their shine. You look real close and ya see that light comin' right off their skin."

"I don't believe you!"

"It's true, mark my words, when ya see one you'll believe me. It's like this. Yellow ones done drank themselves to death. Green ones drank Boryarshnik, brown ones shot dope."

"What's dope?"

"Heroin, stupid!"

Lana paused.

"What's heroin?"

"Don't ya know nothin'? Heroin's a drug! Ya take it and ya get all whacky," Tima said, leaning over with his eyes rolled up, his mouth hanging open and a trail of drool hanging out of his mouth.

"Ewwwwwwwww, stop it!"

"What? Ya don't like that? Then ya won't like dope! Dope makes ya look like that!"

"My mom said drugs and alcohol are bad. They turn people into zombies."

"Well, your mama is more right than she knows! Hell, I reckon' some of 'em would be lucky to be zombies. At least zombies get to stay up there. But it ain't just the junkies and drunks."

"What's a junkie?"

"People who do drugs, silly!"

"Oh."

"But like I said, they ain't the only ones down here. Why, the light blue ones simply died from the cold. Maybe that hurts most of all. They ain't even numb before they go numb. And ya wanna hear 'bout the red ones?" Tima asked, leaning in with devilish eyes glowing under the lamp.

"Wha … what happened to the red ones?"

"They got murdered," he said in a low, ominous voice.

Lana's eyes grew to take in the terror.

She leaned toward Tima's underlit face and whispered, "Who killed them?"

"Old folk say the capitalists. But I figure the same ones who killed 'em were killin' people long before 'dem capitalists ever came."

"What's a capitalist?"

"Jesus, girl, you ask a lotta questions. A capitalist is someone who'll gut ya for a buck and say it's just business. They drive around in black boomers, wear black jackets, have heads like turnips and pockets full of cabbage. Better 'dan a comm-u-nist I guess. They'll kill ya simply so ya can't have a buck to begin with."

"My grandma says the communists were good. She says they built a lot of things."

"Built a loada' crap!"

His blue streak left Lana red in the face.

"I see ya don't like how I talk. Sorry 'bout that. A boy's bound ta' get some dirt in his mouth livin' underground."

"Then why not come up? That way, you won't get any dirt in your mouth."

Tima was tickled by her earnestness. And then all that innocence struck him somewhere deeper. He stepped back from the lamp until the devil in his own eyes dimmed.

"Look," he said with a sigh. "I live in the tunnels 'cause I ain't got nowhere else to go. My dad, my dad was a bad man. He done me real bad. Did things to me … I can't even tell a little girl like you the thing he and his friends did to me. One day I couldn't take 'dem things no more and I stabbed him, right in the belly. I wanted to kill him, I swear I did! He didn't die, though he sure squealed like a pig. I ran out the door then and there and never came back. In the summer ya can live above the streets and under the sun. But then ya ain't gotta worry 'bout the cold. It's the grownups that get ya above ground. Some monsters out there catch a kid and do things ya don't want no part of. In the winter, it's usually the cold that gets ya. No. Living in the tunnels ain't so bad.

"Just us kids down there, bunched up like pups on a pipe. Ain't no grown folk comin' down there to get ya. Maybe some city worker from time to time, but they just shoo you away like a dog. Normal folk don't know what to do once they catch ya other than cut ya loose. That is, unless they the kind that wanna cut ya. But most tha' time most folk'd rather not look. You show them too much of what they don't want to be seein' in 'demselves, how little they care about the things they think they should be carin' for. No, the tunnels are good, the tunnels are safe. You get to be what good folk want ya to be: Invisible. And ya learn quick enough ya wanna be invisible too. 'Cause it really is better to freeze than to let one of 'dem lookers get 'der mits on ya."

Tima turned his face away from the flame. Lana stepped forward and took his hand.

"It's okay, Tima."

Tima shuddered, pulling his hand away from Lana's.

"Come on now, don't get all gooey on me!"

"I'm sorry."

"Forget about it. Now look. I gotta get back to my pack and you gotta find, what was that, yer little bird?"

"Yes."

"Well, ain't no way ya comin' back the way ya came 'less ya can hold yer breath for a long, long time. But that's okay, there's all kinds of ways to make it in this place. And I'll be damned if ya don't have a lamp. That's sure gonna make it easier. Just gotta find a way outta' here, that's all."

Tima snatched up the lamp, which swung wildly in his hand.

"Be careful," Lana squeaked. "If you drop it the light will go out!"

"Relax. I come from 10 generations of jugglers," Tima teased, dancing in tandem with the flame, feigning to drop the lamp, as he bandied it from hand to hand like a hot potato.

"Stop it!" Lana shouted, charging up to the adolescent elf playing keep away with impish delight.

Suddenly the rumble of rock against rock stopped them both in their tracks.

"Did ya hear that?" Tima asked with a slight tremor in his voice.

Lana slowly nodded her head.

The chamber rumbled again, followed by the sound of moving earth crumbling to the ground. Tima coughed as dust showered their heads.

"That's not good," Tima said, trying to suppress his dry hack. 'That's not good at all."

Chapter 14

THE RUMBLING CONTINUED TO GROW and grow. Tima waved the lamp over the circular stone. Fissures were forming along the edges. Water bubbles percolated through lightning crack lines. Then the sound of a water-sprung leak punctured the fictle gnar.

"Oh no, it's 'bout to give! We gotta get outta' here!"

Tima frantically ran around the room flashing the lamp every which way looking for an exit.

Lana stood in place as the room growled like a belly before bedtime after dinner had been skipped on account of deficit, trying her best not to eruct her growing sense of panic with a scream.

The sound of splintering stone intensified as water bubbles kept kissing until they became leaks. Lana's eyes followed the wavering hurricane light as Tima rounded the wall. She lifted her boot and put it back down with a shallow splash.

"Tima," she cried, running in the direction of the orbiting light.

"Lana, over here!"

On the other side of the chamber a semi-circular alcove was cut into the wall. Surmounting the semicircle, the gaping mouth of Anubis protruded from the rock. In niches on each side, statues of a snake and nursing jackal lay.

Tima hopped up on a statue-less pedestal in the hollowed-out space. A large, rusty grate had been fitted in the stone slabs. He crouched down to place the lamp back on the ground. Standing back up, Tima grabbed onto the bars and pulled. The rusty metal flaked under his fingers. Working from side to side, the worn-partition soon popped out with a screech. Tima tossed the rusty grating to the ground as Lana held a light down below.

Tima planed his elbows on the edge of the ingress. After kicking off against the wall several times, he finally managed to pull himself up.

"Lana, give me the lamp. Then I'll pull you up!"

Lana hopped up onto the pedestal and arched up on tiptoes until Tima got a grip on the handle.

The next great crack was followed by a crunching pop as a piece of stone shot across the room and water started gushing in. Up above, the eyes of Anubis glowed red. Jackal pups wriggled; a snake slithered.

"Pull me up, Tima, pull me up!" she cried.

Tima looked down at Lana, washed in the coral light of oculus canid. There was something cold and baleful in his gaze.

"Tima, please, please!" Lana squealed as the first wave of water lapped at the soles of her boots.

"Tima!"

Her blood-curdling scream snapped the cold out of his reptilian eyes. The red-eyed burn above faded to afterglow. Tima shook out the hesitancy with the wag of his head, got down on his belly and slithered until his arms were dangling over the ledge.

"Here! Take my hands!"

More cracking. Soon the stone was set to completely give, letting the uninterrupted rush in. Lana made a splash every time she hopped up to put her soft hands in Tima's grimy paws. When Tima got a hold of her, pull as he might, he didn't have the strength to lift her up.

"Whew! You're too damned heavy. Lana, you gotta walk up the wall. Don't just hang there like some fat kid on the monkey bars."

Lana grabbed hold of his hands again and frantically kicked her feet against the wall.

"Not like that! You ain't some dog tryna' bury his bone. Plant yer feet and walk up!"

"I can't!" Lana cried, water now up to her ankles.

"Well ya better damn well learn 'cause I don't know where this here shaft goes, but I sure as hell know we're both gonna' drown like rats if we don't book it! Ain't no time for cryin' now. Now's the time for movin'. Ya get up here and you can do all the damn cryin' you want! Now grab my hands and move!"

The water was nearly parallel to Lana's pedestal perch. Her tears now falling into the flow, Lana shot her arms up, which Tima grabbed with rabbit-snare resolve. He cursed Lana something fierce when she let herself momentarily dangle, before returning to her scampering ways. He finally got her to bend her back enough to plant her feet and wall walk as he reeled her in. With more than a bit of strain he managed to pull them both back into the passage. But just as he was laying there panting on his belly and hoping for a rest, the stone below completely shattered. Total inundation ensued.

"Run, Lana! Run!"

And run she did, until the chamber filled up like a bucket under a broken village hand-pump well. Lana kept screaming, "Wait up!" as Tima's longer legs took him and the swinging light to the edge of Lana's sight.

But then the lamp suddenly stopped swinging and Lana ran right into the back of Tima's legs.

He yelped at Lana's nearly perilous push as he girded himself against gravity.

She called out his name, only to be silenced by the dread flashing in his eyes.

Without a word, he waved the lantern beyond, showing Lana there was no place for his next step. Beyond, the whole world gurgled in darkness.

"Oh crap, oh crap, oh crap!"

"Tima, what are we gonna do?"

Tima stuck his head out the end of the culvert and lent his ear to the void.

In the unseen expanse he heard rocks groan. From up on high, water dripped into a vast plunge pool, like nature's own suikinkutsu formed by chthonic hands.

He turned back and listened to the waxing of the freshet flow.

"Okay, okay, okay, okay," he nervously repeated, steeling his resolve.

Tima took a deep breath and sat down. Pulling off his down-at-the-heel boots, he tied the strings together and threw them over his neck.

"Come on, Lana, get yer boots off."

"Take my boots off? Why?"

"There's water down there. We gotta jump and wet boots are gonna make ya sink like stone!"

"Are you crazy? I'm not jumping down there!"

"Either yer jumping down there or all that water rumbling behind us is gonna blow ya down. So, get yer damn boots off!"

"No, Tima!" Lana shrieked.

Tima got up on his haunches and looked at Lana, holding the lamp between them. The insuperable surge roaring like time and tide personified and intensified in the rear.

Lana's bottom lip quivered uncontrollably. Her wet eyes glistened under the lamp, lambent tears falling like sap down a spruce.

"I know yer scared. Hell, I'm scared! But sometimes life don't give ya no good choices. We're goin' down one way or the other. Better we make that choice how. Now please. Get yer damn boots off before I yank them off! I ain't playin' no games, Lana … NOW!"

Lana sobbed as she dropped to her backside and pulled at her boots.

"Faster dammit, faster!"

The second she wrangled her boots off, Tima snatched them up, tying the laces together. He then pulled his own boots off his neck, tied up both pairs in a bow and tossed them down. Soon thereafter, he heard a splash resound throughout the grotto.

"Well, that sounds deep enough … I think. Just hope we can find the damn things floatin' down there … if we make it down there. Now I'm gonna toss down the lamp. Think of it like a star falling to the bottom of a well. And we'll be chasing that star's tail down. I mean, at least we'll have a bit of light before it all goes black."

Lana shivered. The rapids neared. Tima took Lana's little hand, gripping the lamp in his left. Lana squeezed with quiet desperation.

"Now keep your body straight. Before ya hit the water, point your toes and keep all your muscles real tight."

Lana's breath caught a cool air current of ephemeral calm.

"Okay. On the count of three ... one ... two," Tima said, tossing the lamp down, "three!"

Their sight sailed a sky-fall lantern. With a spring in his legs and a pull of Lana's hand, the kids followed the shrinking aureole into the deep.

Their tandem scream resounded on the richter scale, kicking up microseisms on a spinning drum. The cool air rush of darkness caressed their skin as epinephrine shot through their blood. Then the lamp hit the water, setting all that moving blackness alight.

Tima and Lana hit the amber lake foot first, shooting like bullets into dazzling depths. Their body splash ripples turned the surface of the plunge pool into a seal of reticulated gold. Lana continued to sink down and down, like an ancient insect in a sea of tree resin. She couldn't think to fear as she floated down the golden fire deep, 10 million years of inclusion excavated by immense wonder.

Who knew one could descend into Heaven? Euphoria quickly took the place of air. It was all so beautiful. Darkness lapped at the edges of gilded deep.

Chapter 15

WHILE TREADING GOLDEN WATER, TIMA spotted their boots floating like a four-squid foxtrot. What he didn't see was Lana's golden hair flowing above the gilt.

Panicking, he dove into the blinding light. The seconds counted down as the depths failed to produce the outline of a water-fall angel. Running out of air, he expelled a sea of opalescent bubbles like an eructing Oyster. Up, up, up, he surfaced with a gasp.

Steadying himself, Tima took a deep breath and plunged back into the brilliance. He went deeper and deeper, until the burn began settling in his lungs. He fought the panic. Then, just below, what appeared to be a bluefire jellyfish jacket was undulating in the water.

Tima darted downward until he saw tiny hands stretched out beneath the pulsating bell. He grabbed Lana's hand and pulled her up from the pyrite paradise. His lungs were pumping bullet ant venom on the ascent.

With one final thrust their heads surfaced the amber lake. A blackwater fall rushed unseen from the culvert above.

Tima held onto Lana as he gasped for breath, struggling to keep her above water. Each flap of the arm sent El Dorado gold across Lake Guatavita.

Despite being weighed down by wringing-wet winter clothes, the water was surprisingly buoyant. How on God's Earth did that little girl sink like a rock? Tima wrapped his arm around Lana's chest and swam in search of a bank, as gilded cat paws traipsed across the glowing water in their wake.

He was practically floundering by the time he found a rocky outcrop and managed to drag Lana up, depositing her on the cold, wet stone.

He couldn't tell if it was just the reflection of her jacket and the golden light, but he caught a hint of blue in her small lips. He put a hand to her cheeks, which were rubbery wet and filled with chill.

"God dammit, girl, God dammit!"

Tima blew air into Lana's little lungs just like he had seen in the movies, but she didn't move.

"Not like that, not like that," he fretted, tilting her head back and blowing more panic into her.

Breath after breath after breath, she failed to stir. But just as Lana appeared ready to give up the ghost, one more go she convulsed, hacking up luster from her lungs.

She shot up a shaking cough machine, expectorating liquid sunshine every which way.

Her spittle mottled Tima's face in golden glitter shine.

"Ewwwwwwwwww," he cried out, immediately jettisoning Lana's brush with death. "Cooties, ya gave me cooties!"

With her final cough of saffron mist scintillating in a dank cave, she looked at Tima with beaming eyes.

"You saved me! You saved me!" she cried, jumping up to give him a hug.

Tima immediately tried to peal her paws from his neck.

"Get off of me, will ya? I'm starting to think I shoulda' left ya down there!"

"You're my hero!"

"I don't wanna be yer hero, ya goof! Ya shoulda' told me ya can't swim! Ya sank like a damn rock."

"But I … I can swim. My dad taught me when we went down to the sea."

"He sure as hell didn't teach ya good! Why, you could just 'bout walk on that there golden water it's so floaty!"

"I don't know, really I don't! When we hit the water it was like 'SPLASH ' and then I just felt so good and warm I wanted to be there forever and ever and ever!"

"Well, ya just 'bout stayed there forever, ya nut!"

Lana's arms slid off of Tima like seaweed.

"I'm sorry, Tima."

Tima looked at her all wet and pathetic.

"There, there, that's all right now," he said, patting her on the shoulder. He proceeded to reach into his pocket and pulled out his packet of cigarettes, which were soaked through and through.

"Rats!" he exclaimed, throwing them to the ground. They slapped against the rock with a spongy plop.

High up above, the black water continued to empty up into the plunge pool. A barometric breeze moved through the grotto, filling their wet clothes with cold. The pair shivered in unison.

"We gotta find a way to get warm before we freeze to death!"

Lana nodded her head as her teeth chattered.

Tima scanned the dimming water and caught sight of a small bit of fortune.

The foxtrotting shoe-knot octopus caught a wave and headed for the bank. The falling water pushed it closer and closer to the outcrop.

"That's right, that's right, come on over!" he hooted, running back to the plunge pool. As the falling water pushed the shoes toward the bank, Tima waded into the water, playing tag with the ebb and flow before finally hooking the knots with his fingers and pulling them in.

"At least we got our shoes back. Though they're even soggier than my damn smokes!"

Tima struggled to undo the tight, wet knots before putting on his right boot with a squish.

He groaned, slipping the left one on.

Lana plopped down and cringed as sock-clad toes mashed soles of moss.

As more and more water fell from above, the liquid lake of gold was slowly adulterated to burnt sienna. Steam rose above the surface. Haze plunged the room in gloom.

"We should get outta' here," Tima said, walking up the slip-off slope and along the ridge. Lana followed on slick heels looking for any excuse to slip.

Their wet suction feet made an off-tempo plunger duet sans trumpet. The plangent pops echoed en marche.

Unlike the previous escape tunnels cut with mans' hands and filled with dark, they had now entered an underworld of nature's will and unearthly wonder.

Flower-shaped drop stone glistened like frost. Phosphorescent algae created day-glow walls marbled in motley strokes.

The two carefully carried on, spellbound by the subterranean gleam of Persephone's palace.

But the brume grew with the stygian waterfall, throwing a wet towel on the grotto glitter and cutting down their visibility to the tips of their noses. Lana instinctively latched a hand onto the back of Tima's hoodie. Tima had nothing to hold onto but himself.

At first they could merely move around the dimming pool. But then an underground passage revealed itself on the bend.

Pushing through, once the water was obscured by the meander of rock and earth, the two were thrust back into darkness. The passage narrowed until Tima found himself squeezing sideways through jagged spaces.

What was left of the glitter was nothing but a memory in the pitch-black crack. The creep of claustrophobia sank in. Smaller, Lana moved more easily through the rock, but the atmospheric pressure of crushing small spaces weighed on her imagination.

Every time heart beseeched lungs to breathe at a hyper-speed clip, she kneaded Tima's pullover, forming 33 knots in her makeshift prayer rope.

In the lead, the darkness turned Tima into an inverted synesthete. Black was no longer a color, it was something he could bump his head on, breathe in, taste and hear as the thrumming of blood in his own ears. Darkness was the color and shape of memories forming in the bubbling tar pit of trauma. And Lana's clasp was his unseen anchor of light.

Time itself was blotted in blackness as well. The meter of sidesteps squeezed through crevasse cut the quarter note beats per minute to single digits. The whole world was chopped and screwed in the black chasm warp.

So, for seconds, or perhaps centuries, after tracing every zig-zag cut through stone, in a flash a crack of lighting became apparent on the other side.

"There, there, you see that?" Tima said, barely containing his excitement at the prospect of space and light.

"I do, I do!" Lana joyously squealed.

The two squirmed through the space until it opened up, letting in more and more light. Finally, they were able to make a sideways exit through the rift.

Chapter 16

BEYOND THE EGRESS, WHAT THE young explorers saw, in spite of all of that space and light, was categorically grey.

The sweeping catacomb was an open-plan office with rows upon rows of desks. Every imaginable variety of riff-raff rushed about, while innumerable lines behind numbered windows cut into the walls snaked every which way. Through glass scratched to abstraction and over intercoms that translated angry cries into static crackles, the wretched shouted back and forth under the earth.

Surmounting each window, an archaic take-a-number system of pulleys and levers spinning metal plates snapped absurdly high digits into place. Dead, shuffling souls held numbers so long they appeared printed on ticker tape.

Lining the walls, cataloged skulls in glass cases evoked Parisian catacombs and Cambodian chambers of torture on Strychnine Hill. The endless clacking of keys, dings and sliding carriage returns blended in with the flapping wings of bats and the cacophony of underground paper shuffling. Hundreds of hanging Edison bulbs kept the entire operation alight.

A massive wicket gate lay shut on the other side of the room. Interspaced throughout the cavern, massive stalagmites some 50-feet high literally held up the world.

"Where are we?" Lana asked.

"Ya got me," Tima replied. "Maybe we should ask somebody for help."

He looked around the red-tape labyrinth and tentatively headed to the first window on the left, cutting in front of a crooked queue.

A man with a yellow hue practically adorned in mummy rags screamed at Tima: "Hey, boy! Wait yer turn!"

"Wait my turn for what?"

"To get in line, ya knucklehead!"

"To get in line for what, Gramps?"

"You got a lip on you, don't ya? I had a lip on me too before I ended up down here. Just you wait!"

"Spare me the sermon. Just tell me — what the hell is this place?"

"This place," he said, pupils spinning in bisque-colored sclera,"is the place where the dispossessed and possessed go to repossess themselves of their possessorship so that they may be disposed of!"

"Say that again?"

"The possessed are dispossessed and taking numbers to repossess! The possessed are dispossessed and taking numbers to repossess! The possessed..." the man continued to chant like a malfunctioning mechanical parrot.

Tima and Lana took several steps back as a mad cackle accompanied the ramped-up pupil spin.

"Pssssssssst," whispered someone with a blue-glow in the corner.

Tima and Lana hesitantly walked over to the man, who appeared in his 50s with a moth-eaten red sweater and a pair of bent spectacles. His wild hair was a salt-and-pepper swirl of cotton candy suspended in pomade.

"You wanna know where you are? This is where us snowdrops go to get our bury bindles."

"Does anyone down here talk a damned bit of sense?" Tima said with a huff.

"Simply put: We go here to get permission to die!"

"What do you mean by get per-missing to die? Ain't ya already dead?"

"PERMISSION. And technically yes, we are already 'dead'. But seeing as we got taken out and buried under the snow, we aren't officially dead, as no one has found us yet. So, we need to get our death certificates. Until we get

~ 80 ~

our death certificates, we cannot be officially buried, and until we're officially buried we can't cross to the other side, whether there even is another side. I've yet to meet a man who can give you a straight answer on that question. Apparently 'the other side' is on the other side of that wicket gate. But for all my time here, I've yet to see anyone go through it."

"Wait, yer telling me a buncha' dead people under the ground gotta get told they're dead so they can be buried?"

"That is correct. Even the dead and buried are not officially dead and buried without the correct paperwork!"

"That's some crazy talk right there."

"Welcome to death, lad! The madness never ends!"

"How long ya been waitin'?"

"Hard to say. Thousands of years I reckon."

"Come on now, yer just pulling my leg. How ya gonna tell me ya spent thousands of years down here? Were ya up there wandering around with the dinosaurs or somethin'?"

The blue-hued interlocutor laughed.

"Boy, it doesn't work like that here. We're not on the same clocks. You ask me how long I've been here; the answer is both forever and a flash. There isn't a difference between those two things. Right now, it feels like 10,000 years. Other times it feels like 10 minutes. And then other times 10 eternities. And when you step outside of all space and time and hold it like a glass globe filled with myriad galaxy spin tacked to eternity on appliqué pin black, you see there isn't a difference between a moment and all moments — it's all perspective."

Tima gave the man a bemused look. Lana couldn't even begin to feign his speech had any more to do with human language than bird song — but it seemed like a pretty song all the same.

"Mister, do you think they can help me find my little bird?" Lana chimed in.

"Find your little bird?"

"Yes."

"Well, I don't know about any lost and found around here. Maybe the information desk can help you," he said, pointing to a window on the other side of the room.

Tima took Lana by the hand and ruffled more than a few feathers pushing his way to the front of the line. An enormous woman in a ruddy blue jacket with epaulets was seated behind the glass. Her garrison cap had a hammer and nail stitched in gold thread on the side.

"Hey lady," Tima shouted.

She shot Tima an irritated look.

"Number please."

"Number? I ain't got no number. Ain't this the information desk?"

"Yes. And you need a number for the information desk."

"What kinda' crazy is that?"

"Young man, there's nothing crazy about it at all. It's protocol."

"What's PRO-DI-GAL?"

"The way things are to be done! And more importantly, the way things are not to be done!"

"And what's your PRO-DI-GAL?"

"Our P-R-O-T-O-C-O-L-S are as follows:

"Upon arrival a visitant should go directly to The Numerical Assignment Section Number 1."

"What do they do?"

"They give out numbers to get in line for the Information Desk. When your number comes up, the Information Desk will help verify that you are a post-somatic being waiting in line to be assigned to the relevant department for further query. They will send you to the Post-Somatic Inspection Department, determining your post-somatic nature. Upon confirmation of your post-somatic nature, you will then be given a spravka, which you then take to the Office of Notary Commissions and Authentications.

"It is their job to determine that your post-somatic spravka is genuine. Once confirmed genuine, the Notary will stamp your spravka. You then return to The Numerical Assignment Section Number 2, from which you will be assigned a number to queue at the Information Desk and Notary Commissions and Authentications' Authentication Center.

"They in turn determine that the stamp used to authenticate your spravka, as well as the spravka itself, are genuine. You cannot even begin to imagine how many times we end up with genuine stamps on fake papers, or fake papers with genuine stamps! During that process, you will further be asked to undergo a post-post-somatic non-physical, to determine that the findings of the first post-somatic inspection itself, which provided the basis for the documentation being subjected to further verification, were themselves genuine. Just in case the documentation was in fact correct, but the findings of the first post-somatic inspection were errant.

"Once the Information Desk and Notary Commissions and Authentications' Authentication Center has confirmed that the stamps and spravka and post-post somatic check are authentic, you can then head to the Numerical Assignment Section Number 3, which will give you a number to queue back up for the Information Desk, who, after a final check of your non-somatic nature and verified documentation therein, will finally assign you to the appropriate department to process your request."

Tima looked at her with chagrin.

"I don't understand a damned bit of what ya just said. What does that even mean, Post so .. so…?"

"POST-SOMATIC."

"Yeah. What the hell is that?"

The matron shot him a withering look.

"It's for people who have passed away."

"Passed away?"

"Died!"

"But we ain't dead!"

"Then what on Earth are you doing here?"

"We're looking for my little bird," Lana interjected.

"Your little bird?"

"Yes!"

"We don't deal in birds here, little girl. Perhaps you could ask the Miscellaneous Department," she said, gesturing toward a window in a dimly lit corner of the cavern covered in cobwebs. A florescent light flickered above. Tima squinted hard and could have sworn he saw a skeleton's outline behind the glass.

"As you can see, their services are not in high demand. What is your little bird doing down here to begin with?"

"I asked her the same thing!" Tima interjected.

Lana looked down at her feet.

"I opened a door. I didn't know it would take me here! I promise! And then the shadow man came from the dark water. And my little bird got scared and ran away. And I think if he gets to my little bird before I do, something very, very bad will happen."

"Dark water you say?"

The underworld apparatchik scratched both of her chins.

"Do you see that?" She pointed to the ceiling where water dripped.

"Last night, somewhere up there in the darkest corner of the sun-touched world, someone let the devil of the deep black sea in. We've always suffered snow-melt underground, it's how we get our applicants! But this is something altogether different. Why, we've had to seal off half of the catacombs to keep the dark water out. The pressure is building all the same. We don't know how long the stoppers will hold. We've even had to close off the gate to the other side out of fear we'll inundate the after-after life. So, you're the one who opened the gate and let that water in!"

"I didn't mean to!" Lana squealed.

"What you did or didn't mean won't change a thing. As for your little bird. You said the 'shadow man' is after him?"

"Yes! He chased us down here!"

"Well, if I were looking for a little bird, one perhaps touched by a magic hand, I might go to the highest bird bath on Earth."

"Where's that?" Lana asked.

"Gamayun's Tear, a lake situated in a cirque atop Mount Rod, just east of Vyraj. All of the water falls from God's frozen tears, so dark water cannot creep death into the terminal basin."

"There's a lake in a circus?" Lana asked, imagining Uncle Yura directing motley Macaws in aeronautic acrobatics above the water.

"Not circus, but cirque," the matron corrected, "although you're not exactly wrong. Think of it like a big pot on top of the Earth catching water from the heavens."

"I think this place must be very beautiful."

"I imagine it is, being so close to Vyraj – where souls go after death and birds fly for winter. I guess Gamayun's Tear is the last pit stop for fowl traveling south for winter, where birds big and small alike flock for purification before finding perch on the edge of the cosmic tree."

"What is p-u-r-i-f-i-c-a-t-i-o-n?"

"It means to make yourself clean."

Lana paused in thought.

"Wait a second. I thought people came here when they died!"

"Oh no, we only handle the melted snowdrops. Though I must say, this is the only underworld passage to the sky. On that point, we are quite proud. But that also makes our place a risky one. Like I said, dark water could never flow so high. I guess we are the one chink in eternity's armor."

"Wait a minute," Lana said, looking to both allay her own concerns and pour oil on troubled waters.

"My little bird lost its wings! How will it ever fly up to your circus?"

"Cirque."

"Yeah, there."

"Well, the path to Vyraj is straight — right through that gate. Perhaps your little bird found a way through before we had to seal it off."

"But if we can't open the gate, how will we ever get there?"

"Well, there is one more way, please follow me."

So the matron led Lana and Tima down a series of corridors whose walls were made of skeletal remains. Hanging brass oil lamps with red votive cups that above ground would shed light on orthodox icons hung in regular intervals between skulls and bones.

Lana instinctively huddled closer to Tima as they traversed the ossuary.

"Why ... Why are all of these bones here?"

"They don't fit through the gate," the matron replied.

"They give me the heebie jeebies!"

"Don't worry, everything scary about those bones is long gone," she consoled.

"She's right 'bout that," Tima said. "I spent a long time livin' in a place like this. Underground. Dark. Dank. Even less light. 'Cept those bones walked around sucking air and covered in skin. Most of 'em were filled with murder. Everything scary in this world has blood in it, if not on it."

"Not everything," the matron replied starkly, sending a chill down Tima's usually sturdy spine.

After a few turns and several straight lines down chilly corridors, the catacomb opened up into a high-ceilinged room held up on colonnades and illuminated by Yablochkov candles — an atrium without sky to look upon. A grand chandelier hung from the ceiling.

To the children's eyes, it looked much like the lobby of a fancy hotel cast in Stalin Empire style. Not the kind they'd ever stepped foot in, as neither of them had ever actually seen the inside of a hotel at all. Rather, it was the kind whose grandiosity had seeped in through televised dreaming – the backdrops to perfect winter holidays they had never had, where cheery men shook off snow from foreign clothes under New Year's lights before settling down for cognac and cigars at the bar.

At the end of the marbled hall, seemingly out of place, was a red-padded door with a golden frame. An attendant with obsidian-colored skin in a double-breasted maroon jacket with golden epaulettes stood by steadfast like a stone Easter Island sentry, staring inland in watch over centuries of progeny.

Six soles alternated echoes on the march toward the only other soul in the gallery. When they reached him, the attendant turned his head and smiled ivory at the matron.

"Good evening, madam. What floor can I take you to this evening?"

"I won't be going anywhere, Gönpo. But if you would be so kind, please take my young guests to the 83,999th floor."

"Oh, I see, they will be visiting Indra's eye?"

"Indeed they are."

The matron turned to the children.

"As I said, there is no direct access to Vyraj apart from the closed gate.

This lift, however, will take you right to the edge of the Valley of Death. Now don't be afraid. I know the name sounds scary, but it's actually quite a lovely field of wildflowers and bear grass blowing in blissful breeze. To reach Gamayun's Tear is another matter. To get there, you must cross a treacherous ridge called Veles' Spine. You cross that path, and you just might find your little bird."

And from atop that mountain pass, a frigid wind sailed down, delivering doubt to Lana's heart.

"But I'm just a little girl! How can I climb over a mountain? Why, I only have one glove! Won't I be cold? What if I slip and fall?"

"Up there's always a path for believers. No matter what you see before you, all the stumbling blocks are within. A wise man once said a man could see a mountain taken up and thrown into the sea if he had faith. And you don't even need to throw a mountain into the sea. You simply need to cross a mountain to step onto a shore."

"Why does everyone talk so funny down here?" Lana asked.

"'Cause they're all nuts!" Tima interjected.

"Let me put it more simply, my dear: If you believe you can fly, you will find your wings."

"That's s'posed to be simple lady?"

"As simple as I can put it," she snapped. "Now if you are ready, Gönpo will take you up."

"Right this way, sir and madam," Gönpo said, addressing the pair as if they were middle-aged and upper-crust rather than Rag without Tag and Bobtail.

He pulled open the red door and rolled back the scissor gate before the elevator cab.

The inside of the elevator appeared a tiled Tibetan Thangka depicting blue-skinned Vajrabhairava breaking the cycle of Samsara. Red ball socket bulbs ran the length and width of the walls like a Hollywood vanity mirror in Sañjīva.

But all the two children saw was a hodgepodge of eastern nightmares.

"There are monsters in there!" Lana squeaked.

"No monsters ma'am, none at all. Perhaps this will help," he said, flipping a switch that turned the bulbs blue like Egyptian lotus petals, casting a clam cloud over what the kids still peeped to be hellish scenes.

"Lady, let me ask you a question," Tima asked brusquely.

"What is it now?"

"Why do we gotta ride up some nightmare elevator for God knows how long, only to have to take a crazy trip over some mountain, when we can go right back the way we came, open the gate and head straight to that damn bird bath ya keep talkin' 'bout?"

"As I already said, if one drop of that dark water follows you in, Heaven is lost. Just one drop is enough to poison eternity. I really must get going. I have a department to run."

And with that she made an about face, her heels clicking and clacking down the corridor.

With the last of the matron's echoed steps dissolving in silence, Lana hesitantly stepped toward the cab. But it soon became clear her feet weren't the coldest on the marble floor, as Tima remained frozen in place.

"I say you forget this nonsense about that bird and go back home! Your mama and papa must be worried sick 'bout you!"

Surprised by Tima's reticence, Lana stopped in her tracks and turned to him.

"Yes, but … he needs me!"

"If he needed ya, he never would have run off!"

His logic cut Lana like a knife. The pellucid blood of pneuma poured forth from baby blues. But there was no going back. If not exactly Amor Fati, something in her bones would not allow her to oppose the turn of the whirling wheel.

"We have to go, Tima," she said, an earnestness glistening crystals in her eyes. "I met the nightmare man once before. He did something terrible to my little bird. I think he wants to do the same thing to all of us."

"Just who the hell is this nightmare man?"

Chapter 17

Once upon a time, when Lana was even smaller than she is today, her parents took her down to the sea.

Before departing from Moscow Kiyevsky railway station, they took a stroll across Krasnaluzhsky Bridge, with rail tracks running right down the middle.

Her father scooped her up in one big, sturdy arm as they took in the Moscow River at night. Lana noticed the moonlight sparkle on the water and said it was so pretty. Mama pressed against them, voicing agreement. Dad told her the Turks even had a word for that — yakamoz — which made her giggle.

To her ears it sounded a lot like "utkonos" — platapus. He said her mom was a lot like the moon light, something sparkling and beautiful that danced on the darkness, giving it life. Mamma laughed and said daddy was silly, just like a platypus.

Lana then asked Dad what a Turk was. He told her they were people who lived in a land far, far away, on the other side of the Black Sea.

She asked him why they called it the Black Sea. In her mind she saw an ocean of ink and a midnight sky where the only light came from electric platapuses swimming in the water. He told her he wasn't sure, but the water was anything but black. She asked if they were going to the Black Sea, to which he said no, they were going to the Sea of Azov, which was above it, though the two kissed at the bottom.

She asked if they swam too far, would they end up in the Black Sea. He laughed and said that would be quite a feat. She told him he'd have to hold onto her tightly — she didn't want to float away into that dark, scary place.

He gave her squeeze and said she'd never leave his arms.

As their departure time neared, they walked back to European Square, where the clock tower loomed large, just like the one in London.

Stepping inside the station, they navigated their way to the platform, where shuttle traitors with checkered plastic bags too big were struggling through doors too small, creating bottlenecks that the more impatient sought to break with shirt fronts and shoulder tackles. Some of those assorted wares stuffed would end up in bazaars beyond the Black Sea.

But while the mad traffic created disgruntled dispensers of sharp elbows and the occasional fist, Dad was not one of them. He was content to slow his pace to a penguin's waddle, even when the less scrupulous continually took his turn for him. Those were calmer days.

By the sheer force of inertia, the hustle and bustle eventually carried them down to the vast, parabolic platform.

Lana felt like she'd ended up in the belly of a whale, just like the one from Grandma's tale.

The great, glass arc structure was pinned in place by triangular trusses suspended way up in the air.

As Lana looked up in wonder, a train pulled in, running the length of the whale's spine until coming to a jerky halt. The platform was soon awash with people, some hauling large canvas bags, some smoking cigarettes, others rushing to friends, family and lovers — anchors of embrace in the human flow. Echoes of laughter and conversation at every clip and pitch caromed from steel rib to steel rib.

The platform was a place where the great drama of the country had unfounded millions of times across millions of lives. The love from a hug in Moscow could travel six days and infinite tracks until reverberating in a Vladivostok heart. Every platform, like every soul, was connected on a single, contiguous line.

Through the now dissipating explosion of life, Lana's small family settled into their space on Platform 3. Fifteen minutes later their own southbound train arrived.

They piled into platskart and found their space in the open-plan sleeper. Dad put their luggage beneath the blue-bottom berth before sitting down to rest his back against the faux-wood partition. Mamma pulled out her thermos and poured them all cups of tea.

A middle-aged couple who looked like they'd been married longer than they'd been alive exchanged pleasantries before settling into silence across from them; staring off into distances that can still be found in the closest of quarters.

The train eventually pulled out of the whale's mouth. The ticket lady came by, brusquely handing out linen, taking her fee, and otherwise making sure no stowaways had gotten by on her watch.

Mamma pulled a container of sliced fruit from her bag, along with a bag of cookies, laying them out on the table. The couple across the way declined Mom's offer without a word, as the laughter of young men drinking vodka filled up the wagon.

Lana nuzzled in between her parents and munched on an apple slice. Dad watched out the window as Moscow retreated one building at a time.

As the night wore on Dad eventually climbed up onto the top bunk and Lana nestled in with Mom, the steady motion of the train rocking her to sleep. At some point deep in the night when everyone was fast asleep, the border had been crossed and passports checked, she awoke in a perfect place between her mother's warmth and a tiny flow of cool air seeping through an unsealing window.

Lana had never felt so safe. She imagined that instead of a train she was on a large ship sailing down the big, black sea. The lights that blinkered in and out in the distance were the electric platypuses frolicking in the distance. The moon smiled and blew a wind kiss ripple across the waves. And then she felt that even in a big, bottomless sea, when creatures of light come to play, under the water it glowed.

From that point on she was no longer afraid of the Black Sea. Her mamma and daddy were always there, as well as the moon, who knew all the secrets of the light and the night, as well as the electric guardians who knew no depths for which their luminescence could not shine.

She fell asleep feeling that life itself was a big, beautiful dream, that there was nothing to fear in the darkness that came with closed eyes.

But for a girl so young, the nearly 14-hour trip to Kyiv did come with stultifying stints of boredom. After waking up, they often drank tea, ate sandwiches of sausage and cheese, or picked up smoked fish at the many stops on the 600-plus mile route to pass the time. Dad even went off to the dining car to drink beer, not even waiting for midday.

Mom, not so happy with that, knitted her brow. Dad laughed and said, "We're on vacation. A beer won't hurt!" Over the next two years, Dad seemed to go on vacation more and more, albeit in their own kitchen. And for a while he carried the same smile and jocular manner, until he didn't.

Mom tried to knit or read, doing her best to keep Lana out of everyone's hair. Lana likely ran up the wagon 747 times, dodging stinky feet and outstretched hands of slumber which would remain asleep even after their owners had woken up. But the lifetime on the train and the world watched through green curtains, in the end, would come and pass.

They'd roll into the rolling green Kyivv plateau, meadow sliced and diced by ravines and gulches. From the ancient withdraw of the Kharkiv Sea, wind-blown loess formed vertical bluffs along the Dnieper upland. It was the most beautiful thing Lana's young eyes had ever seen.

On and on, single structures floating by windows grew into settlements and then industrial outskirts before blooming into a full-blown city. At last, the train pulled into Kyiv station — a monument to Ukrainian baroque that had seen better days. They then took their places among a different mass flooding out onto the platform, watching all the familiar themes unfold, looking for a space to divest their bodies of the motion before they did it all again.

For their final destination was the port city of Berdyansk — the gem of the Azov Sea. Galya's older brother had been a Soviet sailor who'd found his way to the city in his youth, found love, and never found his way back.

The time between trains didn't give Lana's family a chance to strike out into the city. Rather they pushed through the motley crew of travelers and tramps to find a canteen and have a meal. Perhaps it would have been better to go without.

Viktor was pretty sure that whoever was running the place had previously worked at a prison cafeteria. The surly staff certainly took to treating customers like convicts. At some point someone had squeezed the fruit from the kompot, cut the meat from the cutlet and skimmed the beats from the borscht.

When Lana said her food tasted like cardboard Galya couldn't even feign a message imploring her to appreciate what she had. Galya herself was certain there was cardboard that tasted better.

After chewing on the same pieces of meat for an hour, they left feeling hungrier than when they had arrived, hoping something better would be found at a random station down the line. Just search out the kiosk with the biggest babushka and the biggest line. It was one of the many unwritten rules of the track.

Eventually the train to Berdyansk arrived, and the city between the hills was left far, far behind.

And if the first leg of the voyage had lasted a lifetime, the second one was an eternity.

Youth had amplified the fetters binding Lana to the endless wheel. There was nothing but the moment, and the moment was terrible. Her mind could not form a future to escape into southern shores, succulent meat on the spit and kodachrome sunsets.

Some killed the time with spirit shots and plastic jugs of beer. Teetotalers drank from glasses cradled in filigree-adorned glass holders, keeping shaking hot liquid in careening carriages from burning arms, legs and feet. Tin foil was unrolled from table to table, cuts of sausage, fruit and cottage cheese scones nibbled on incessantly.

Thousands of cigarettes were smoked in the spaces between wagons as a scape of gravel, tracks and tussocks sailed by.

Lana would lie on her mother's lap, blonde hair running like Virginia creepers down the floral pattern dress, staring at the sky rushing by too fast for cloud animals to take form in the window frame. Beads of sweat formed on her brow. The heat inside the window-sealed wagons was stifling. Lana herself had lost the will to run the gamut of stinky feet and sleeping arms.

Around the wagon, some stripped down to their underwear and tank tops. A big ol' man in a blue-striped telnyashka propped himself up majestically on a bunk like a beached walrus, snoring a sonorous response to a siren's song, keeping sailors and ships alike at bay.

If Dr Aybolit ventured to ask what ailed him, he might have responded he'd eaten Barmaley and was attempting to sleep it off.

For a few unable to fall under the soporific sleep of their own weight, they laid on white linen, heads held up by elbows, thousand-yard stares above mouths left agape, putting the cattle in the car.

Lana herself had no choice but to let that slow summer dullness seep in, the full oppression of unrelenting heat and boredom taking over.

But somehow, hours into the second 14-hour stretch, beauty, unlike fresh air, managed to seep in. At a stop in Korsun-Shevchenkivsyki, as the first draw of dusk scattered sparkles on the Ros River, Mom secured syriniki from the biggest grandmother with the biggest line as street dogs played on the platform and illegal vendors dodged in and out of pockets of people, a lumbering security guard not far behind.

Back on the train the sun reached the window line, slowly moving down as everything else sped forward. But Lana's mind slowed, and between sips of tea and bits of crispy cheese, raisin and sour cream, the boredom evaporated, and contentment took hold.

Around that time Dad came back after hours on the lam, a bit too giddy but good-natured enough to escape rebuke from Mom. All three sat on the bench, watching the raspberry swirl in the sky — a triptych of family bliss.

Later on, Chronos would harvest the good memories and discard the tedium like chaff. That seemingly endless trip, with all its suffering, would be refashioned into an endless well of nostalgia.

Random spots of light would be refashioned into a constellation, the great black vacuum beyond nothing but backdrop.

The night came with the setting sun, the dull yellow light of the train switched on, people who had been dozing all day prepared for sleep while the party was just beginning for some.

Dad kept on Mom's good side by waving off a few companions from the un-dined carriage, climbing up into the upper birth and counting sheep on the ceiling, mere inches from his face. Those sheep, granted, often appeared two at a time.

Lana tucked back into Mama's arms and waited for the rock of the train to sink up to her circadian rhythms, until she fell into a deep, dreamless sleep.

Morning came, breakfast was made, chatter was idle, bodies were stiff. And then, as if by magic, they arrived. Half the passengers had scrambled for their luggage and were already waiting in line before the train even came to a stop. Mounds of linen had formed on nearly every berth.

Her family remained on the shelf, watching Bredyansk roll in. Lana asked Dad where the sea was. Close, he promised her, it was close.

Finally, they joined the line of passengers shuffling out onto the hexagonal stones lining the platform. The mint green and white station in subdued Russian neoclassical style could strike a sixth of the world with a sense of familiarity, or, at least, those spread out across a sixth of it.

That was the strange trick of the monolithic uniformity in Soviet style and its imperial antecedents: however far one had gone, they often ended up somewhere that looked just like home.

Midway down the platform stroll, a strange looking man with his hair pulled back in a pony tail and a jean jacket thrown over his narrow frame began to wave.

He drew everyone's sunlit eyes like fireflies in a jar.

"Andrei!" Mama called out, before running to embrace him. He gave Galya a big hug, rocking her to and fro.

Dad slowly approached with Lana in tow. Andrei released Mom and shook Dad's hand with almost formal salutation.

"My, look how Lana has grown!" he cried out, kneeling down to look her in the eyes. Lana saw in his diamond cut face and coal black hair a male variation on a female theme. And those eyes, pinched between tiny crow's feet, were lighter than Mama's, but equally kind.

"Lana. Say hello to your Uncle Andrei," Mama said.

And Lana did say hello to Uncle Andrei, even if her eyes turned from his to look at the shadows his knees cast on her feet.

Andrei stood up, a gentle smile rising to the sun which had already sailed 70 degrees upon its northeastern arc.

"Let's go!" he said with cheer.

— — —

When they pulled up to the little wooden home of warm timber cladding sometime later, dusk was beginning its initial descent. Crickets began to chirp as a soft glow washed over the iron mansard roof and surrounding trees.

The windows were lavished with ornate woodcut trim in a gothic style, whose symbols were meant to ward off bad spirits and attract the envious eyes of neighboring aesthetes.

Far less care had been taken in providing order inside the home, as the smell of stale cigarette smoke poured out the door. It was the type of place where even the dust bunnies had asthma.

Andrei flipped on the lights, handed over the keys, and gave them a brief tour across creaking floorboards. Apart from a living room, connected kitchen and two bedrooms in the back, there wasn't a lot to see. Andrei said as much, leading them back to the yard.

There was also a summer home, which was little more than a den and bedroom.

In the small walk of half sunken slabs between them lay a garden long since overgrown with weeds and fenced in by stones. Wooden strips from a once-white trellis hung in downward slopes as desiccated tomato vines clung to the arc in death.

While Andrei insisted that they stay in the main house, Viktor assured him the smaller, less-lived in outbuilding was more than enough for a family of three. What he didn't mention was the spartan style which Andrei found uninviting, what with its lack of clutter and cigarette stench, was far more appealing to his family's sensibilities.

Apart from the outhouse out back, flanked by a stack of wood to the right of the main house was a banya, where the grime and dirt of summer fun could be lifted off with steam.

Giving out hugs and promising to bring his boys back at the weekend, Andrei doled out smiles one more time and headed back to his own box called home in the city.

The second he pulled away was a literal breath of fresh air for Lana. He was a kind man, but the smell of cigarettes clinging to his jacket and oozing from his pores didn't settle well in her small nostrils. While years older than his sister, he seemed so much older still.

But Lana would soon learn that Andrei was earnest and smiled a lot, never far from a guitar and often breaking into song. He had all of Mom's joy and none of her worry, for better and for worse.

But on that particular evening, Mom's soul was featherweight fluff. She sang the sun a lullaby and set Lana to sail above the grass, perfect pirouette bringing flight to life on outstretched arms.

Lana's laughter was the answer to the ultimate question. And around the arbor of maternal love, she spun 42 times.

From somewhere not far away, a sea breeze came rolling in to season the sunset with salt. A dog began barking in the distance. After Mom set dizzy legs to pratfall plop on the grass, lightheaded, Lana asked Dad if they'd go to the sea tomorrow.

We'll go to the sea every day, he replied, chasing after Bambi legs with a faux roar and earnest glee.

— — —

During many an evening sunset that would follow, the smell of grilled shashlik would spirit her away in the wind. In her little world a backwater village turned into a land of fruit and berries, bumblebee friends and towering sunflower wonders. And then there was the unassuming sea, an ocean of grand proportions on her own small scale.

And while Andrei and his wife Masha visited infrequently due to work and whatever toll the previous night's drinking session had taken on them, their boys, Pasha and Sasha, were there more often than not.

Pasha, a year older at nine, was pensive and slightly pedantic. While muscles had yet to accumulate on his beanpole body, he already had the contours pointing toward a sturdier future. Sasha, by contrast, was overweight and easygoing, even with two left feet.

Pasha always felt protective of Sasha, who tended to take everything at face value. He was slow to pick up on jokes and left many questions in a permanent state of unanswered ellipsis.

Sasha's demeanor left him an easy target for bullies. Pasha shied at rising to his brother's defense, even if barbed words and rocks followed.

One afternoon when Andrei had brought the boys down, they decided to head to the store for ice cream. They initially protested when Lana looked to tag along, arguing her tiny legs would hold them back. But Andrei slyly appealed to both Pasha's sense of duty and a child's sense of play, convincing the boys they were members of the Imperial Guard tasked with protecting Grand Duchess Anastasia.

Warming to the game, the boys escorted Lana out of the gate before shutting it behind them. To accommodate her less-than-speedy pace, Pasha kicked out his long legs, one after the other, enacting a slow-motion march. Sometimes he'd hush Lana and Sasha, imploring them to stay still. He'd then run up the trail and out of sight, only to return in a huff and a puff, telling the convoy it was safe to continue.

Along the dirt road, huge, corrugated sheets of metal formed the perimeter fencing for most of the homes to wall off (or perhaps in) the world of the living.

But nature still reigned behind towering borders. Further on down the strip where houses became less sparse and the fright of snapping dog snouts lunging under gates less frequent, the insects turned up their percussive pitch along the heat wave. In the fields dotted with trees, feather grass attempted to take flight in the breeze. Spindly flower fingers like inverted purple sea urchins bloomed on abundant nap weed.

Pheasant's eyes formed blood drops on the soil. Sandpipers sailed over sedges. Weasels wriggled around reeds. Dandelion clocks sat atop stems without a thought to departure times.

When the trio eventually arrived, the word "produkty" was painted in red above the clapboard building. Lana felt the wonder that all children feel entering new places and spaces. And yet Soviet standards persisted in a post-Soviet world, leaving shelves filled with the same fare, from Carpathian hamlets to Siberian steppes, Moscow suburbs to Black Sea valley depths.

The woman behind the counter was in her early forties, with bleached blonde hair, black roots, and a welcoming smile.

Knowing the boys from years gone by, she inquired about their mother and father, to which the boys mustered up a pithy "fine".

Then her eyes turned to Lana.

"Who is this pretty young thing?"

Lana looked up with big blues eyes but retreated into herself without a reply.

"This ... is ... our ... cousin ... Lana. She ... lives ... in ... Moscow. Her ... mom ... and ... dad ... are ... visiting ... us. We ... are ... here ...to ... protect ... her ... because ... she ... is ... a princess ... and ... we ...need ... ice ... cream," Sasha said in a hair-too-loud, syncopated clip.

"Ice cream for the princess, why of course! Tell me, Lana, do you like our little village down by the sea?"

Lana twisted on her own vine, letting out a "Yes," with downcast eyes.

But the kind lady above knew a thing or two about kids and strangers and was more than happy to take her time drawing the princess out of her carriage.

"So, what kind of ice cream will we be having?"

The boys rushed over to the freezer, pulling out three Lakomkas.

"We'll take these, ma'am," Pasha said, running back over and sliding a few bills across the counter.

After settling up, legs small and smaller marched down the wooden steps, cold bounty in hand, right back into the heat.

Before Lana had half pulled off her wrapper, Sasha went to work devouring his ice cream before the sun had a chance to act. But in his haste, the lion's share of chocolate ended up smeared on his face.

"You're a mess!" Pasha shouted, in a tone voicing both frustration and acceptance of Sasha's fate.

"Slow down. You won't even taste it if you carry on like that!"

"I … can … taste … it," Sasha stammered, nothing but a conical numb left pinched between two sticky fingers.

"Come here!" Pasha said, taking his brother by the hand. "Lana, let's go!"

Having barely torn off the foil on her own, Lana trailed her cousins as the tall one pulled the round one back behind the shop, which opened into a field with a few abandoned buildings set amidst the scrub grass. A football pitch away, the track was hemmed in with concave diamonds not shining along the plate fence concrete wall.

A sink set in a white, wooden desk was pressed up against the back door. A bucket was placed underneath to catch the water. A metal canister with a spigot that had to be manually filled was screwed to a board that was in turn screwed to the wall. Flies buzzed around the nearby outhouse.

Pasha pulled Sasha up to the wash basin, let the water flow and began wiping his brother's face with a wet hand.

Lana, still nibbling away at her ice cream, noticed something rustling in the grass over by one of the half-built Soviet homes never to be. Carrying on in the path of Curious Varvara, she ventured to see if her nose would fall off in the field.

Her feet parted a sea of white and purple topped weeds. A single Scottish pine who'd somehow found a home far away from home cast a tattered net of segmented shade on the lorn domicile. A few steps from the trunk, an overturned hubcap had turned orange with rust.

As she got closer, she began to hear a tiny chorus of tweets.

In a small depression surrounded by a bed of imported twigs and leaves, a brood of baby birds called out blindly for their absent mother.

Lana settled into the marvel. She bent down to get a closer look, animated balls of fluff sounding out an all too familiar message to the heavens. One in particular seemed out of place, with snow-white feathers standing out against sandy down. It stared up at Lana with big, black shining eyes. Basking in sunshine, the little chick's plumage shone with pearlescent splendor.

Lana slowly extended her free hand toward it. After several cautious steps, the little white orb planted shaky legs on a soft palm.

"Aha!"

The small, fluffy thing shrank into itself.

Lana peered up. A man, a strange looking man indeed, had emerged from the ossature.

"I knew I'd find you!" he boomed, pausing to sniff and wipe his nose.

"And what do we have here? Who do you think you are, little girl, trying to take my runagate! Why, it hopped down from the moon and punched a hole in my roof! And it's going to pay!"

Lana slowly stood up, failing to muster a response. Every man is tall for a five-year-old girl, but this man was taller still.

To her mind he was dressed like a circus clown, his sartorial choices fell on the spectrum between gentleman of leisure and vagrant vaudeville.

Despite the weather he was decked out in a pea soup green blazer, a grimy, wrinkled guayaberas, rosewood-colored trousers and plain-toed brown derbys that were more than slightly scuffed up and dustier than a sparrow post-dirt shower. A Cheshire smile was stretched across his shadow-cast face.

His fingers were as long and twisted as silk cotton tree roots wrapped around a brown pharmaceutical bottle shaped like a Khmer Prang. Something hot and clear sloshed around in bottle and slightly distended belly alike.

His rough skin was a smoked, ribbed rubber sheet making a mask on something once human. His face seemed shaped by haphazard candle melt. Dichroic eyes peered from underneath the wax in pie-sliced irises of hazelnut and lemon. His smile, strangely, remained pearly white, with the exception of a single gold cap filing in for a front tooth.

He filled the awkward silence with fire from his bottle.

Lana stood petrified. The man sneered, arms too-long dangling on slumped shoulders, meeting her pace.

"Are you deaf? Put it down!"

With shaking hands Lana lowered the little bird back into the nest.

Buzz of bugs and boys' voices from behind filled the air. The steps got louder.

"So, you've come here with friends. Do your friends know you're trying to steal my dinner?"

Pasha reached Lana and put his hand on her shoulders. His lucid eyes met the two-tone glaze with a start.

"Mister, I don't know what she did, but we're sorry. We'll be going now."

"Going? Did I say anything about anyone going? She's put her stink all over my hors d'oeuvre!

"But who knows. Maybe she's a delicious little morsel as well! Finger food? I do like the sound of that," he said, smacking his lips.

As more of his big white teeth were revealed in a twisted smile, a strange sort of darkness fell upon his yet-to-congeal face. Three kids turned to goose flesh as the madman began to laugh.

Sasha took Lana by one hand; a half-melted ice-cream cone fell from the other. Together, without signal or command, they all started stepping backwards.

The buzz of bugs returned to fill the silence still pulsing with heat and menace. For the first time all three felt a place called home that was terrifyingly far away.

Then, with unexpected deftness, a long arm snatched up the quivering ball of fluff.

"I must say, little girl. This little bird is no bird at all. He is something far more terrible, something just like you! And you know what I do to such despicable things?"

He grabbed the bird by its wings, with a bottled tucked between pinky and ring. Then, before six wide eyes, he ripped little wings off in a ruby red pop.

Lana screamed bloody murder. The wingless bird fell to the ground, followed by Sasha's jaw.

"You know what?" he snarled. "I think my appetizer is in fact dessert. But you sweet thing are going to be my main course!"

"You leave her alone!" Pasha shouted, slender shoulders hiked, chest puffed out. Something in his chemistry had converted all of that percolating fear into anger. Afraid still, but not frozen, with a heart beating like worn tappets, the twisted face screwed up further in dark recognition.

The buzz of bugs returned to ride the pulse of heat and menace.

"So, you're a feisty little boy, I see. You can show me just how feisty you are."

Stepping back, Pasha noticed an old beer bottle discarded in the weeds. He reached down to pick it up. Grasping the glass club, his hand immediately began to shake. His mind fought his quaking hand to a standstill, planting his feet as Lana and Sasha continued their handheld retreat.

"What do you think you're going to do with that? Trust me, little boy, you don't want to make me angry. It gets very, very bad when I'm angry."

He began to saunter their way, long limbs moving like a slow-motion squid underwater. Getting closer, the kraken's ever-expanding shadow swallowed them, pulling high noon to chthonic depths.

Lana and Sasha froze in terror as the monster stopped several feet from Pasha.

"Now you're going to put that down and say you're sorry for being such a naughty little boy! Otherwise, I'll rip off more than your wings!"

Tentacles lunged at Pasha, looking to suck him into the deep.

Pasha's arm hurled a glass baton at the kraken's beak, finding its mark with surprising force. The latter cracked, the former failed to break, a river of blood flowed, followed by a stream of expletives the likes of which the kids had never heard. A small brown bottle carrying a monster's poison hit the ground. A bleeding little bird free of wings fell as well, fleeing into the weeds.

The kids began to run before flailing tentacles could cut them off at the pass. But little rabbit legs moved at terrapin's clip. Something called murder was awakening from its pain and starting its pursuit.

Pasha faced the fear of that monster's retaliation with tactical flight, zigzagging in the field until coming upon another pile of garbage left by day drinkers and depth sinkers. With the die already cast, another missile followed, falling short, skidding off the dirt and smacking the lunatic in his shin.

"You little son of a…"

Another bottle sailed but missed.

"When I get my hands on you…"

The two-tone eyes hovering above a blood drip scream were burning as passion met with pain and power turned to impotence. Now there was nothing left in the beast but murder.

The madman ran at the boy, swinging an Oxford shoe Pasha's way. Pasha feinted as the foot whizzed by, losing his balance, planting his hand on the ground, and pushing off into a sprint. Tips of tentacles tore at his collar, but the shirt gave before Pasha fell. That lunge sent the man with a screaming shin and rotgut burning ulcers in his maw to fall face first onto the ground. The itch of dirt and ants stung his eyes, which were already electric with the second smack to his now smashed snout. He spit out dirt as his nose filled an anthill with ferritin flood.

He tried to stand up but the bottle in every sense of the word had left him tipsy on a spinning world. He tripped up on his too-long legs, hitting the ground again. The maniac melted into a puddle of pain and profanity as insects ran from the river running red through their land.

Pasha turned and stared at the screaming pile of rage. He thought about stomping a wax seal from a splayed hand on the dirt but opted instead to take his hard-fought seconds and catch up with his slow-running kin.

The kind lady in the store, having heard all the commotion out back, stepped outside to see the three kids fleeing an enraged ringmaster whose diabolical big top had fallen down.

When the man-beast dreaming of murder and worse made his way back to his feet, he smacked dust clouds out of his trousers and jacket.

His eyes met the shopkeeper's as the kids kept running until their tiny legs had taken them under her arm and through the back door.

The pea-coat predator said, "Good afternoon, madam," offering her a slight bow before hobbling off with a hand keeping his gushing nose in place. She could have sworn the flowers wilted in his wake.

There was no phone in the shop, nor Andrei's datcha, so she had the kids wait inside until a teacher and former classmate stopped by for lazy Saturday small talk. Instead, she was treated to a story whose dimensions had yet to come into focus.

The shopkeeper herself had yet to piece together what she had really seen in stepping out to a scene of kids running and a queer man bleeding. The kids weren't too keen on having answers elicited.

When she asked Lana what had happened, all the little girl could do was wail about a wingless bird.

After the teacher agreed to escort the kids home, Lana pleaded for them to help the injured creature.

But neither the shopkeeper nor her schoolteacher friend had the gall to go back out to the field and gather up the nestlings when a weasel was roaming the land big enough to swallow a person.

So, the teacher escorted lacrimal Lana, silent Sasha and pensive Pasha back to the datcha.

Galya scooped up her red-eyed cherub and pushed her big damp cheeks to her chest. Following a teacher's fractured summary of what had transpired, Lana would never again leave home without her folks that summer.

— — —

Lana's first encounter with darkness and the loss of her little bird was balanced by a new world of color and light. Long family strolls on slices of the Berdyansk Spit, triangle-shaped strips of sand, silt and shell formed by river flow and giving break to the sea, all this became the stuff of timeless memory.

Stretching out for over 10 miles, lagoons formed on the western side of the spit to face the setting sun. Seagulls, geese and swans found rest from migration among stripped-down primates seeking redress in the mud and mineral springs at the mouth of the Berda.

Lana was fascinated by the creamsicle-striped, orange sherbert and white lighthouse perched up on a hill, which was among the oldest on the Azov Sea. A smaller, older beacon could also be found on the edge of the gulf, where the line between land and sea blurred.

On the lower lighthouse the words of Paustovsky were inscribed: 'Lighthouses are the shrines of the sea'.

Showing the way to port from times of kerosene beacon burn, both towers served the most dangerous spit on the sea, which waned in the middle on the southward stretch and waxed again in the southwest, forming a natural snare of shipwreck.

Lana loved the idea of a light shining from up on high, signaling safety to those making their way from that big, black beyond. Viktor took to the idea too, finding poetry in a little girl's wonder.

He even convinced the long-serving lighthouse keeper to let him carry Lana up the 99 steps of the smaller tower to watch ships below bring in the summer harvest. The custodian of the light told them a story of how the Germans had tried to destroy it, though through a stroke of luck they only managed to blow up the tower's dome. He told Lana that dolphins could be seen dancing in the early morning. He said he'd spent decades of his life watching sunsets and sunrises to the endless lullaby of swell and sea.

Lana shouted she wanted to become a lighthouse keeper too. The lighthouse keeper laughed and told her she was so bright, no other lamp would be needed to guide the ships.

As she left, she imagined dolphins dancing on the water at dawn break. She had no idea that the world here froze over too, forcing icebreakers to serve as seafaring Sherpas. This, to her mind, was a land of endless summer.

There were also long evening strolls down the boardwalk. She was tickled by the eclectic monuments to fish, frogs, plumbers and poets.

There was joy to be found in all the schlocky structures, from creaky Ferris wheel rides to circles run around the rusting sundial.

Hopping along the boardwalk, she enjoyed taking shelter in the golden-domed rotunda, skirted by tram tracks inlaid in cracked concrete. She watched as men of every shape and size cast lines in search of dinner.

She was wowed by the cranes scattered around the seafront by the port, which to her eyes looked like raptorial legs in northern mantis style. She imagined cannonballs roaring from the ships dotting the horizon to beat back the giant monsters in prayerful procession.

Lana was enthralled trying to climb terrace vines, running circles around gazebos and through yards, hearing her uncle sing songs as lamb roasted on the spit and warming herself in long sunsets which wrapped the world in mandarin skin.

But more than anything, Lana loved the sea. Further down the split, on the comma-like curl of the shallow, southwestern gulf, there were sparsely populated beaches with khaki-colored sand and water in an aquamarine hue. Perhaps it was modest compared with tropical beaches she had never seen. But for her the world's most shallow sea, which was sometimes seen as nothing more than an extension of the great black briny deep beyond — without coconut trees, thatched huts, horseshoe shaped atolls or waters deep and ultramarine — was still some great big, beautiful expression of everything.

Dad told her those shallow waters were the perfect place to teach a little girl how to swim. On her first day, leading her beyond the knee-high breakers, he put his big, steady hands beneath her back as she floated in water for the first time.

She gazed into the endless blue sky feeling weightless and without fear. Her mind returned to the warm amniotic fluids before her eyes had ever opened to the world, safe, oh so safe, from harm. It was her first feeling being in the hands of God, a being of light riding a crepuscular ray up through a stratocumulus cloud and beaming off into Heaven. She was buoyed by boundless love, awash in agape.

She spent many days in those waters, feet kicking, little hands splashing as Mom and Dad took turns teaching a rabbit to be a fish. When it got dark they would watch the world awash in water colors.

Lana built a castle in the sand and then in the sky, locking memory away in a tower with a princess. For in lifetimes are created those that are both forever and never more. And in times of Moscow snowstorm and familial fury, Lana would dream of the shore.

And deep underground, remembering all that was light in the world and all that was dark, she knew why they had to go after the bird. For once upon a time the nightmare man was a lone figure of dark cutting out a small corner of dark in all that bright. And now her wingless little bird was the last speck of light in a dimming world.

Chapter 18

LANA'S STORY WAS ENOUGH TO convince Tima that the little bird was worth braving the perils ahead. Something in that monstrous man reminded him of the many nightmares he had faced in his own waking life. Little bird or not, he told Lana he'd gladly kick that S.O.B. in the teeth if they met him along the way.

So the two stepped onto the carpeted elevator floor and took in the scene of ancient dreams.

Gönpo stepped in behind them, closing the red door and pulling shut the sliding scissor gate.

The children felt an uncanny calm, basking in Nefertem's light.

Gönpo pulled the lever, and the trio began their slow ascent. Tima thought he caught shadows flitting across the wall; perhaps it was the figures adorning the walls themselves which were starting to wriggle and writhe. The elevator tottered. Claustrophobia and the fear of unseen heights crept in.

"What floor did you say we're goin' to again?" Tima asked.

"To the eighty-three-thousandth, nine hundred and ninety-ninth floor," Gönpo replied.

Tima felt the elevator wobble again as it slowly crept up impossible heights.

"Christ," Tima huffed. "At this rate it's gonna' take us thirteen thousand years to get up there."

"I was going slowly so as not to startle you and the young lady. Would you like to go faster?"

"Yer damn right I would!"

"And what about you, madam?"

Lana was more doubtful about expediting their journey.

"Is it safe?"

"Oh yes, perfectly safe. Though some have described a slight feeling of exhilaration when moving at faster speeds, we haven't had an accident yet!"

"What's e-x-h-i-l-a-r-a-t-i-o-n?"

"The butterflies in your belly when you ride a roller coaster."

"But I've never ridden a roller coaster!"

"Would you like to take a ride to the stars?"

"I … I guess so."

"Hurry it up already!" Tima demanded.

"As you wish, sir. Please hold on."

"Hold onto wha…?"

But the second Gönpo's hand hit the lever, they took off like a rocket.

The young kids coughed up butterflies from their stomachs as the tapestries became fully animated, acting out a universal dance of Yama being trampled underfoot at an increasingly frenetic pace.

Gönpo appeared to grow 34 arms pulling 34 levers in circular spin, twirling round and round like a Catherine wheel.

They continued to pick up speed until all they could see was a lattice of light. Gönpo sailed to the ceiling a pinwheel galaxy.

The children reached out and gripped his spiral arms, riding the merry-go-round of vastitude. Faster and faster, until even that galactic spin blurred the boundaries between myriad stars, turning all of creation into one big blanket of blaze.

Behind closed eyes Lana felt the warmth of summer sun — the force of propulsion gripped her like her father's sturdy hands guiding her over an Azovian wave.

All of existence, it seemed, became nothing more than a single shard of memory, where youth, light and life vanquished death. And Lana no longer cared if she were a star sailor or merely an angel face caressed by Helios' hand.

One mantra floated through her mind in infinite reprise: 'I just want this to last forever, I just want this to last forever...'

And that voyage did last forever. And that voyage finished in an instant.

And just as suddenly as it had started, with the pull of the lever the ride came to a halt. A long ding resonated in the cab. Tima and Lana looked each other in the eyes, which were still swimming with constellations.

The tapestried-tiles had returned to stasis. The rows of bulbs buzzed blue.

Gönpo pulled open the scissor gate.

"Your floor."

He pushed open the red-padded door and stood to the side. Nothing was visible on the other side beyond blinding light.

"What's ... what's out there?" Tima tentatively asked.

"Why, the Valley of Death, of course, just as you requested."

"And there ain't no way you can just take us right up to that bird bath?"

"Oh no, the 84,000th floor is restricted."

"But I mean, there's no shaft? Nothin' to crawl through?"

"Oh, no, sir, the emergency exit is quite firmly locked."

"Why would ya do a thing like that?"

"Well, it could be quite dangerous leaving it open on our ride. Why, were the hatch to fly open during the trip to the higher floors, I do believe you might end up floating in space forever. God himself might not be able to find you out there."

"Tima," Lana asked, pulling on the bottom of his jumper. "Are you okay?"

"What's dat' supposed ta' mean? Of course I'm okay! I just think there's a lotta shady dealin' goin' on 'round here! Now this goon's tellin' us we gotta go through some Death Valley rather than take the elevator up just one more floor. Why I bet if I..."

Tima suddenly grabbed onto the lever.

"I wouldn't do that if I were you."

"And why not?"

"For one, the gate is open, so we cannot move. And even if we did move, the only way is down. Do you really want to fall through three thousand realms in an instant with the cab open? I wouldn't recommend it. You just might get flung out into Avīci by accident. While no one stays forever, it's practically long enough to feel that way. I can promise you, kind sir, you do not want that at all.

"Now, if you'd like me to take you back down, I'd be happy to do that. But if you want to go up, well, the first step you must take is right out that door."

Tima scrutinized Gönpo's unvexed visage and felt his bluff called. His hand slowly slid off the lever.

"Right. After you finish your business here, come back, ring the bell, and I'll return in a jiffy. Oh, and one more thing," he said, reaching into his jacket pocket. "The color doesn't exactly match, but you'll need this."

He handed over Lana a glove the color of an Egyptian lotus petal to replace the one she had left above.

"A flower of this color was the first piece of light to rise from the abyss. Keep this on your hand, and under dark waters you'll never sink."

"Thank you, Mr. Gönpo!"

"At your service, madam," he said with a slight bow.

Lana turned to Tima, who looked sullen.

"Are you ready, Tima?"

Tima stared down at his boots.

"It's okay if you're afraid."

"I ain't afraid!"

"I know. But even if you were afraid, it's okay."

"I told ya," Tima growled, baring his teeth, "I ain't afraid of nothin'!"

"You cannot be brave, sir, if you are never afraid," Gönpo told Tima.

"What kinda crazy talk is that? Only cowards are afraid!"

"No, sir, that is not correct at all. You'd have to be crazy not to be afraid, sometimes. What makes a man brave is what he does when he's afraid. If you are scared to death and then take death head on, why, that's the bravest thing a little boy or a girl can do."

Tima looked Gönpo in the eyes.

"You're a smart man for someone runnin' an elevator."

"And you're a good boy, Tima, no matter what they did to you."

Tima's amber eyes went wide, the orange flecks in fiery sunflower iris glowing like wind-blown embers.

"What does he mean, Tima?"

"Nothin'," Tima said, looking away to hide the dousing of blossom burn. "Are you ready to go?"

"I'm always ready!" Lana exclaimed, channeling the pioneers of a previous time.

Lana took Tima's hand. Steeling himself one more time, they stepped into effulgence until all the lines separating life from light were erased.

Chapter 19

"IN ALL MY YEARS, I'VE never seen anything like it. His face looked like Herring Under a Fur Coat that had been crushed in a hydraulic press. That's the last time I answer a noise complaint at 4:30 in the morning," the tired man said, exhaling sharply and dragging on his cigarette.

Major Kuzminov had the unenviable task of being the quarter militiamen for the worst quarter in the worst district of the city — Kapotnaya. It was his job to keep tabs on all of the filth in the second quarter, who'd been given an extra coat of soot on account of the Moscow Oil Refinery.

Junkies, pushers, pimps, prostitutes, pipe-sleeping bums, Central Asian migrants, street toughs, ex-cons, Caucasian mobsters, glue-sniffing punks and the occasional working stiff were his wards. He relied on a motley network of prevaricating informants and half-blind eyes to keep the peace in a city sinking in chaos. And the second quarter had sunk more than most. Overdoses, abused wives, curb-stomped street vendors, stabbings and gangland shootings were part of the beat.

He wasn't just supposed to respond to crime, he was supposed to prevent it.

But in truth, he spent more time stopping crimes from being classified as crimes than fighting them, a reality whose blame he promptly shrugged off his own slumped shoulders.

The 'ticking system' guaranteed a paper trail longer than the Silk Road. A cop who failed to solve a crime had meticulously documented a case of self-incrimination along the way.

And failure, not to police, but to solve the crimes one attempted to police, was all that mattered. That's how murders became suicides and high crimes were covered up for the lowest common denominator — saving one's own skin.

But last night's case of macabre ultra-violence would soak blood through any rug it was swept under. It had given pause to the most jaded of militamen.

"Is anyone talking?" asked Sergeant Vitaly Novoselov, a longtime friend and academy mate who worked far down the ladder in an uneventful public safety beat in the northwestern district of Schukino.

Major Kuzminov sucked too hot black tea between his teeth before taking another puff.

Normally such a disparity in rank would made such a discussion, let alone friendship, impossible. But having swum in a shark tank for so many years, Major Kuzminov knew the value of a good friend, and, if a few too many drinks were had, was sentimental for the time when they had been equals, when none of the things that had transpired had put so much space between their respective places on the table of ranks.

"His friend got head kicked into a concussion. When he came to he was drunk and disoriented, took a swing at a cop — the kid had no idea where he was. He probably got a few more bumps than he needed being restrained until the ambulance got there.

"Paramedics hauled his ass off after giving him a sedative. A sedative right to the ass with the biggest damned needle I've ever seen. Turns out there was a lot of cranial bleeding, and he went into a coma.

"There was another one on the couch whom we thought had drunk himself to death. Needless to say, he slept through the grisliest murder I've ever seen. Maybe the bastard got lucky on that count. No one, not even those punks, should have to see something like that."

"What about the neighbors?"

"They heard everything and saw nothing. Seems to have gone on for a good while. Front door was left wide open during the whole melee."

"And no one came to see what was going on?"

"No. People hid behind their doors. They were scared. Let's just say these three had kept their neighbors living in a state of agitation. We've been called in two dozen times on account of those idiots fighting, drinking and otherwise engaging in acts of hooliganism.

"Sources on the street say they formed some sort of skinhead crew. They're not affiliated with any larger organization from what we know, though they meet up at underground rock shows from time to time with other 'boneheads'. The extent of their criminal activity seems pretty diffuse. Basically, small time local punks causing mayhem for their own amusement.

"Those three knuckleheads used to rob migrant street vendors for money. Other times they just kicked the crap out of 'em for fun. Something tells me they won't be doing that anymore. The deceased even had a big swastika tattooed on his chest. Can you believe that? A Russian man, getting a swastika tattoo on his chest. This country is losing its mind."

"You think the murder was connected to Chechens, Georgians maybe? Could've robbed the wrong guy."

"Maybe. The little pit bull who had to be put down was mumbling something about a 'taximan'. Maybe they robbed a driver, and his friends came back to collect. Maybe things went south from there. We'll canvass the area and talk to the gypsy cab drivers but that's a bit of a needle in a haystack.

"For now, our best hope is for the one in the coma to wake up. But I'm not holding my breath on that one."

"Good Lord," Sergeant Novoselov said, nervously tapping his fingers on the metal table in the bare bones stolovaya, creating tiny whirlpools in his sugar-filled tea.

"We live in a city where a violent murder can take place in the middle of the night, door wide open, and not a single person comes out to check on it. This is not the Moscow we grew up in."

"Welcome to the free Russia, comrade!"

Major Kuzminov bellowed, but something came over his eyes and he fell silent. He took the last drag from his cigarette, stubbed it out in the ashtray, and immediately went fishing in his pack for another.

He turned and stared out the window pane onto the fading light of

Tsvetnoy Boulevard. The black bags under his eyes were heavier than the clouds outside.

Families walked back and forth down the damp streets. Cars whizzed by, sending pedestrians fleeing from puddles in flight.

"We talk about crime of passion," he said, turning back to Sergeant Novoselov. "But there was no love in this."

Sergeant Novoselov stared down into his spoon-spun whirlpool, fingers locking in an arch around the ceramic.

"You know, I think we're the only country in the world that has two different words for people eaters — those who ate the dead and those who hunt others. Such is our history, to need to come up with two different words for that," the sergeant ruefully replied.

They sat there without a word as the revolutions slowed to nil, leaving a sugar bed to settle at the bottom of his cup.

"You are terrible at cheering people up, Vitaly," the major finally said, breaking the silence.

"Yes," he chuckled, "but that's why you called me. I am an expert at feeling terrible with people."

"I know no one better … or worse."

Sergeant Novoselov laughed, looking up with dark eyes that were still lighter than the conversation.

"It's one thing when people feel like the world is falling apart. It's another thing when they act like it."

"Well, someone's world was smashed into a million pieces last night," Major Kuzminov said with a sigh, cigarette half turned to ash and dangling from lips in suspended disbelief.

"And now I gotta go find a hammer in a stack of hammers."

"Good luck with that."

Major Kuzminov cracked a wry smile. He downed the rest of his tea in a single gulp, stubbed out his cigarette and pushed a metal screeching chair against the tiles, standing up.

"I should get going."

"Of course, Major Kuzminov, you've got a murderer to catch."

Chapter 20

THE MARCH WIND BREAKING ON his face, Viktor pushed his way back between the cars and onto the pock-marked street. A black Chaika M13 with tinted windows crawled down the road and stopped 30 feet from Viktor, idling in place. With only a few thousand made for bigwigs of another era, to see it pull up on his street was an absolute oddity.

A mobster in a Mercedes was one thing. This was something else altogether.

After gawking at the once-luxury ride, Viktor took off in the other direction. The driver kicked it into first gear. Seeing the car inching forward, Viktor squeezed between two bumpers to let it pass. But as soon as he did, the car came to a halt. Viktor returned to the road, and once again the car began trailing him. Viktor squeezed between yet another pair of bumpers. Once again, the car stopped.

Agitated, Viktor stormed over toward the car.

"Hey, buddy, you got a problem?"

The car sped off with no thought to puddles, potholes or the sole pedestrian on the street, leaving black water spray in its wake. Viktor nearly rolled over the hood of a car diving out of the way. He watched in shock as the vehicle disappeared in a cloud of exhaust, a maniac's laughter echoing in his head.

Someone, something was clearly out to get him. But how? How could that shadowy man have instantly known about something that went down across town? None of it was making any sense. Viktor needed answers, but none were coming. And then the chill set in his bones. If whoever was in that car knew anything about last night, he knew where Viktor lived. More importantly, he knew about Lana.

Without a second thought, Viktor hurried to his garage, got into his car and sped off.

He drove up and down every road and side street. But neither Lana nor the black car fell on his radar. He must have stopped a dozen people, asking if they'd seen a little girl in a blue jacket come their way. No one had seen a thing.

Without so much as a lead, his fears continued to grow. Viktor needed to talk to someone. He needed someone with an ear to the street. He knew just the man.

Chapter 21

BY LATE AFTERNOON, WITHOUT WORD from Viktor or sight of Lana, panic took hold. The walls of their small flat began closing in. The melancholy of winter's valediction was amplified by so many months without sun. Dark thoughts left to fester were a boon to madness. Galya had to do something, even if that something was in vain. Anything to offset the vagaries of the mind.

So, she got dressed and headed down to the police station. And like a cherry tree in December, this trip was not bearing fruit.

The moment she saw the kid behind the counter with sleepy eyes and a uniform two sizes too large, she knew all was for naught. Just getting him to engage beyond disinterested replies was a challenge. Compelling him to actually do his job — forget about it.

"She's just a kid, kids go out to play," the young constable said with a yawn.

His insouciance riled Galya to no end. It wasn't that he didn't have a point. It was the fact that he couldn't have cared less either way. He just wanted Galya to leave so he could sleep off his hangover.

And out of nowhere she snapped, dressing him down like he was one of her students. Barely removed from school, her reprimand worked like a charm. Maybe he was a cop now, but a lifetime of being bawled out by one homeroom teacher after the other would not be shaken so easily.

He pleaded with her, saying they couldn't do anything until it had been 24 hours, swearing up and down he'd tell the boys to keep an eye out for her daughter.

Galya stormed out, knowing he'd settle right back into inaction once the blush had left his cheeks and the ribbing had run its course.

After she slammed the door shut behind her, inciting hooting and hollering from his squad, an older cop approached the constable, asking him what the commotion had been about.

"Oh, it was nothing, Sgt. Novoselov. Just some crazy woman who's scared 'cause her kid went out to play and hasn't come home yet."

"What's nothing today is a tragedy tomorrow, Constable."

"Yeah?" he lazily replied, picking up the sports section of a newspaper. "Well, it ain't tomorrow yet."

Chapter 22

VIKTOR CIRCLED AROUND SAVELOVSKAYA SQUARE in search of the Georgian's car. He didn't even know what to ask, but something, anything needed to be released from his pressure cooker head. Looping through the parking lot where men lined the concrete like birds on the wire, sending smoke signals into the night, he drove a few hundred meters to Sushevsky Val. There, a massive neoclassical apartment block ran parallel to the flyover, where cars whizzed by on their way toward the airport.

Viktor pulled his car around the tail end of the 10-story monolith, which incongruously broke into Corinthian colonnades. On the other side of the road, Viktor noticed a car that looked just like the Georgian's maroon Volga. Parking behind it, he got out with aching joints. The temperature had dropped a hair-below freezing. Tiny wisps of snow spiraled under unlit street lights, though the road remained wet and muddy.

Viktor headed back to the rush of traffic running low and high, turning left down the main road beneath the brutalist concrete facade with the most superficial application of Grecian glory.

He walked along the monolith until reaching double doors without a sign, pinned between arcade windows whose lights had already been turned off for the night.

He pulled the doors open and stepped inside, descending a narrow staircase which opened into a dingy, windowless, 'ryumochnaya' dive.

Standing behind high, circular wooden tables, men of every class in a society that once had none billowed out smoke, took in spirits, drank flat beer from sud-stained mugs and contributed to the indecipherable den of muzhik love and loathing.

A surly 30-something with red hair, an ample bust and greater contempt for her clientele resentfully slung out shot glasses, beer mugs and oily chebureki half-filled with food poisoning behind the back counter. If a customer inquired about a drink while she was smoking a cigarette, he'd likely end up with a mouthful of ash in his room-temperature lager. That is, if he were lucky.

In the back corner, Viktor spotted the Georgian, who let out a bellow that rose above the commotion. A wrought-iron man forged in the shadow of Ararat joined in the joviality, slapping the big man on the back.

The Georgian, whose mother had named him Irakly, was 15 years Viktor's senior, 30 kilograms above his weight class and 10 centimeters below his nose. That corpulent cabbie really got a case of the tingle toe, gut shoved up under the steering wheel, constant swirl of cigarette smoke giving stimulus to stillness.

They shared stories of the night, shared drinks, shared sorrows wrapped up in grape leaves to make them more palatable. He also got involved in a lot of business that Viktor had never thought he'd sully his hands with. And yet it had taken Viktor one night of digging to surmount a lifetime of dirt.

Irakly saw Viktor making his way through the cancerous fog and beckoned him over with a heavy hand.

"Viktor, Viktor! Good to see you join the working man for a drink at a reasonable hour," he guffawed.

But once Viktor got closer and the Georgian saw his eyes, the jolly man's mirth escaped him. Even in the low light haunt of high and low lives, the cordierite-colored contusions on his friend's face clearly made the dichromatic shift from black to blue.

"My friend, you've seen better days!"

"Don't worry, Irakly, I feel much, much worse than I look."

"You look like hell."

"Like I said."

The two shook hands. Viktor tried not to grimace as pain shot through his elbow.

He extended a hand to the man with the black cap and Emil Babayan rose on the other side of the table.

His mitts were sandstone rough. His eyes were harder. Black searched blue for understanding. The shadow on the sea found it.

Hard hands unlocked. The two exchanged nods.

"Tigran this is Viktor, Viktor, Tigran."

"Pleased to make your acquaintance," Viktor said.

Tigran nodded again.

Viktor turned his gaze to the big man.

"Irakly, we need to talk."

"Why of course! Stay, have a drink, the day is young."

"No, we need to talk alone."

Irakly studied his eyes, then leaned over and whispered in his friend's ear. Without a word, Tigran nodded at the Georgian and walked off.

"Quiet, that one, but a good man. He fought in the Nagorno-Karabakh War. He's seen his fair share of hard knocks. Speaking of hard knocks, it looks like you've taken a few since I last saw you."

Viktor looked down at his feet. Despite the droopy lids, the Georgian's gimlet-eye caught sight of his crestfallen companion on the way down.

His smile slumped into a more somber expression. He drank from his glass of cognac and sighed in satisfaction.

"Viktor, you really don't look well. What the hell happened to you?"

"I had a disagreement."

"With a moving bus?"

"Something like that."

"How much did they take you for?"

Viktor almost said "everything" before stopping himself.

"Enough."

"What about the gun? This is why I got it for you. But it won't do you much good if you don't use it."

Viktor hemmed and hawed before mustering up the resolve to start asking questions.

"Have you heard anything?" he said in a low voice.

The Georgian shot him a quizzical look before taking another sip from his drink.

"Heard 'anything'? I've heard everything, Viktor. Which thing are we talking about?"

"I..." but Viktor fell silent, not knowing how to go on. He was trying to hedge his bets but didn't even know what game he was playing. Yet he had to know, something, anything, about what was already known, on the streets, as well as the station.

"Does this have anything to do with the sad state of your face?"

Viktor answered in the affirmative with sinking eyes.

"What part of everything do you want to know?"

Viktor furtively scanned the dimly lit room for eavesdropping ears, but he himself could barely pick a word from the cacophony of clinking glasses and endlessly overlapping colloquy.

"Last night sounds like a good place to start."

"Clearly. Apart from the usual muggings, stolen cars and drunken brawls?"

"Apart from all of that."

"Well okay," the Georgian said, breaking into a fit of coughs and, upon collecting himself, adding to the congestion with the strike of a match.

"A guy got shot in the kneecap during a dispute in Richnoy Vockzal with some pissed off Aver. A businessman got shoved into a black Mercedes kicking and screaming coming out of the Metropol. I figure he'll be sent home one piece at a time any day now. Either that or he's already made his peace beyond the pines. There was a gunfight or two that led to nothing. Oh! And this is a rich one," he said, sucking on his cigarette.

"A crooked narcotics cop from the 18th precinct. His favorite game is planting drugs on girls to coerce them into coitus. Well, turns out he pulled that trick on the wrong girl last night. They were at a club in Kitai Gorod. Dropped a baggie of blow right into the girl's cleavage and pressed her to plead her way out of the charge. Turns out the girls were with a couple of heavies, 'former' kontraktniki types, who didn't care much for his charms. One of them knocked his eye right out of his head. Not exactly eye for an eye, but close enough. Something tells me he won't be seeing much action for a while!" the Georgian bellowed hoarsely before breaking into a hacking cough.

Viktor's head started to throb as he tasted the violence. Something in the smoke and chatter magnified, the pressure grew, and then a dizzy spell came on.

Only then did he realize he'd barely eaten a thing all day, and whatever he had managed to put down had long since come up on a forest's edge.

His stomach began to contort like a man trying to bite his own elbow. He braced himself against the table.

"Are you okay?" the Georgian asked, himself barely recovering from his coughing fit.

"Yeah," Viktor groaned. "I just need to eat something."

"Oh, well I wouldn't eat here. That is, unless you have the urge to spend the next three days on the john! I wouldn't be surprised if they were using what's left from the polar bear meat that did the Nazis in at Schatzgraber!"

Despite his discomfort, Viktor couldn't help but crack a smile. Irakly's soul was iridescent even in this dark watering hole.

"I think I'll take your word on that one," he said, his grumbling belly subsumed in the sea of grumbling men.

"So apart from crooked cops getting their eyes punched out and all the usual madness of this city, have any other stories hit the streets?"

The Georgian paused, taking a final drag from his cigarette before extinguishing it in a half-cut beer can ashtray. He then began scratching the side of his face.

"There was something in South Moscow. A decadent American horror story, as it were. Apparently it was a senseless act of violence. No one I know knows anything about who's behind it, nor do their people. It's the one real mystery of the Moscow night."

Viktor's heart sunk. He could feel what was coming. He tried to steel his resolve, but he already felt so weak in the knees he risked dropping to the floor like a sack of potatoes. He arms tensed, anchored on the table's edge.

"What ... what happened?"

"From what I understand, down in some god-forsaken suburb, not far from the oil refinery, some wanna-be crew got the life stomped out of them. One of them got his head clean bashed in."

Memories of a hammer fist hitting a nail until it went straight through the board, splitting the wood into a thousand splinters along the grain, flashed in Viktor's head. A glottal stop sent bile burning down even hotter than it came up. It had taken most of his will not to blow battery acid all over the table.

Viktor broke into a sweat.

"You really don't look good."

"I'm fine!" Viktor unconvincingly replied.

"Anyways, the pigs have been rounding up every Caucasian cabby and vendor, giving all of 'em hell. It's clearly one big fishing expedition. Clearly, they don't know a thing."

"They don't?"

"No. But here's the thing. The bratva don't know either. Word on the street is, this wasn't sanctioned by anyone. Not that anyone cares, mind you. These punks were Nazis. Seriously. Russian Nazis. Never thought I'd live to see that! A bunch of cowards too. Robbing random migrants, fruit vendors, working men. It's unsurprising a group like that would rub someone the wrong way."

"So, no one has any idea who was behind it?"

"Like I said, no one."

Viktor became pensive. He wanted to talk about Lana, the maniac who chased him, but it was all simply too crazy to put into words.

"Thank you," Viktor said. "I really should get going."

"Sure you won't be staying for a drink?"

"I really can't."

"I understand. Just one more thing, Viktor."

"Yeah?"

"The gun. Get rid of it."

Chapter 23

GALYA STOOD OUTSIDE THEIR BUILDING, realizing there was no point in going back up to let her ugly thoughts pile up like old newspapers. The impotent rage from her visit to the police station had yet to dissipate.

She knew the whole city was a den of tragedy. So many missing kids, there was no point in raising an eyebrow until a body was found face down in the river or stripped and bare in the forest. That was their logic anyways. But it was the sort of logic that left hearts in ribbons.

So, she set off to look for Lana. Heading down Aviatsionnaya Street, Galya took a left past the corner store where a circle of gruff men in black leather jackets drank from a two-liter bottle of Okhota beer beneath a shroud of cigarette smoke.

One of them leered at her, but Galya met his lecherous look with a reproachful stare. Perhaps triggering a flashback from his own disappointed homeroom teacher who saw him then just as he was today, he grumbled a few four-letter words and stared at his square-toed shoes. The others paid her no mind. They were her neighbors, even if they were strangers.

She made her way on down to the Moscow Canal, trash-strewn and otherwise abandoned.

Beyond the woods on the other side of the bank lay the Khimki River. Beyond that, Spartak Stadium. The melted ice had retreated into a jagged brim extending several feet out from the sloping concrete bank.

A gathering wind hurried along straggling clouds across the sky.

Grey, diffuse light fell on the un-iced waterfront. Memories came forth from the shapeless gloom.

Viktor with Lana in one arm standing on a bridge over the river. Galya by his side. He told Lana about a Turkish word to describe just this thing — moonlight dancing on the water — but she couldn't recall it.

Lana had thought it sounded like duck-billed platapus. Perhaps it didn't, but that was no matter. It was the limited associations of a young mind following rivers, reaching out from her small pound to find the beauty and bounty of the ocean. Her love of the world was bigger than the words that all the big people had for it anyways. They could name it — she could feel it.

Galya leaned over the rusting rail and exhaled. Grey concrete, grey sky, grey water, grey lives. Everything of color was a thing of memory. What she wouldn't give to see Lana's sky-blue eyes cut holes in the granite sky. And yet somehow, shapes took form in the dense block of clouds. A rabbit in the mist. A hedgehog in the fog. A leopard outrunning its spots. A mountain rising to Heaven.

Out of nowhere, tears began to well. Footsteps fell.

Galya looked up, inconspicuously whipping her eyes. A tall man walked down the promenade, shrouded in darkness.

Closer now. A wide smile seemed stretched across his shadow-cast face. He was laughing to himself. He seemed positively insane.

She reflexively wiped her nose and began casually walking away. His laugher grew louder. Galya slowly picked up her pace. He did not fall behind. Anxiety, then fear followed.

She furtively shot him a glance over her shoulder. The shadow man was gaining on her. Galya widened her stride to a gazelle's gait.

When he followed suit, she knew. She ran. He pursued.

Shoulders down and arms at 90 degrees, Galya propelled her light-as-a-feather frame with pumping arms and driving legs, bolting across the strand.

She ran up the slight embankment and back onto the streets, empty of people and bathed in blinking peach light.

He was right behind her. She could feel his movements — precise, powerful, unwavering. And yet somehow the boom of his laughter grew in the pursuit. She couldn't figure it out amidst that maddening din. How was he even breathing?

He wasn't gaining, nor falling behind. He was stuck in a five second lag.

One slip up on a patch of ice and she was finished. But her fear was subsumed in flight. All there was was the run.

In a minute's time, running in the middle of the street, she approached the grocery store on the right-hand side, the circle of carousing men still holding court outside.

She cried for help in a cloud of condensation and lost a second to her pursuer. She cut back onto the sidewalk and ran past the bemused circle of storefront revelers. One of them tried to cut the madman off at the pass and was smashed into concussion on the curb with a stiff arm.

She got her second back. A stream of invective tore through the night. It was soon drowned out by the lunatic's howl. She cut a left around the corner back onto the aviator's street. The burn in her lungs grew but she refused to relent. She'd rather run to her death than let this bastard get his hands on her.

She was praying for a neighbor, someone to step outside. She was praying to run into Viktor. Where was he?

She nearly crashed into the main door outside her block. But as she tried to pull it open he came bounding at her at a breakneck speed. She ducked as he lunged at her, slamming into the door. His airborne boots scraped across her back as she pivoted in her crouch. Springing up to dash, he grabbed her by her ankle. She smacked her face against the pavement.

A warm wet trickle poured down her face. His grip tighten as he pulled her in. It felt like vines were wrapped around her ankle. His gaping mouth seemed big enough to swallow the world. She pushed up on her palms and kicked him right in the teeth. More laughter. Another strong thrust and her hard heel landed with a crunch.

His grip loosened with his teeth. She managed to break free from his impossibly long-fingered grip, sprung to her feet, flung open the door and bounded up the stairs. A lunatic's laughter followed. Reaching her apartment, she fumbled with her keys, as madness was heard but not seen.

Unlocking the door, she practically dove onto the floor before slamming it behind her. She pressed her shoulder to the padding, shaky hands struggling to turn each lock and slide the chain. She slid down on the floor, struggling to slow her breath. Wide-eyed, she ran to the telephone to call the police.

When she picked up the receiver, the static shower was so loud she had to hold it away from her ear. And then a mad cackle rose above the crackle. Galya slammed the receiver down. She looked back out into the foyer, dim in the ashen light of early evening.

Heart in her throat, she tiptoed toward the door, eyes fixed on the band of light rounding the peephole. And then she froze. The ring of light was eclipsed in darkness.

Chapter 24

W<small>IND</small> <small>BLEW</small> <small>GREEN</small> <small>GRASS</small> <small>TO</small> rustle down the parabolic backside of the glacial trough.

Bell flowers and cranesbills mottled the meadow; Beargrass watchtowers rose five-feet high in fragrant-white flower, frozen-firework bursts of bloom. A lapis blue river ran through the malachite waves of green. The morning sun turned gossamer threads to gold.

At the valley's head beyond, a ridge shaped like the ashen jaw of an ancient god filled the distance, salivating over its manger in water fall. Snow-capped, the canines of Anubis rose. Way down below, two tiny figures skirted those white-flower watch towers and sent petals of purple and pink sailing, leaving evanescent impressions on verdant lea.

The larger of the two, a porcupine of nettlesome demeanor, languidly pulled his bundle of quills through the valley grass and floral affluence. He panted, struggling (and failing) to keep up as a much smaller rabbit with sky blue eyes and cloud-cotton tail exuberantly ran circles around him. Some distant memory of another world pointed toward him being the rabbit, and not the tortoise of the twosome.

The pair, soft and prickly, pushed on toward the impossibly high mandible cutting its teeth against the sky. From a distance, every twist and turn of mountain pass and sharp slope of arête, every crag to be climbed and frost-bound chasm abetted by rock fall and still little fingers faltering grip sprawl, every snow slide aiming for life to be buried in ice and scree, all were turned by distance and separation into inexplicable beauty.

The babble of brook filled their ears as sunbeams shattered into tesserae waves on water, a mosaic of movement, fluid but still. A mountain breeze blew over. The apex of life rested in the Valley of Death.

On a slope overlooking the river, a birch tree grew horizontally in search of light. Atop that tree, grey eyes fixated on the odd couple pilgrims aspiring to great heights. Long claws from thickly furred paws kneaded the bark. Bushy tail waved like a prayer flag in the wind. The cat's back twitched, sending black rosettes sailing down rippling grey fur. Ears perked up and eyes dilated. Instinct propelled by belly rumbles impelled the feline fatal.

The snow leopard jumps down onto the grass, stalking its prey posthaste.

At first prickly and soft don't see the razor wilding cut-throat bounding down the valley. But the rabbit in yet another victory lap around the porcupine caught the charge on their periphery.

The bunny stopped dead in its tracks, prompting the porcupine to spot the reason its partner's patter went silent. Four feline legs on the double was the only answer he needed. How strange to see such ferocious beauty at a distance, charting a murderous course.

But stand too long and the lovers of rare beauty would soon be its martyrs. So sharp spines and cottontail did the only thing leporidae and rodentia do when caught in the crosshairs of panthera pursuit – they ran.

At this distance the rabbit still had a successful chance at flight. But the porcupine's shot at outrunning the approaching cat was deflated by its terrapin clip. Rather than leave its slow-moving friend in the dust, the rabbit directed them toward a rock garden parallel to the river bank.

On the cat's approach, the two managed to disappear in the lithic labyrinth. They zigzagged through the stony maze until taking shelter behind a boulder. The rabbit had to hold in a scream after instinctually huddling up to his prickly friend's backside, nearly being deflated in the process.

Beyond the sound of their beating hearts, they could hear paws shift pebbles as the cat tried to sniff them out amidst the rocks. Slowly, the antipode pair slinked around the stone to catch a peek at what might be on the other side. Tip by toe, they rounded the perimeter. In a flash, they caught the leopard's body bounding between stones. The leopard stopped. A breeze carried a whiff of blood trickle from quill prick into its nose. Pressed against the rock, the pair pulled back and out of sight, though the leopard was being guided by another scent.

The hunted circled the boulder and veered left toward the river. The tranquil burble of water over bed and rock cut such a sharp contrast to the life-and-death tension in the air. The lullaby rush nearly lulled them into a false sense of respite.

The calm was snapped with a panther pounce into pebble slide somewhere behind them. Unseen, the pair rushed off until sheltering behind another redoubt of rock. The leopard, on the scent but inexactly, continued its meandering pursuit.

This game of cat and not-quite mouse could not go on forever. The outcrop was a temporary shelter in green expanse. The choices were hide and seek forever or make waves in the river.

Pressed up against their presidio, the pair pressed up against the cool stone and unanimously exhaled. Then a breeze blew, sending quills to tap against the rock. The leopard ears perked up. Triangulating scent and sound, it dashed toward the source of unintentional tap code.

The rabbit and porcupine kicked up dust and gravel in flight. They cut around opposite sides of a boulder and barreled face-first into each other. Smarting from the smack, the rabbit at least was lucky it wasn't a rear-end collision.

They listened for their predator in motion. Silence. A shadow eclipsed them. Looking up, they saw the mighty cat perched to pounce. But between spikes and stones, the cat had set its sights on the softest of landings, leaping at the rabbit. The rabbit darted out of the way just in time, as outstretched paws were steeped in pebble and dust.

The rabbit made its way through the rock and out of sight. The snow leopard shifted its eyes to the prickly remainder. In all its days it had never seen such a strangely barbed brunch. The two, in fact, were nearly the same size, though the leopard had never been made to count fear as a factor in its calculations, underestimating the variable all that pointy plumage would play.

The cat crouched down and wiggled its hind legs, sending the transmission loud and clear down radio tower quills. The porcupine responded by rattling its sabers and clacking its teeth.

The threat went unheeded as the snow leopard lunged, prompting the porcupine to respond with a sideways charge. A swinging set of razor-sharp claws got a paw-full of pain. The cat reset as the porcupine skirted sideways around its attacker. The cat looked to pounce again, but the porcupine spun its thorny backside, stopping the assault in a cloud of dust.

The porcupine once again ran off, prompting the cat to pursue out of instinct. The prickly pig howled in fear.

With the snow leopard hot on its heels, the porcupine knew its tortoise legs were no match for the gainful gait descending on its flank. So, the prickly prey stopped dead in its tracks and flared out its quills. The cat crashed into the pincushion and winced as it withdrew with a quiver-full of quills.

The pain of fiery thistles radiated through his face. A yowl echoed through the valley.

Smarting from the much-worse-than nettle sting, the rumbling in its belly kept the snow leopard from completely giving up. There would be plenty of time to lick its wounds later, on a full or empty stomach.

And yet the hot stove had been touched more than once. The pain wasn't even a memory – it was pulsing in a bloody maw. The next series of lazy jabs were tentative, with the prickle under paw producing immediate retreats. A murderous pursuit turned into a half-hearted sparring session. The cat finally gave up, wandering back toward the river to plop down next to the cool water and extricate the quills with pressed paws.

Left alone in the rock garden, the porcupine jogged off into the grass. It looked everywhere for the rabbit. She was nowhere to be seen. Pressing on into the green, the creature with anything but a barbed heart began to whine.

The slow march through the valley from there on out became a grim affair. Alone, and knowing death could come bounding at any moment, the bucolic frolic of before, even with all of the teasing from his infinitely faster friend, was gone. Now there was nothing left to do but make the trip up top, to the suppressed memories of a mystic lake filled with gods' tears.

— — —

The porcupine trudged on the rest of the day toward the valley head, a hint of terror from the snow leopard in the sunny field underscoring every step. Fear was the black ink on a blanket of flowers, the versicolor splendor of 300 fragrances spread across open fields dimmed down to the black edges of tunnel vision.

Every wind-blown blade of grass and parasol of pollen spin was cause for concern and perked up ears, lest a spotted predator be on the prowl. But apart from driving a terrified marmot back into its hole or watching a couple of red-crowned, black-necked cranes regally dance to take on the mandate of Heaven, the long excursion was a lonely one.

And there was something in that solo-sojourn which made the mid-afternoon sun beat down that much harder – the bug song that much louder. At such a slow speed, it took the out-of-place creature all day to cross the valley.

Finally, on exhausted legs, the prickly pig ascended the final step of the valley slope.

But unlike the jagged teeth seen cutting the sky from the distance, the gums of the incisor ahead was a lush broadleaf canopy, covering the seemingly impossible ascent from the setting sun.

From the woodland of impossibly high oaks, eerie birdsong filled the still dusk air. A blue fog rose between the big trees. The porcupine caught a chill that rattled its quivers. It turned around and saw a saffron river flowing through bucolic bliss. His eyes ran over the eventide valley again, searching out friend and foe alike. But all he heard was avian elegy to the fading light.

To his left, a massive oak is split open like an open zipper at its base.

The sun dipped further as blue mist gloomed the forest floor. Something like the shape of a man seemed to form in the distance, watching him from beyond the limen. A nebulous lapin ran smoke circles around his feet. The mournful moan of the ghost of the mountains sent shivers through living and dead.

The porcupine balked at a dark-wood trip and sought shelter from the night. His eyes were drawn to the split oak. Another wail from the mountain ghost sent the porcupine jogging over to the tree. Inside the hollow, bioluminescent mushrooms cast an eerie glow. The porcupine took a tentative step inside the sanctuary and hunkered down in a ligneous nook.

The spherical caps of bitter oyster mushrooms began to pulse and shift shades. The lights blinked in segments, ascending the right-handed helix of the cavity. The firefox-run up the inner tree got faster and faster, the kaleidoscopic pulsations more frequent. The porcupine was lifted up within the thrumming helix like a tractor beam.

His quills took on all the colors of the rainbow. And then boom! He was shot out of the tree like a barbed cannonball of light, star sailing above impassable heights.

Chapter 25

" TIMA, TIMA," A VOICE CALLED from the dark. His ears tingled with the chill, as well as the tickle of a familiar timber. Something cold and damp was stuck to his face. He breathed in the sylvan dewiness of dead leaves and damp ground. He breathed his own life back into the brume.

"Tima," the voice called again with the shake of a shoulder.

Then the memories of a snow leopard giving chase flooded the wooded calm.

Tima's eyes shot open as he sat up straight in a sloping forest bed. Lana was at his side. He patted himself down to make sure he was feeling what he had always known to be himself. He pulled away the leaf pressed to his face in clammy kiss. He looked up and saw 10 million more stitched together like Devana's umbrageous baldachin thrown over the roof of the world. The remains of the day poked through the closely spaced holes.

Where are we?" Tima asked, the afterglow of transmigration fading.

"A forest, silly."

With a bit of salt thrown down on the slippery plane of reality, Tima stood up, brushing the grime from his knees.

"I knew that, stupid!"

"I'm not stupid!"

Tima sighed.

"I know, I know," he said, pulling in the defensive barbs of his human avatar. "I don't mean to talk so mean to ya, it's just the way everyone talks on the streets. I don't know so many nice folks like you."

Lana's eyes lit up.

"But you are nice, Tima! You saved me, not one time, but two!"

"Yeah, yeah, yeah," he said, awkwardly accepting her praise.

Tima looked up, scanning the majestic canopy formed by thousands of countless tree crowns holding court well over a hundred feet above ground.

"I'll tell ya, I just had the strangest dream. I was some prickly critter runnin' 'round a field with a rabbit. And I'll be damned if a cat wasn't tryin' to eat us. That thing came after me, but I was just too prickly for 'em. But the rabbit ran off. So, I spent the whole day goin' over grass 'til I got to a mountain. And then I got spooked 'cause it was gettin' dark. So I hid inside this old tree covered in all these glowin' mushrooms. And then BOOM! I was shot right into the sky like a bottle rocket. Then I woke up … here."

"I know, Tima, I know!" Lana exclaimed, clapping her hands in excitement. "The same thing happened to me. But I was the bunny! I remember you! You were so funny! A big, slow hedgehog, that's what you were," she giggled.

"I wasn't no hedgehog! I was too damned big to be no hedgehog. I was some other kinda' critter."

"Hedgehog hedgehog hedgehog!" Lana teased.

"Whatever, whatever, I was a hedgehog. But I mean … you really was there, with me?"

"Um-hum!" she voiced cheerfully.

"And you remember that cat?"

"I do!"

"Then why the hell did ya run off?"

"I don't know. When rabbits get scared they run. And when I stopped running you were gone. So I just kept on going. Then I saw the same old tree. And ZOOM! It sent me right up into the sky!"

Lana abruptly became pensive, her eyes scanning the trees.

"The kind old man I met down there, before I met you. He told me it's not a dream. I was a bunny before, and these scary wolves chased me. And a big bear too. And then the bear and the wolves had a bad fight. And a bird picked me up and I went up in the sky. Whoosh again! And he says it's all me. He said we are all music. I didn't really understand. How can I be me, and be a rabbit? How is that music?"

Tima stuck his hand inside his beanie and ruffled his already tousled, damp hair.

"Whoosh," he said under his breath, "whoosh," looking around as the lights of the ancient forest dimmed.

"Well, that old man was right about one thing. It didn't feel like no dream. It felt as real as this, real as pinching my own skin."

Tima took a hold of forearm and squeezed.

"I said it felt like pinching my own skin," he repeated.

"Hey, Lana!"

She didn't reply.

Looking her way, Lana had clearly stiffened up, her eyes wide.

"What's gotten into you?"

"Do you hear that?"

"Hear what?"

But then 'what 'caught his ear as well.

In the distance, an ethereal chorus of whispers echoed in ghostly lament.

"Yeah, I hear that," Tima said with a gulp.

The cries of the unhallowed choristers was getting closer.

"We gotta get outta' here!"

At first the two began walking at a fast clip, but as the wailing got closer, they took off through the darkening forest, feet pressing leaves into muck. Their breath blew cloud crystals over the shin-high fog. The big trees seemed to sway like ancient gods. Terrible voices continued to culminate in some unspoken horror. Even from afar, those spectral screams of the damned blew ice over skin.

Closer and closer, the echoing whispered cries inside the forest walls resonated with wicked revenge. Tima with wild eyes impelled Lana to speeds hindered by a lack of years and height. But run she did.

The two felt the whips and trips of the bit players of the boreal understory — sapling-branch smacks, trip-roots and midair vine snare. Downed wood covered in moss and decaying into top soil looked to set bodies to flight.

The unseen sun dipped further still, filtering the world in navy-blue.

The choral caterwaul was drawing near.

The lateral run was becoming increasingly steep. Little legs burned as their phantasmagorical pursuer made a frictionless glissade over rough terrain.

Running down the shoulder of the earthen giant, gravity seemed set to trip up legs. And then the land leveled off. But firmer footing was a false friend. Exposed rock covered in moss caught Lana underfoot, sending her tumbling down into a gully.

In shock she took several panicked breaths, her body caught in a bassinet thicket. Tima slid down between slanting saplings whose roots had lost a battle with gravity, laying down their lives on the other side of the divide.

"Ouch," Lana moaned pitifully, piercing something soft beneath the surface of his hardened heart.

"Lana, are you okay?" he implored in a whisper, taking her by the shoulders.

"It hurts, Tima, it hurts!"

"I know, I know," he said in a consoling voice.

"'Do you think anything's broken?"

"I don't know," she sobbed.

"Hold on," Tima said, sticking his head out from the trench. His eyes grew wide. A black mass was barreling through the broadleaf. Closer, the darkness began to take shape as a black-wind rider on a thunderclap steed.

Tima slid back down the dirt toward as Lana continued to weep.

"Lana, we gotta hide!"

Tima grabbed Lana who winced, tears freely flowing as he wrenched her from the deadfall and dragged her beneath the overlapping trunks.

The earth was cold and damp to the touch. Trees continued to sway above the water-cut trench.

The phantom rider moved like black clouds on a jet stream, the ungodly wails reaching a fever pitch.

Tima pulled Lana to his chest and scooted the two beneath exposed roots and vines hanging overhead. He hastily buried them in dead leaves. The ground beneath steeped his legs in chill. Leaves took their final breath through stomata, filling young lungs with retro redolence. The ozone smell of chlorine asepsis poured forth from the dead and rotting vegetation. With an ear to the ground, Tima heard the wails through the filter of earth.

Lana's warm breath fanned his chest as muffled weeping filled the space between them.

"Shhhhhhhh," he whispered in an unexpectedly tender voice, rubbing her back.

The soft-shell fabric of her jacket was cold and smooth beneath his exposed fingertips. Their exhalations blew wisps of steam from between the leaves.

Lana put a cork in her hurt as she silently sobbed. Her out-sized bravery further battered Tima's ramparts.

After so many years of street and subterranean life, Tima almost feared an angel's affection more than the devil dancing his way. But somehow Lana found a way through the hard, dark spaces like a ray of sunshine pouring through the Newgrange roof-box on a Solstice morning.

And in that remembering of a self that had long since seen the light, the aerial marauder was imbued with menace, sending shivers through the tiny droplets holding the world in a fog of fear.

Despite the cold, pain and dread, Lana fought the quiver in her lip to a stiff standstill. Her pinched breath came out in a wheeze. Tima's nuzzling hand halted on blue polyester. He suppressed a cough induced by a tight diaphragm squeeze looking to put a sock in his full-mouthed respiration.

On the black rider's approach, a cold wind blew through the gulley, turning breath to hoarfrost and tears to icicles. Every shiver came with the fear they'd shake off their shelter like wet dogs.

Lana grew so still Tima nearly had to fight the urge to shake her to make sure his embrace wasn't suffocating. But holding his own breath, he faintly heard her muffled exhalations continue on the increasingly warm spot on his chest. He didn't want to be afraid. It had been so, so long since he'd genuinely felt fear – he'd become too feral for fear. But that part of Lana that unlatched long-shuttered places let fright in with the light.

Tima closed his eyes. The sounds of snapping twigs turned to floorboard creaks.

A preternatural mist filled the trough. The incorporeal carolers' wails came to a halt. And without taking a step, something both weightless and infinitely dense planted itself above the open grave. Up above, his father's legs were seen from beneath the bed – a wrench in hand, booze on his breath, hate in heart.

A tremble settled in as he became something much smaller than Lana and the rabbit too. Seven layers of nesting doll shattered, leaving an irreducible core of dread in an imperfect hiding place.

He broke into a cold sweat. The wraith's refrain became his father's baleful blues played at the expense of his whipping boy. Tima heard his own bestial wails unmelodiously pitched against the percussive downbeats. The crushing pressure of darkness seemed to press them further into the dirt.

He gnashed his teeth as scars running the length of his back seemingly split open like sausages on the spit. Lana felt his agony flow through her. She forgot about her own stinging spill. She pressed her tiny hand into his back, kneading a communiqué of calm. Tima was stuck between his father's blows and Lana's caress. Lana pulled away and looked him in the eyes, wet with tears for the first time in years. The part of him that had long since recognized himself as a child cried: 'It hurts, it hurts.'

He fought to control panicked breaths that verged on hyperventilation. Fiendish lament blew on the backs of his neck.

Lana's touch signaled knowing that salved suffering. It was suffering of a kind that broke skin and bone, while turning spirit into a vessel of shame.

Slowly, Tima returned from the clutches of frenzied filicide. He breathed in the dead leaves as the dust from floorboards settled in another world.

He opened his eyes. Lana looked up at him, her own pain subsumed. Tima awkwardly craned up his neck, looking to peep something between the overlaying leaves.

Hovering up above, the specter appeared as a flowing black shroud draped over colossus — two scalene eyes cut from cinnabar peered down into the trough. Another cold wind blew, threatening to deep six the leafy sanctum. Tima locked onto those red shapes and saw the mélange of wailing souls burning behind the furnace grates. And somewhere in the furnace, he saw his own father being battered with hot irons from the fire. And fatherly howls seemed to cry out: "You did this to me, you did this to me!"

And in that lament, Tima felt the sting of hellfire on his father's flesh before the truth turned gas-lighting will-o'-the-wisp to waste.

"You did this to yourself," Tima whispered, "you did this to yourself."

The monstrous mare snorted as the wraith's red eyes flared and faded.

The black rider pulled back from the gulley and galloped off, until perdition's song abated.

Nightfall had pitched the world above in black. Lana's pitfall had turned into as good a shelter as they were going to find.

So, a little girl with a sore body and a young man tracing the fractures of a broken heart each drifted into their own uneasy sleep, where the line between waking and dreaming was equally blurred.

Chapter 26

THEY AWOKE TO THE SOUND of birds chirping, bathed in light diffusing through leaves. Lana was still in Tima's arms. He slowly disentangled her from his gangly limbs, prompting sleepy murmurs and roly-poly retreat into self. He decided to let her catch a few more winks as he rose to his feet, shaking off all the shades of autumn. The air was crisp, all the fright of the previous night having dissipated like dew under the rising sun.

The morning tide benediction had absolved the Earth of sundown damnation, though thoughts of his father in the furnace burn lingered like embers from a smoldering campfire at dawn.

But even as those embers kindled empathy, no sense of guilt at his father's fate could burrow into Tima's heart. That man had spent a lifetime building his own corner of Hell on Earth, and not only for himself. In the end, he had walked to the end of the bridge he himself built.

Tima traipsed down the gulley, periodically looking back to see that the rabbit's nest was undisturbed, until her supine body was nestled behind a bend.

After ten minutes of treading through the trough, he heard the faint sound of water burbling nearby. He took another step forward and nearly got caught on what he first thought was a snare. But looking down, rather than finding a booby trap, a half-buried strap was sticking out of the earth like an uncovered root. Tima worked at digging it out.

The snare, it turned out, was the crownpiece of a horse bridle.

Tima pulled and pulled, until finally unearthing the reins. Dusting it off, he noticed a small cross etched on the headband. Tima awkwardly swung it around his head like a lasso a few times, nearly smacking himself in the face. Figuring it could come in handy, he tied it around his waist and turned back to fetch Lana.

When he returned, he found her slumbering right where he had left here — beneath the natural dream catcher. Rousing her from her sleep, Lana hugged the air with a big stretch.

"How ya feeling?"

"Sleepy," she said with a smack of the lips, followed by an out-sized yawn.

"No, I mean, ya took a pretty bad tumble last night. Can ya walk?"

"I don't know," Lana said, slowly rolling herself into a sitting position.

Tima extended a hand, gently helping her to her feet. Up, down and side to side, Lana reached for every point on the windrose. Apart from a number of knots and ripe-plume contusions, she couldn't find a sprain or break.

"I'm okay," she said matter-of-factly. "But I bet my legs are all purple like an aubergine!"

"You're one tough lil' girl!" Tima, hooted. "I'll give ya that."

"But I don't want to be tough!"

"Tough luck!" Tima said with a chuckle, the head gear sagging around his waist.

"What's that?" Lana said, pointing at the bridle.

"I dunno. Looks like some sorta' thing to drag an animal 'round with."

"Where did you find it?"

"Right over there," Tima said, pointing down the trough. "There's some sorta' stream down that way too. I figure we should head that way, if you're feeling up to it?"

"I am!"

So Tima led Lana down the gulley until the sound of flowing water returned, right above the tiny pit where he had extracted his wares. They walked further on until the trench was shallower, pulling themselves up by exposed roots before doubling back.

The pair pushed on through the woods as the burbling grew and grew. Up ahead, the earth sprung a leak that flowed downstream. They followed the increasingly steep gradient downhill, guided by the calming morning vespers of the babbling brook.

Over there," Tima directed in a muted shout, leading Lana down the ridge of an interlocking spur. Through the serpentine riverbed, eroded green banks shaped like frozen waves framed the flow.

The two angled down the slope as if tracing the back of a sidewinder snake. They finally touched ground on the bank, basking in the river breeze as the full rush of cold water over rocks filled their ears.

Tima and Lana walked along the rapids as a convex river cliff rose above the outer bank. Mist rose from the cool water. In the shade of the wave of cresting earth that was crashing in the slow motion of lateral erosion, they spotted a pale horse lounging near a rock further down the shore.

"Ya see that?" Tima asked. "That horse has a saddle on it."

"Where do you think its owner is?"

"That's a good question. I say we check it out."

"I don't know, Tima…"

"Look, I reckon after what we saw last night, this gotta be a good horse, right? Just look at it – don't seem like it wants to hurt no one."

"If you say so…"

Tima struck off down the bank, with Lana tentatively following from behind.

On their approach, it swung its head around to take in the pair, greeting them with a nicker. It was clearly dripping with water, as if it had been bathing in the river.

"See! That there ain't a bad horse at all! Why, I reckon if we ride him we can get to where we need to get goin' double-time."

"Where are we going?"

"That's a good question. Up I guess. That bird bath gotta be somewhere over there," he said, gesturing uphill.

Lana gave the horse a once-over.

"He's wet. I don't want to get on a wet horse."

"Come on now, Lana, don't be a baby. He ain't that wet," Tima said, slowly moving over to pat the horse on the neck.

His hand made a smacking sound as the mare's mane was soaked. Tima pulled his hand away, wiping it on his track bottoms.

"Okay, it's a little wet. But he'll sun off in no time."

Tima remembered the bridle around his waist and untied it. Tentatively, at first he rubbed the horse on the whither, and then moved down to the nose. The horse reacted with a gentle neigh and lowered its head.

Having never haltered a horse, it took Tima a hot minute as he attempted to put the headgear on any which way but right.

After a spell he finally snapped the last buckle strap into place. The recumbent steed repositioned its body, seemingly offering its saddle to Tima.

"Will you look at that! He's more or less tellin' us to get on up!"

"I don't know, Tima. If he has a saddle, he must have an owner. We can't steal someone's horse!"

"We ain't stealing it," Tima said, grabbing onto the saddle horn and pulling himself up. "We're just…"

Suddenly, the pale horse cut and run like a bolt out of the blue.

Tima held on for dear life as the steed charged right toward the river, dangling reins well out of reach.

"WHOA, WHOA!" he cried out in fright as hooves smacked against the water.

The horse roiled the river's surface with pounding legs before its tail sent a roll of thunder through the rapids. Lana shrieked and ran as a tail-whipped wave gave chase. Tima tried to abandon ship but felt stuck to the colt as if by the force of magnetism, if not magic.

The horse's gait only increased as it glissaded across the rocky river waves, heading off to the middle-most point between banks. Reaching the latitudinal center, the mare began its aqueous descent.

The chill of the water hit Tima like an electric shock as he was quickly submerged. The horse cut through the water like a shark. Stuck to the saddle, Tima nearly screamed before catching the escapee breath, extending the window between life and death by a minute.

He could hear Lana's dampened shouts rattling in his skull. Then, her pleas were completely muzzled by the murky depths. The ambient tones of red, orange and yellow were swallowed in watery fall. High up above, the sun broke through a shifting cloud shape, filling the river with cathedral light. Tima desperately grasped at a sunburst straw as he rushed to a watery grave.

Chapter 27

AFTER THE HORSE'S TAIL THUNDERCLAPPED upon the river, rushing water brimmed over the shore. Each thrash intensified the flood, as Lana ran from the growing surge. Beyond the unbroken wave of earth perched above the outbreak, Lana found a naturally-made ziggurat of rock buttressing the bank. She scampered up the craggy steps as the water smacked and frothed at stone. Reaching the peak of terraced outcrop, she struggled to catch her breath as the river surge grew in her ears.

"Tima!" she shouted above the din.

"Tima, Tima!" she cried and cried again.

The raging rush offered no reply. Lana began to cry her own river. But interrupting small and big flow alike, a harum-scarum half-pint on an oversized white steed broke the surface of the water in towering hurdle. Lana's glistening eyes looked up in amazement as the white mare sailed under the sun and crashed upon the river's surface.

"Yeehaw!" cried the faux Russian-gaucho, channeling Americana gusto fed with Italian spaghetti.

Lana cheered as the horse galloped to shore. The gallantry of the half-point rider was undeniable — his heart could fill a ten-gallon hat.

Tima himself felt electrified by the flight. The adrenaline turned the cold-air caress on sopping wet clothes to bliss. Just after hitting the river bed, the horse was set to devour him.

But in that heady swivel, the reins took to the water like kelp, swinging in Tima's direction. He lunged out in slow motion, getting a single hold on the hope of control. The horse thrashed about to break his cinch, but Tima held strong, reeling in the other strap and securing a grip. That turn of good fortune happened just in the nick of time. Tima's lungs were about to burst as the growing burn became unbearable. He stared up at the sunburst diffused through rapid rush.

Freezing, seconds from involuntary exhalation, inundation and expiration, Tima squeezed his hips against the sea horse, lifting the reins up and forward. Letting out a shower of bubbles, he screamed, "UP!" with a watery burst of long held-breath. And while all that was heard was a frantic burble, the horse obediently carried out his command. Tima barely managed to take in a gulp of drowning before shooting up to river's surface like a harpoon. Flying through the air, he spit out a stream of water like a statue perched over a Peterhof fountain.

And now riding along the bank, sopping wet and still panting for air, he guided the horse to Lana's stony retreat from the flash flood.

Lana descended the terraced-rock toward the high-water rider who had averted the onset of hell.

"Tima," she shouted with a mixture of joy and relief, smiling ear-to-ear as their eyes met.

Tima shot her a cocksure smile, a poker face hiding the fright of a narrowly-averted fate.

"Get on, little lady!" Tima hollered above the rush, hamming up his idea of a cattleman's argot.

"I'm not getting on that horse! It tried to kill you!"

"Don't you worry your lil' head," Tima said with bravado, masking over nearly-averted calamity.

"As long I keep my hands on these here thingamajiggies, this horse will do whatever I say," he announced triumphantly, snapping the reins as the white horse brayed.

"Here, watch!"

Tima commanded the horse to take two steps forward and two steps back.

He then led it on an awkward six-count foxtrot, spinning around the end so that the saddle was level with Lana's feet.

"You see!" he said with a smile, directing it to press its side to close the remaining gap with the rock. "You're in safe hands! And besides, with all this water, I don't see any other way down!"

Seeing the tide rise, it was difficult for Lana to argue with him. So, with shaky legs, Lana crouched down and gingerly slid onto the saddle, immediately wrapping her arms around Tima's waist.

Tima shifted around in his seat, pulling his shoulders back and holding his chest out high as small arms strained to connect around his ribs. The street kid who had never known a patch of green not surrounded by concrete was still beaming with his perilous victory over the stallion.

"So listen here, horse. The way you ran on that water, I figure you can go just 'bout anywhere. We need to get up the side of this mountain to some big ol' Bird Bath up there beyond the pass. You know the place I'm talkin' ' bout?"

The horse neighed.

"So, ya think you can get us up there?"

The colt once again whinnied in the affirmative.

"So, Lana, you ready to walk on water?"

"Like the man in the Bible?"

"You and your…"

But his ribald was interrupted by a gale so cold it nearly turned white caps running down the river to icicles.

The sunlight was suddenly eclipsed by a fast-spreading shadow. Up above, a massive black-wool blanket of stratocumulus had been rolled out above the land. Boreas blew another stinging kiss down the mountain.

Uncanny wailing echoed in the distance. Then a peal of thunder. Tima looked back as Lana dug in. Maybe a hundred yards down river, a shadowy apparition on night-mare descended from dark clouds upon the water. Burning black hooves turned white caps to mist. Pounding legs of atramentous steam spirited the dark wind-rider up stream.

"Oh crap!" Tima shouted.

Too afraid to turn her head, Lana quavered at the swelling chorus of the damned.

"Get us outta' here!" Tima bawled with a superfluous kick to the horse's side in imitation of silver screen reflection.

The white mare instantly bolted from the flooded bank and up the river. Lana pressed her face to Tima's back as Beira's icy lips smacked on her wind-whipped cheeks. She fought to control the chatter in her teeth. Tima winced with the sting in his exposed fingernails and face as he squeezed the reins in ice nettle sting.

The black rider continued to advance, hooves incandescent like irons from the fire, punching holes of vapor in the river underfoot. The white horse kicked up a blue streak on the rapids, taking a hairpin turn into a concave meander, deftly navigating the anfractuous course and falling out of sight behind a spur.

They flew up the graded serpentine path toward the blanket of black sky.

Tima looked back down the zig-zagging ravine cut with white-water rush and almost breathed a sigh of relief as their pursuer had fallen out of sight. But then the nightmare rider came around the bend in a shroud of mist. Its hooves white hot, the inner flames of Hell raging in infernal black umbra, the blazing wraith was gaining on them. It seemed that the greater the furnace burned, the faster the black-rider cut across the water, a razor of evaporation parting the river.

Lana made the mistake of looking back to catch hell bent on setting Heaven ablaze.

"Faster, Tima, faster!" she squealed.

But no kicking and crying could push the white horse into a higher gear. The internal screams of the damned grew and grew as the wraith's heat engine gathered steam on burning souls.

The rising river vapor was scalding hot. White steam hit black cloud and fell as blood rain.

The green valley slopes grew higher and higher until soon they were sheer cliff faces of stone.

Up ahead, a massive waterfall cascaded down from a hanging valley, shrouded in condensation.

The black mare was now 10 yards away. Nine ... Eight ... Seven...

Lana and Tima screamed as they hurtled toward the thousands of tons of falling flood. They were caught between the devil and the sky-diving sea. Thousands of steam-whistle cries dissipated into the mist. Blood red continued to fall from black death.

But rather than take its chances on the approaching curve, the white horse veered toward the sheer cliff, running straight at the water wall.

Tima tried to muster a diversionary command but sanctified excrement instead. Lana's wail was loud enough to drown out infernal screams.

The second they hit the wall, the white horse shot up the water fall. Lana's feet took to flight as she squeezed her arms around Tima for dear life.

"TIIIMAAAA!" she screamed as the pair rocketed up the water face.

The black rider followed in a rage. But as it began the vertical climb, the water too quickly dissipated in ruptured heating pipe, leaving the wraith treading, and then falling, through a cloud of mist. The fall of the black rider seemed to snap his spell over the sky. The red rain stopped, the black clouds parted, opening up the heavens as Lana and Tima screamed into the blue.

Lana felt her fingers beginning to slip away under the strain.

"Hold on!" Tima shouted. Hold on!" feeling her shift in weight.

The second her fingers unclasped, Tima twisted back and grabbed her arm, letting loose one of the reins. The white mare began to falter, feeling freedom within its grasp. Tima desperately gripped Lana's wrist as she dangled over the plunge pool hundreds of feet below.

And while the mare was only half-tame, it seemingly had no desire to join the black rider in the rising steam pit below. Despite subtle efforts to unburden itself of passengers, it sailed over the bed rock and splash-landed onto the river. Lana fell over the side of the horse. Tima's faltering grip was the only thing keeping her from being swallowed by the rapids.

They sped up the river as the hanging valley opened up mountainous majesty before them. But facing so much beauty, all Tima could feel was the agonizing strain in his arm. It was either lose Lana or grab hold of the other rein.

Tima commanded the mare to head toward the bank. The beast half-heartedly obeyed.

But approaching the shore, sensing its rider was off-balance, the mare bucked, sending them head-first into the rapids.

Lana immediately went under, but Tima managed to hold on. Fighting to tread the infinite flow underfoot, Tima pulled Lana toward him, drawing her onto his chest. With her winter boots and clothes waterlogged, the extra drag sapped Tima's resistance to the current's drive toward fall. Lana coughed up water as Tima fought to keep them from going under.

It was a losing battle. The pulldown stream was just too strong. He whipped his head around, seeking out a life line above the swell. Some 20 yards from the cascading crash, the exposed branch of a felled tree reached out to touch those in need of salvation. Caught in the downstream drag, Tima fought his hardest to steer their bodies toward the timbered limb.

He was coming in fast and off course by several degrees. But a few well-placed kicks helped shift their bodies toward the undrifting wood.

Tima reached out his hand, just barely securing a grip on the branch. Dangling from a bough of peeling bark as the rapids raged their course, Tima felt like a piece of flotsam stuck between the teeth of a giant that was trying to spit him out. Exhausted, with the water still beating down and the current working against them, he struggled to see how Lana could somehow shimmy her way up the sodden tree trunk.

Lana heaved against his chest. The two shivered as the cold waters washed over them in icy epiphany.

"Lana!" Tima cried out over the din of the rapids. "You gotta turn around, climb up onto my shoulders and get a holda' that branch."

"I can't!"

"You can, and you will!" Tima screamed, his voice snapping in adolescent crack. "I can't hold on much longer … I can't pull us up with one arm. Listen to me! You gotta go and you gotta go now! I'll be right behind you!"

"What if I fall?"

"Then I'll catch you! But if you don't get up there right now, we're both goin' down!"

Lana fought the cold and terror as she tentatively wriggled around under his arm, recoiling every time a momentary surge of water pulled at her feet. On the final turn they were chest to chest.

Looking at him with a quivering lip, she was shocked to see so much fear in his eyes.

Somehow, all of the barbs that had accumulated over time had been washed away, leaving the boy before her in fear and trembling.

"Tima," Lana said breathlessly, probing the incredible pain in his eyes.

"Lana, we ain't got no time," he said turning away as tears poured down his face and into the stream. "We ain't got no time…"

"We're gonna be okay, Tima," she said, "we're gonna be okay."

Seeing it was her turn to be strong, Lana tried to grip his shoulders, but her wet gloves stole her grip. She looked at the right glove Gönpo had given her, giving off a subtle blue glow. He had told her if she wore it they would never sink. Whatever he had said about that glove, she sure felt like they were going under. Another slip and the jolt sent sparks through her heart. A rush of adrenaline dashed her faith against the rocks. She tugged at the glove with her teeth, wriggling it off of her hand. But on the final go she pulled a little too hard, flinging it with a whip of the head into the water.

The glove hit the water like a ton of bricks. She had just abandoned her one safeguard against the abyss to the maelstrom. As it floated down the rapids toward fall, it pulsed blue light.

"Lana, come on!"

Feeling the heat despite all the cold, she worked the other glove off and almost slithered up his chest, as he tried to stabilize her with his free hand. Unsteady as she went, she eventually planted her feet between his chest and shoulders, practically bending forward in bakasana. Tima half-wanted to scream from the added strain, but was barely keeping his head above water.

Lana rose on shaky legs several times, only to squat back down and grab onto Tima for dear life. But she saw his arm begin to tremble as he clearly winced in pain.

'Time to be strong', she told herself, 'time to be strong'.

She took a deep breath and centered herself. On shaking legs, she rose until the branch was at chest level. She balanced herself as if against a wall-mounted barre at her mother's school studio, placing her biceps and forearms atop the bough. Taking a deep breath, she swung up, pinning her elbows onto the other side, straining with all her might as her water-soaked clothes pushed her to the very limit. Slipping and squirming for dear life, she eventually pulled her stomach against the wood, swinging her legs up to straddle the branch.

Mounting the bendy limb, she cried out ecstatically, elated with her victory over fear and death.

"I did it, Tima, I did it!"

But there was no reply.

Lana looked down, only to find that Tima was gone. The rush of the water continued unabated. Not a soul was seen between shore and fall.

— — —

Cold, wet and in shock, Lana shimmied down the branch, onto the trunk, which she crossed like a balance beam to the river bank.

Soaking wet and breeze blown, she stared blankly into the flowing water as her teeth chattered uncontrollably. There were no feelings, no thoughts, just dry eyes and numb ears taking in the rapid rush and fall. The white horse watched her from the other bank before finally running off.

Lana laid down on her side and pushed her face to the damp earth, blankly staring sideways at a world veiled in mist. Blood rushed from her extremities to keep warm her quaking core.

The praxis of Pratītyasamutpāda was made manifest. The being Lana had become in this world was seemingly not a node on a network, but the motion made on a standing wave she had surfed in tandem. And now that he had been washed away, it seemed the music of dependent origination had come to an end – the taut string left unplucked in a world now without music.

And a heart too broken to feel let the cold seep in as the stream susurration became its own sort of silence. And without her own wavelength, Lana fell into the lull of steady erosion. She closed her eyes and drifted into the dark without resistance.

Chapter 28

WHEN VIKTOR PULLED BACK INTO his garage, he popped up the glove box and put his gun in his jacket pocket. He would heed the Georgian's advice and dump it. But not yet.

Before heading up to the apartment, he decided to check out the backside of the block just to make sure Lana hadn't somehow wandered off there.

As in every other corner of the city, the worst manifestations of man often drank there during the summer, perched on gas pipes, howling at the moon. But this time of the year it was a blackwater basin that even the most intrepid alcoholic wouldn't tread. He couldn't think of a reason why Lana would ever go back there this time of year, but decided it was best to leave no stone unturned.

Viktor took a corner around the panel, skirting the building under the balconies on a narrow strip of pavement that rose just above the muck.

A cold wind blew hard, setting off waves across the black water sea. A murder of crows were gathered on a muddy island poking out from the dark water, arguing over something dead.

Viktor thought of Lana, Lana with lambent eyes, whose laugher rang out as stichera after psalms and lingered like sweet incense from the censer, lifting one's soul to Heaven. It was not clear as day how he had risked her, risked everything, for nothing.

A leak sprang in dry eyes.

Fighting the crush of guilt, he rounded the building, only to stop dead in his tracks. There, by the stairs leading down to the maintenance room, he saw a small glove. It was tiny and blue. He reached down and picked it up.

He knew it before he knew: It was hers. He squeezed it in his hand before shoving it into his pocket.

Then the faint echo of a child's laugh on the other side of the door. It didn't seem real. Was he just hearing things? Was he losing his mind? There was only one way to find out.

He took the handle, slowly opening the door with a creak. There was nothing but darkness before him. The wind cried anew. The branches rattled.

He took a deep breath and stepped inside.

The room was dank and musty. Viktor waited for his eyes to adjust until realizing there was nothing to adjust to. There was not an outline to be formed in the pitch-black basement. He felt as if he'd ended up in an oubliette whose sole window had been bricked up and built over. He ran his rough hand over the wall in search of a switch.

Somewhere, off in the darkness, he heard breathing.

The hairs on his neck rose. His eyes got wide to take in the light that wasn't. A chill once again settled in his bones.

Keeping his hand on the uneven wall, he took several steps forward, tracing the perimeter.

A few drops of water fell from a pipe overhead, echo expanding in the silence. Then the breathing again.

"Hello," Viktor called out.

Nothing. He waited. He could feel it in his bones. He was not alone.

'Why didn't I prop open the door and then look for a light switch?'

He turned back.

Out of nowhere, hurried footsteps getting closer. A flash of panic as Viktor defensively raised his arms. A body crashed into his shoulder, knocking him to the side, but not down. It wasn't the worst hit Viktor had taken lately, but he still felt the sickening thud of bone on bone.

The footsteps stopped with an explosion of faint light, spiriting someone, something up the small staircase.

"Hey!"

Viktor ignored every last ache and bolted through the swinging door to beat the retreat of sky. Adrenaline rush drowning out the pain, he bounded up the steps. Ahead of him, a man in a snow camouflage jacket worn over a white hoodie ran along the muddy shore of the snow-melt tidal basin. He then cut right through the muck without missing a beat, lost in flight like a man possessed.

Viktor chased the white shadow from one end of the bog to the next until hitting the street. The hooded man dashed out into the road without a second thought. A car horn bleated upon impact. He was knocked to the ground, only to jump back up to his feet and keep on running. Viktor was dumbstruck, the driver apoplectic. Viktor shook his head in disbelief before running across the wet street.

The pursuit continued past the police station and up over the small wooden bridge traversing the railroad tracks. They continued running down the sidewalk lining Ivanskoye Highway until reaching an underpass. A few homeless men huddled up along the wall barely noticed the hot pursuit cutting through their cold refuge.

The running man cut a right and ran up the stairs. Viktor pounded feet up the wet concrete and soon popped out onto the street.

He spotted the hooded man heading toward Pokrovskoe Streshnevo Park. The park, in fact, would have been indistinguishable from a forest if not for the unpaved path cutting through the woodland. The nimble figure ran down the muddy trail, not missing a beat despite the clumps of mud clinging to his boots. Despite being increasingly weighed down by the muck and his body's pleas to the contrary, Viktor clumsily followed.

Deeper into the forest, fog rose from the ground and shrouded all the big trees. Not a single hedgehog was to be seen. The running man stuck to a pair of rabbit tracks overlaid by canine prints, moving straight down the miry path before veering into the forest.

Viktor doggedly followed, branches smacking him in the face. Between the brush and brume, his visibility was cut down to nothing. Viktor was flying blind. Eventually he reached a small glade. Exhaustion forced him to stop.

Hands on knees, he huffed and heaved. All the pushed back pain took center stage. He dry heaved several times as the blood was drained from his stomach.

"Christ," he mumbled when finally being able to form words through his gaping mouth. "I need to get into shape."

He slowly rose and circled the clearing, surveying the trees.

Somewhere, in the shroud of fog, he could almost see the apparition of a bear at war with three wolves, a small rabbit frozen in their midst, serving as the axis around which the violence stormed.

Those apparitions collapsed back into the blanket of mist before reforming as a man on top of a man, pounding gunmetal grey into an evaporating face.

Viktor couldn't believe his eyes.

Gaining depth, color and shape, he saw primordial ooze breath in bursting bubbles of snot and blood. He saw a man who looked just like him painting the forest with murder.

He lurched forward in vertigo. Footsteps fast approaching. Viktor reached for his gun. But before he could even get a grip, a resounding crack was followed by a white lightning flash. And just as quickly, the darkness came.

Chapter 29

GALYA REMAINED FROZEN IN FEAR by the front door. Someone, something was on the other side, stopping up the peep hole light. A hand gripped the handle on the other side. The door began to violently shake. She ran to the kitchen and grabbed a knife before taking shelter in the bathroom. Faded daylight from the kitchen poured in from the small windows above the bathtub.

The feverish pounding intensified. Peals of mad laughter resounded in the stairwell. Her neighbors had to hear what was going on. Someone, anyone had to call the police.

A spray of sparks from the grinding wheel of consciousness set fire to her heart. Each white-hot spangle cooled with the countless specks raining down in a slow growing slag heap.

Galya only noticed her hand was shaking by the repetitive sound of the blade clanging against the blue tile. She tried to steady her hand. She slid down to the floor, holding the knife like a prayer candle.

And then the banging stopped. She searched out the silence, punctured by her own rapid breaths. She slowed her breathing. The light dimmed outside, taking on the dark shade of storm clouds. Galya slowly rose to her feet and crept over to the bathtub and stepped inside. She slowly rose on her tiptoes to see what was on the other side of the glass.

Chapter 30

WHEN VIKTOR CAME TO, THE sun had already dipped below the horizon. The wind droned mourning from an Alanian necropolises. Spirits' susurrus rose to a haunting refrain from Sibyl of the Rhine. A chill settled in his bones from cold and fright.

Before his blurry eyes, wisps of mist formed rabbit feet, running off into the woods.

He was wrapped in a nesting doll of fog.

Then it all start coming back to him. Disoriented, he staggered to his feet.

He felt the knot on the back of his head. Fingers touched a warm, wet, patch of blood.

"That bastard got me good," he mumbled.

But who was that bastard? What the hell was going on? And Lana? Where was Lana?

A spectral laugh erupted in the woods. Fog filled the spaces between the trees as the red sky dimmed in twilight shades.

Viktor reached into his pocket and pulled out the gun.

"Who are you? What do you want?" he cried out into the forest.

The mad cackle erupted again. Viktor couldn't tell what direction it was coming from. It seemed to be coming from all directions all at once.

He tightened his sidearm grip.

Behind him, footsteps fast approaching.

'Not again!'

Viktor swung around and fired off several rounds. The shots resounded throughout the forest. The bullets cut through mist. There was no one there. With fright-filled eyes, Viktor set off through the dark woods, looking to outrun the fading of the light.

Chapter 31

LANA AWOKE WITH A WOOD-POPPING crackle in her ears. She felt the heft of itchy wool blankets draped over her aching body. The bubble of broth filled her nose. Opening her bleary eyes, a fire burned in a dark cavern. Soup steamed in a metal pot.

Before the fire, an old man in a fur hat sat on a small wooden chair, humming to himself.

He was wearing a long, faded blue robe of home-spun wool tied off with a white sash. His face had the color and texture of a walnut shell.

Lana was too wiped out to ask who he was or how she had gotten there. The chill had moved from her skin to her bones. Beads of sweat formed on her pallid face. She shuddered uncontrollably.

And in the grips of fever, thoughts of Tima hit her like the rush of rapids which she had miraculously escaped, and he had not.

She drew into herself under the blankets and began to sob uncontrollably. The old man continued to hum his haunting melody, leaving Lana to weep undisturbed.

Lana cried until her own consciousness slipped out in tears.

Somewhere in the selfless hollow between the world of wake and dreams, Tima's face surfaced from the void, only to sink back into nothingness. Then the trip beyond the void began.

Thoughts of rabbit run through the snow and up mountains. A little bird's wings rendered by a nightmare man. Mom and Dad laughing and crying within hemmed-in Soviet dimensions. An unknown man battered through the floor. Wolves howling at the silver moon. A bear tearing a hawk apart. Dolphins dancing on the lighthouse beacon. Metal-blade waves cutting ribbons out of the sky. Earth rattling. Sky falling. A bear setting sail. A hawk taking flight. A rabbit huddled in Heaven. A wingless bird riding a sunbeam to sky.

For days and days, Lana came in and out of consciousness, sometimes being fed from that pot or led off in a shaky amble to relieve herself, only to return to dreamless dark or hypnagogic kaleidoscope.

But in time the shakes settled, the fever abated, and delirium's hold subsided.

And then one day she awoke fully herself, firmly outside of the dominion of dreams and dying. Just as before, the crackle of fire was still in her ear. But this time she was alone in the cave. She waited for her eyes to adjust. She felt grimy and hot.

The restlessness of a body too long in rest compelled her to cast aside her blankets. Although her cheeks were slightly sunken in, some color not cast by fire had returned to her face. After wriggling her toes and a stretch or two, she was ready to stand up on her own two feet, although she had to steady herself from step to step until finding her legs again.

Lana moved through the chamber, whose walls were ordained with weather-worn murals of animals, nature scenes and the Sage of the Shakyas' journey to enlightenment. Her bare feet pressed against the cold stone, collecting dust and hard impressions on soft soles.

And as the light from the fire receded, the sun spilled in. Up ahead, a reuleaux triangle of light was cut out of the darkness.

Lana approached the egress. As her eyes adjusted to the light, the alpine vista took shape on the approach. Reaching the opening, she soon realized a sloping threshold led to a three-foot wide ledge. From there, a sheer cliff dropped down into the valley floor. Lana stepped onto that ledge and gazed out over the land impassively.

She watched the blue ribbon of river cut through the marbled land of grey and green, which dangled down from the hanging valley, exploding in a rush of white foam. Somewhere deep down she knew she was looking at the self-same flow that had carried Tima away. But her mind refused to follow that stream of thought.

While her body seemed on the mend, emotionally, she was drained. Like leached earth after deluge, matters of heart had dripped down to subsoil well beyond her roots.

A breeze blew through golden hair further gilded by the sun. Sky-blue eyes were clear following a relentless storm. Lana could hardly remember how she'd gotten there. The snowy world of Moscow March and parental bickering now seemed nothing more than a dream.

What strange affection had led her on this wild-goose chase from the underworld to the ceiling of Heaven in search of some wingless little bird?

What folly had pushed her down a perilous path lit by ignis fatuus, drawing Tima in and leading him to certain death? Lana spread out her own arms and stepped toward the ledge.

Feeling the sun against her skin and the wind under her palms, she felt no fear of falling. She took another step, pushing pebbles to plummet. Another step now, so close to the edge, an edge that felt just like all those spaces between light and darkness in her fevered dreams.

Tima was beyond one such space now. What if seeing him again was nothing but a threshold away? What if the answers to her questions were all written in the sky? What if one merely had to let go to embrace those high-flown words?

What if…?

Cauliflower-like clumps of cloud overshadowed the sun. The light on her skin was no more. Was it the wind that wailed in her ears, promising the gift of flight? Was it God's prayer composed in clouds?

She began to take another step forward. Sky was under her sole.

'This is where wingless birds learn to fly', she told herself, 'this is where wingless birds learn to fly. Let go. Just let go…'

Her suspended foot untensed and fell forward. A rough hand gently gripped her shoulder, drawing her back to solid ground.

"Where are you going, little girl?" a gentle voice asked.

Lana felt as if she'd been yanked out of a trance. Taking in the external's intrusion on internal movements, she recognized the voice of the Sherpa who had pulled her from the fires of fever. And in place of fear, shame began to creep in.

"I ... I'm going to fly."

"But you don't have wings. I'm afraid you can't fly."

"A man, he said, no, he told me ... if a bird loses its wings, it, it has to go to a place where it has to fly. And maybe I have to do the same. Maybe I can get my little bird back, I can get Tima back, if I, I..."

"Have faith?"

She turned around and looked at the Sherpa with sorrowful eyes. And he followed everything, even if nothing could be put into words.

I think I understand what that man was saying to you," the Sherpa said softly. "Faith, faith is good. And having faith in flying is a good thing too. That's true. We can all fly if we have faith. But we don't all fly in the same way. And this way is not for you."

Lana clasped her hands over her stomach.

"But what other way can you fly?" she asked in her fig leaf pose.

Thunder clapped as the dark clouds rolled in. The wail of the wind seemed less and less like a natural affair. The Sherpa felt a touch of the uncanny in the air.

"We all fly as our souls see fit. But there is no need to push it. Time will show you the way. Let us see just where your spirit leads you," he said, placing his hand on her back and leading her away from the impending storm.

— — —

Lana sat across from the Sherpa on a cushion, eating from a wooden bowl placed on a small, lacquered table. The meat in her noodle soup was strangely sweet — the pungency of garlic and ginger, the spiciness of chili powder — danced on a tongue long accustomed to blander fare.

Delicious dumplings similar to her steamed-Siberian pelmeni, but served with red chili chutney rather than sour cream, filled her with an unexpected sapor. She savored both newness and nostalgia in every bite.

Having barely imbibed anything but broth for a week, her appetite was ravenous, even as exotic seasoning brought buckets of sweat to her brow.

The Sherpa was content to eat with her in silence, as a strong gale could faintly be heard buffeting the bluff.

Although the fire kept him warm and a fortress of rock kept out the wind, a chill settled in his spine all the same. He could feel the darkness raging against the light.

"Outside, you talked about your little bird, and…"

"Tima," Lana said, slurping her soup from a wooden spoon.

"Yes, that's it. Is he your friend?"

"He … he was my friend."

"Was?"

Lana dropped her spoon in the broth.

"He's gone now. We, we fell into the river. He … he saved me, but …"

She didn't have the will to put it into words. She didn't need to.

"A stream moved into a stream."

Lana sat in silence, as the Sherpa searched her with his eyes.

"And what about your little bird?"

She slowly picked up her spoon and pulled in the warmth.

"The lady said if I wanted to find my little bird, I had to go up the mountain to the bird bath. Do you know about this place?"

"Oh yes I do. That's a very difficult climb indeed. One must cross Veles' Spine to get there. Are you telling me you and your little friend were trying to make that difficult journey alone?"

"Yes," Lana said meekly. "But without Tima, I don't know how I can do it. I wish … I wish I could take it back. I wish Tima had never come here!"

"Can I ask you — why would you and your friend come so far to find a little bird?"

"I thought he needed my help. I thought it was the right thing to do."

"Well, was it the right thing?"

"No! Because Tima is gone!"

"So it is only good to do the right thing if you don't lose anything?"

Lana studied his serious expression, but failed to find an answer in the creases of his brow.

"When you do the right thing and lose something, maybe everything, that does not make it wrong. Quite the opposite, that makes your action even more right. Your friend fell in the water to help you find your little bird. And your friend gave himself to the water to save you. I promise you he has gained more from what he did than he could ever lose."

"How can you say that? Tima's gone," Lana shouted. "He's gone!"

"Let me ask you a question, little girl — where do we go when we are gone?"

"Everywhere but here."

The Sherpa laughed.

"You are more right than you know."

"I told Tima to help me. I told him the nightmare man from the Black Sea wants to eat my little bird. I think he wants to eat everything that is good."

The Sherpa listened to the howl of the wicked wind outside and nodded.

"My ancestors told stories of the ancient one who dined on stars, then galaxies' arms, until his appetite grew so great, he tried to eat up every last speck of light. And after a great battle, the custodians of light managed to contain this demon in a deep Black Sea. They said the one-time eater of stars was left to dine on morsels of light from a silver moon. And if he escaped, that would be trouble for not just our world, but all worlds touched by the light.

"As for finding your little bird, I can help you. I know these mountains very well. I can take you to the bird bath."

"You can?"

"Yes."

"But why would you help me?"

"Because something tells me the stories of my ancestors weren't just stories. And something tells me your little bird is so much more than a little bird."

Chapter 32

AFTER WORK, SERGEANT NOVOSELOV DECIDED to go to church. Truth be told he was short on faith but found comfort standing amongst believers in a time of disbelief. At the very least, it kept him away from the bottle, at least for an hour or two.

The Church of the Intercession of the Holy Virgin, located just off the highway on the edge of Pokrovskoe Streshnevo Park, wasn't far from his police station on Aviatsionnaya Street. It was a small church, warm with a tight-knit community at a time when community was in short supply.

Sergeant Novoselov himself only stopped by when he had something weighing on his mind. In this case, it was his meeting with Major Kuzminov. It wasn't exactly the ghastly murder, the state of their country, or thoughts about his own stalled career. And yet it was all of those things, all of those things and more.

At 42, having reached a dead end in the only job he'd ever had, unmarried, with no siblings and ailing parents, it was inevitable that his already lonely life would get lonelier as time passed. Hope as it was traditionally understood was not in great supply. The average Russian man lived to be 59. He found nothing of exception in himself and could only begin to reckon how the last third of his life would pan out.

While he would not exactly say he felt sadness about the matter, he felt himself skirting the edges of a great big void all the same.

'So this is it? Well okay then,' he'd answer himself stoically.

But then came the trickier question. What is 'it', exactly?

He meditated on the unknowable as the Litany of Supplication was sung.

"Help us, save us, have mercy upon us and protect us, oh God by your grace."

After some time, he went to the back, took three candles and placed a modest donation in the box.

Placing each one in the candle stand set beneath an icon to Archangel Gabriel, he found himself at a loss for anything but generic prayer. Sometimes he found inspiration in the ritual. That time was not today.

"I am the light of the world; he who follows me will not walk in darkness, but will have the light of life."

That was the idea behind it anyways. Try as he might, he felt pitched in darkness all the same.

After 20 years of policing a collapsing society, he wished mercy and protection for the people on his beat. But deep down, he believed there was no God standing between men and the void.

All there was were people just like him. And people like him served under what amounted to bank robbing cops, werewolves in epaulettes and otherwise crooked arms of the law.

The wolves were watching the hen house. And he was one hen among many trying to find peace before it was his turn to go. How funny he thought. Just the act of living a life was really an impossible feat. Yet there was no other choice but to live.

After an hour on his feet, Sergeant Novoselov slipped out to meet dusk. Crossing himself three times, he left the churchyard and walked down the road toward the entrance of the park. Under the highway pass bisected by railroad tracks, a small pond was encircled by trees and a muddy track. He walked to the water's edge, where dead leaves and felled trees rose from the last of the retreating ice. Mist rose up over the water. The sun had already dipped below the horizon, the last waves on a red sea broken beyond the horizon.

His thoughts turned to that woman who had stormed out of the station earlier that day. He wondered if she had found her child. If not, she'd be headed back soon enough. Sergeant Novoselov prayed he would never see her again. He prayed a little girl he didn't know would find her way home.

He exhaled and watched his breath rise. He contrasted the chill in his heart with the warmth of the Litany. Tolstoy had once written the Kingdom of God is Within You. Maybe that's why it was Hell on Earth. Man kept looking for Heaven everywhere except the only place they had any hopes of finding it. And then he asked himself: Is there any Heaven in me?

Three shots rang out in reply. Birds scattered. Startled, Sergeant Novoselov looked around. The acoustic shockwave of the slugs dissipated. It had definitely come from the woods. Unholstering his gun, he set off down the muddy path to investigate.

The temperature was dropping with the fallen sun. Dense fog rose up, wrapping around Sergeant Novoselov's legs like a cat marking its owner. The ground squished with each step. His heart beat a sprint despite his slinking pace.

Then came the sound of broken twigs and smacking branches. Someone was charging through the woods. Sergeant Novoselov raised his gun.

A large man bounded onto the muddy path.

"Hold it right there!"

A shot rang out in the dark.

Sergeant Novoselov dove, taking cover in the muck. The man ran off down the path. Sergeant Novoselov raised his gun and took aim at the man's retreating back.

Chapter 33

LANA AND THE SHERPA SETTLED in for the night, waiting for the uncanny storm to pass. The tempest had been inauspicious; peals of thunder roiling through the rock like a madman's laughter. Huddled up against the wall, Lana watched the shadows dance an unsettling allegory above the fire. In those oneiric shapes fashioned by wind-licked flames, animals, gods and men played out creation and destruction myths. But tucked deep into the rocky redoubt against the storm, Lana's heart eventually stilled enough to let her drift into an uneasy sleep. And whether the shadows had followed her into the dark, by morning time she could not say.

Lana awoke to a still world with sleep in her eyes. Even wrapped in stone, her soul was attenuated to the unseen morning light. The Sherpa was already up, all their supplies packed and ready for the long journey ahead. Thoughts that the first steps would be taken down and not ahead filled her with trepidation.

But to Lana's relief, rather than repelling the sheer face, an intricate series of tunnels had been cut through the cliff. Snaking down those series of corridors, they exited a cave farther up the valley that led into a mountain forest.

The two set off on an arduous uphill hike, with the Sherpa drastically slowing his speed to accommodate Lana's lagging. Although it would have been much quicker for him to throw Lana into the bamboo basket on his back along with the rest of their supplies, he knew this climb was one that she needed to endure. And going at her pace would help with the acclimation. But that pace would inevitably slow. She was a soft child born of Eurasian basin and he was a granite man from a skyward abode of snow.

But he thought, perhaps, that which he sought on his own elevated path would better be found at a child's speed. Such was the burden of braving the highest austerity of patience. Such was the way back to his own little bird.

The pair were forced to stop frequently; Lana collapsing into a pile of huffs and puffs, blisters bleeding and cheeks stinging as the friction of the world persisted in its own erosive way. But despite all of the pain and discomfort — the nettle stings, leg cramps, hunger pangs, and chaffed skin — Lana never asked to quit or take a step back.

Such a course the Sherpa could follow forever.

Setting up camp on the first night, Lana was so exhausted she almost fell asleep with a cup of tea in hand as the Sherpa tended to their small fire.

The night, while touched with frost, was otherwise uneventful, though her dreams kept returning to Tima's impassive gaze staring up through running water. Small hands would plunge in to pull him out. But each time she tried to touch him, his visage evaded her fingers, rippling across the water.

And so Lana awoke in a state of ache, which started in her heart and expanded out to the tip of every overextended finger and toe. The thought of taking one more, forget thousands of steps, seemed impossible. But carry on they did.

Uncounted days passed in the zen of toil — no thoughts but the body's focus on its own suffering, and the infinite joy that came from a simple moment of still. Cold nights came and went with loss reflected in dreams lost to ripple at the time of touch. And so those pained periods of rest themselves became a nightly meditation on letting go.

Then, as dawn broke many a sunrise and set later, an all-pervasive pang greeted Lana like a rooster's crow. But despite the now seemingly permanent state of discomfort, she rose with a dancer's grace.

The diffuse morning light spilled down a million feathered veins, as the cool, wet earth exhaled into the medley of pine, spice and honey. There was just too much beauty to be entirely taken in by hardship.

While still suffering, Lana was also more equipped to suffer. Her lungs were adapting to the rarefied air. Her legs, vacillating between states of strain, pain and cramp, were increasingly capable of carrying the load. Her soul almost seemed grateful that all the grief of parents missed, and friends lost could be expressed through the long pull of physical exertion and not idle tears of lament.

The now constant throb in her frame seemed so much more manageable than the ache of heart. But while perhaps not surfacing, Tima was always present in the current of her being.

The Sherpa greeted Lana's rise with shine.

"Close now," he said, "we are close," he said, putting the oversized basket onto his back.

And so they continued their voyage toward the vault of Heaven.

Farther up, the forest canopy was increasingly pruned by altitude as more and more light poured in. Eventually the trees became as thin as the hairs on a balding man's head. And then, late in the morning, the splendor of a new vista opened up before them.

Beyond the tree line was a verdant meadow where yellow Rhododendron's bloomed.

The last of the trees stopped at a grass covered slope.

Shoots and ladders of rock and waterfall went up and up until the green ended and the streaks of snow began, twisting up to the heavens. A v-shaped pass was cut between peaks whose summits were cloud-covered. Beyond those gaps in Veles' Spine lay Gamayun's Tear.

Lana first looked on in awe. Then she gulped.

"Do we have to get up that to reach the bird bath?"

The Sherpa solemnly nodded.

"But how? You need wings to get up there!"

"Make yourself of the way and the way will open up to you. Here, follow me."

The Sherpa led Lana up the hill to a large white stupa planted among a scattering of rocks. Next to it was a prayer wheel under a weathered pagoda of red, gold and green.

"Here's what I want you to do. Place your hand right here," he said, pointing to the cylinder embossed in prayer. "Push it around three times, and ask for a way up the mountain."

"What do I need to say?"

"I can't tell you that, it's your prayer."

Lana looked at the innermost heart of the bodhisattva wrapping around the spinning cylinder in a language she couldn't understand. She watched a tattered prayer flag as it flapped against the blue sky. And across that great expanse, a hawk soared, just like the one which carried her up to Heaven.

"Show me how high wingless birds fly," she said, bringing her hands to dharma's wheel and walking until it slowly began to spin.

"Show me how high wingless birds fly, show me how high wingless birds fly," she chanted again and again, walking in the direction of the sun's spin.

And in that spin, the same throat-sung sound of the universal soul she had heard on a cold March day in Moscow, when her little bird had huddled beneath a gas pipe, resounded through the mountains.

"Show me how high wingless birds fly, show me how high wingless birds fly…"

Rainbow light trails like the tail of a comet followed her.

"Show me how high … show me how high …"

And she felt it happening again, the same growing force of thrust building to transhuman propulsion. And this time she was not afraid as the versicolor beam of light enveloped her body and took her to flight.

For if this was how high her little bird could fly, then this was how high.

Chapter 34

GALYA ROSE SLOWLY AS HER heart ran a race in place. She steeled herself to peer out the windows, to accept the consequences of seeing. What she saw made no sense at all.

An absolutely black has swallowed the entire floor. Somehow, the fading light of day was not coming through.

'This is impossible,' Galya thought.

In that darkness, a shadow shaped like Viktor's hulking figure appeared seated at the kitchen table, hungover head held in hand. Galya pressed her free hand to the glass.

SMASH!

A face made of shadows appeared before her, massive black hands smacking against the pane.

Galya fell back into the tub and smacked her head. The flying knife clanged against the floor. Every spigot handle violently twisted against the clock.

She looked up in a daze as black water rushed from the shower head.

Chapter 35

VIKTOR ROUNDED THE POND AND bounded down the train tracks underneath the overpass, with a shadowy figure in mad pursuit. His feet kicked up mud, gravel and slush.

He looked back and saw his pursuer gaining ground.

Viktor extended his arm back and let off two shots. The figure behind him rolled down the embankment with a grunt. It didn't sound like the mad shadow at all.

His thoughts were interrupted by a series of shots headed his way. A voice called for him to halt. Who was chasing him, the police? Had he fired on a cop?

'Am I losing my mind?'

He pushed on down the train tracks, making a beeline up the embankment, hopping a fence and dashing across a yard and onto the street. He looked back and saw a police officer in pursuit under the peachy glow of a blinking street light.

Viktor cursed himself. There was no talking his way out of this. It was either the psych ward or prison. If he stopped now, it was all over. With the prospect of lost liberty growing exponentially, he snaked his way through a series of blocks before pressing his back to a wall. He peeked around the corner and saw the cop cutting through a nearby yard.

He pulled back and around the backside of the building, came muffled dialogue from too-loud TVs and yellow light pouring out every other window.

By the edge of the narrow pavement lining the building, dark water rose as snow retreated.

He took another turn and spotted a basement door. He bolted down the stairs and shook the handle. It was open. Viktor crept inside and quietly closed the door behind him.

Inside, a strange red light, barely perceptible at first, but then brighter and brighter, pulsed from the floor.

In the intermittent glow, pipes tracing the concrete walls were faintly illuminated before falling back into darkness. An unlit bulb was hanging from the ceiling.

Viktor couldn't wrap his head around the source of luminescence. Isophase flipped eclipses and flashes from the floor. He felt drawn to it like a moth to flame. As the wave got longer, the peak of the red crest before the fade out grew dimmer.

Viktor approached the claret-colored pulse, crouching to get a better look.

He slowly extended a hand to touch the floor. His fingers turned red in the crimson sheen of black-lit blood.

He started into what appeared to be a Rorschach test for murder.

Letting his eyes focus and defocus, the random splashes took on the form of ancient parietal paintings in the Caves of Altamira.

The busy figures were varied in size, all tracing the circumference of a perfect circle.

He squinted to make out the shape of what appeared to be some sort of bird hanging at the 360th degree. Dead in the center stood a small creature. Directly above it a big blob of beast. A smaller canine-like creature stood before it, forming the first of three equally spaced vertices filling out the equidistant pack.

Something in the shape of a man traced an arch of tiny footprints halfway up the radius to Viktor's left. Between 4 and 5 o'clock a tower rose from the bottom. The body of a prostrate man leaking from the face was splashed out before it. What appeared to be a hand holding a large knife stuck out from behind the tower. Aggressive side brushed strokes in the shape of waves lapped at dusk.

It reminded him of the strange scrawls he had seen on the door at the crime scene. What was this? What could it all mean? He had heard news stories about Satanists and occult figures popping up alongside strange Christian sects and doomsday cults. Pretend prophets and psychics versed in mass hypnosis had taken over the airways. Millions held up glasses of water to their televisions on Kashpirovsky's command, looking to receive the charlatan's healing charge.

Soviet belief had shattered into a million pieces. Every manifestation of madness had since flowed in.

Some talked about Mayan prophecies and the end of times. Some claimed to be in communion with the other side. Flying saucers reportedly chased comets in the night.

There had been rumors … only rumors … of child sacrifice.

Viktor closed his eyes, but the image had stamped itself on his eyelids. Blood. It looks like blood. Then his panicked thoughts returned to the cop.

'My God,' he thought, 'I actually shot at a cop.'

And that very cop was much closer to catching him than he was to finding his daughter.

'Lana, my God, what if one of these monsters got Lana? What if I am the monster…?'

His mind was buffeted by visions of a Hell he could not face.

"No, no, no!" he cried, tipping back on his haunches. Lacrima spilled forth. A single drop hit the smallest figure on the floor. The figure took on an ionized air glow hue of electric blue. It shone brighter and brighter. The circle turned red with incandescence and began to spin.

Viktor's eyes grew wide as the blue rabbit ran. Beasts of blood-fire followed. The waves lifted off the floor, inches at first, then feet.

'This is not happening! This is not happening! This is not happening!'

And the words stopped being words, melding into a boiling hiss of fear and disbelief.

The wave crested at the ceiling. Viktor's entire body clinched behind eyes shut tight. Inside, he screamed bloody murder at his own rabbit heart.

But closed eyes could not stop the crashing of the wave. And like a bullet train from beyond, he was washed away in a rush of blood to the head.

He fell off of his heels and hit the floor. A decaying karst rock Soviet monolith he called home collapsed beneath him.

In a sea of debris, he plummeted past iron oxide cliffs, arms flailing against the descent.

He fell and fell and fell, cannonball crashing through the surface of the Red Lake sinkhole. His paralyzed body sank in slow motion.

His body was frozen beneath the water, a marionette held in a tractor beam of retreating light. He sank and sank and sank, until the light shrank to a pinpoint, finally hitting the lake floor.

He laid still in the deep, mind holding onto the last glimmer of light blinking in and out like a distant star. And just like that, the final ray faded out. He was enveloped in total blackness.

A rumbling stirred from beneath. The terror grip sucked the last bubble of air from his lips. Lung-crush-gasp blind-eyed-burn cave-cataclysm-collapse.

The pain called Viktor was suddenly sucked through a waterway drain in a burst of screaming bubbles.

He was breathlessly inhaled by the deep for what seemed like an eternity, crying inaudibly under the surge of moving water. In a faster-than-light descent, choking in a dark water rapid of death, everything that Viktor had and could ever be started to disintegrate in a spray of particles.

And as he himself was torn apart, images of everyone and everything he had ever loved burst into millions of motley specks, only to be swallowed up one by one by the void.

Rage, horror and total despair reached their apex. The surge kicked into overdrive; bone-breaking force pulverizing his last bits of being.

As the dissolution culminated, the dispensation of energy left no wave in the wake of self. And then … calm. The frantic storm of what Viktor had been, became a pacific sea.

He was no longer being carried away in a rush of darkness. He was the rush of darkness, consciousness leaving a terrified boy and possessing the totality of nothing through forever and beyond.

In the center of it all, a glove, tiny and blue, floated beyond the warp speed blackness.

That talisman of touch, laying outside the embrace of darkness, orbited the meridian of Viktor's being. Then and there it was clear. The blue beacon blinked light on a self-enclosed sphere.

And even now, having himself become an embodiment of a drowning pool destroyer of life, the blue glove was everything — even to the darkness itself.

What had been Viktor strained against the countervailing force of his black hole anti-being. And then, off in the distance, in the north winter sky, a hawk perched on Sopdet's arm sees the tiny blue glove and takes flight, flying in frame of the three-pointed asterism, through the celestial sphere, and directly toward the lonely planet that had mistaken itself for the alpha and omega.

Closer. Closer. Closer. With a deep dive, it pierced the membrane and pulled out a piece of man from a black hole grip, a blue-glove lifeline in hand.

The glove in hand tenderly squeezed his soul. Viktor sailed above and beyond the black water abyss of Abaddon. The once black whole of everything shrunk to a point in a fractal picture of not just his life, but all life. Everything that was and is and could ever be danced an infinitely subdividing and multiplying wave into and out of itself in undulating eternity.

Viktor danced atop the waves and saw the dead boy reconstituted one flying piece of flesh at a time. Beyond that breaker, the portrait of the man he killed as a boy fell into the lap of his grandfather, sharing sunflower seeds on the best day of his short and ugly life. And yet even that truncated, brutish existence, a wave too crooked that broke too soon, fell back into the flow and partook in the grand gift of existence in a place beyond life and death.

Further on in a Summerland place high above it all, the ever-moving miracle stood still. In that instant a wave could be a perfect little girl and a man, and he could wrap her in his arms until they both abandoned the middle world shores of hourglass sand.

Flying above beyond and within it all, the essence of Viktor let out a tear that into everything did fall.

Fall and fall it did, on another journey of forever plunging through black, blue and then grey sky, a snowflake melting in mid-March flight, a rain drop hitting the top of a lighthouse from a time gone by, forming as rooftop condescension on a beacon in the night.

Chapter 36

SERGEANT NOVOSELOV HEADED TOWARD THE basement with his gun drawn. A passerby said they had seen a large man take shelter inside.

Taking a deep breath, he slowly opened the door. Nothing but blackness. The hairs rose on the back of his neck. He raised his sidearm and slowly moved forward. At first total silence. And then a maniacal cackle resounded behind him.

When he turned around, he saw a hulking silhouette in the door frame, night sky and clouds filling in the spaces.

He felt dread, dread that some demon was about to lock him up in a crypt. The shadow in the door grew into a black hole sucking in the light; occulting the constellations buried beneath street light cloud bright. The basement blackness massed, the floury texture of basaltic-touched clay edging the contours of his cheeks, seconds from seeping into his mouth and nose.

The fear sucked out his breath. Fingers fumbled at his revolver.

'I can't breathe, I can't breathe, I can't…'

Melting terra-cotta terror fingers sliding off up shoulders and clawed at his faced. His gun hit the floor. The door slammed shut.

Chapter 37

GALYA CAME TO DROWNING IN darkness. Disoriented, she could not tell up from down. She began frantically kicking until her face breached the surface, just a head below the ceiling. She sucked air out of the shrinking space. And then the thoughts came rushing in. The maniac. The fall. The water coming forth.

How could her bathroom have filled up like a bucket? It didn't make any sense. She tried to calm herself in the cold blackness. Her small pocket of air was shrinking.

And then she remembered. The ceiling window.

She dove down, feeling her way along the wall until she found the shower head. The force of the flow felt like a firehose. Other jets of water shot forth from ruptured pipes, the toilet, the sink. Galya pulled herself up by the shower's metal arm. With her nose to the ceiling, the water was creeping up her cheeks. She steadied herself, taking the last of the air into her lungs. Five, four, three, two, one...

She held her breath. The water surmounted the tip of her nose and then touched the ceiling. Still holding the shower arm, she kicked off toward the small window ledge. The light of day just beyond the glass could not penetrate the murk. She grabbed the small handles. It was locked. Working blind, her hands fumbled for the sliding locks. She struggled as they snagged on rust. Wriggle, wriggle, pull. Wriggle, wriggle, pull.

As the ache in her lungs grew, she worked them loose. Turn and slide. She would have breathed a sigh of relief if it wouldn't kill her. She gripped the handles again and pushed. Her hands followed by the force of the black flood wrenched them open.

A water fall erupted in the kitchen. Galya was ejected onto the floor. The knife shot out her way. Galya rolled for cover as it grazed the top of her wrist. She scrambled to her feet as the water quickly rose to submerge her ankles. Running for her life, she bolted for the front door. The darkness followed.

Chapter 38

THE MOUNTAIN GOAT RAN UP the slope, kicking up scree to sky. What would have been a quick-sand trap for a man looking for a foothold in a valley of debris was easily navigated by the adroit undulate.

In a bamboo basket pack saddle, a rabbit rested between woolen blankets and watched the world rush by in woven spaces. It burrowed its way to the back, vista retreating in vertical drop as the goat sailed up and up. Its little heart was skydiving with exhilaration.

But as pockets of snow grew deeper and the streaks of white wider on the banded terrain, a phantasm punched pits into powder. At first the rabbit could not see anything but hole punchers running across paper. Then the pale pelt of the phantasm took shape.

The rabbit's flying heart sank at the increasingly clear sight of a charging snow leopard on their flank. She screamed pained sweetness which caught the goat by surprise.

Looking back, it saw the ghost of the mountain on the haunt for its life. The goat's gallop up the gradient took on a fevered clip. But the undulate was clearly outclassed by the apex beast of prey.

No matter how he zigged or zagged, the cat's cut up the mountainside was unbelievably fast, as if the laws of physics themselves were being devoured.

Losing ground, the goat made a beeline for rough and winding rise that ended in the apparent dead end of a sheer cliff face.

A strong wind rushed down the ridge, fogging their path in freeze. Moments later the rabbit squeaked as grey eyes became visible in the spindrift. The snow leopard picked up its pace. The goat and its cargo were charging break-neck toward a dead end. But the blind alley obscured an ace in the hole.

For the cat's gift of speed in sprint was confined to variations on a somewhat horizontal plane. And what was an impasse for most creatures proved an elevator for the undulate, which took to vertical spaces with a true daredevil's deftness.

Speeding toward the wall, the goat leapt 10 feet into the air, landing on a seemingly invisible ledge as if its hooves were made of glue.

The cat crashed into the rock in a Hail Mary dash at dinner.

The rabbit's eyes grew wide as the bamboo-bottomed basket seemingly levitated up the side of the mountain. Up, up and to the side, split hooves dropped anchor in rocky heights. Before long the snow leopard fell out of sight as the rabbit teetered in terror in the rocking basket strapped to God's own mountaineer.

The goat took a thousand leaps of faith toward the heavens, any misstep meaning certain death. Each second lasted more than 100 years. The rabbit felt every creak and shift of the bamboo strapped to back like an electric zap through every last cell. It almost seemed that each slantwise step willed the unseen foothold into existence, making each rocky lacuna whole.

The basket continued to rock back and forth, the rabbit burrowing away from each swing in hopes its flyweight shift would be enough to stay grounded. After one such jolt the rabbit found itself staring at the drop-off through lattice. Another bump and the sensation of skydive surged through her skin even as the strips of bamboo kept her in place. The touch of death prodded her to panic. Step after step after step. The steel resolve of the ibex was the landing ground for the exposed wire rabbit heart shedding electrons to spark. She stared down the mouth of madness.

The cable-less gondola jounced. But rather than tumble down the face, the goat had deftly leapt up onto the clifftop and immediately bounded up the ridge. The rabbit made its way to the front of the bouncing basket. From her rocking bassinet she espied the col in Veles' Spine ahead.

But on the approach, those cloud-capped peaks did not look like anything of this Earth at all. Rather they towered like the Pillars of Creation rising in the blue, red and magenta swirl of nebulous star creation. It was not the top of the world to which they charged, but rather a place of superposition above all creation.

The goat kicked into overdrive until the mountain climber seemed to fly. Behind them the ghost of the mountain ascended like a rocket burning off its rosettes.

Death was gaining on life in the race to Heaven. Closer. Closer. The pillars rose up like Atlas' hands beneath all creation. The infinitely small pounded its heart 10,000 times a minute to beat out the infinite darkness and claim eternal bliss.

Seconds from the ever. But a final leap from the snow-bounding assassin found its mark. Ibex smashed against the apex. Bamboo crashed against the crest. A ghost dined as a spirit screamed. And a rabbit absconded under the cover of sacrificial murder, run-run-running right into God's heart.

Chapter 39

LANA CAME TO ON A bed of rock. Slowly rising to her feet, she noticed not a single blister, cut, stitch or strain registering anywhere on her body. She felt both solid and weightless, a being free from the pull of gravity and the ache of entropy. Scanning the great amphitheater of stone, she was absolutely alone. The silence was total. No bird song, no wailing wind, no creaks, footsteps, or pebbles falling in or out of place.

Looking up, the vaulted azure sky glistened with star shine. In the center of the cirque lay a perfectly still lake reflecting the scintillating heavens above. She gazed out, and up, taking in the birdless bath without time or tide weighing on her. Whatever eventually willed her to move was not a nudging hand on the clock, nor the mind turning miracles into boredom through familiarity.

Rather it was the ache of loss that had somehow followed her above the clouds. For all those stars above, she could not help but feel the loss of not one, but two lights, so much smaller than the ones above, and yet bright enough to give life to such tiny planets as herself.

She headed down the rocky amphitheater feeling as light as a feather. No grit was ground underfoot, no scrape of stone against sole. Even the temperature was that of a perfect October evening, miraculously free of the biting cold of mountainous heights. Whatever this place was, it was one without friction.

Seemingly the only body in motion, the perfect still of the cirque made it feel more like a landscape painting than real life. The lake and sky looked like cross-sections of an azurite stalactite. The only motion came from the millions of pulsating stars above. Their numbers were simply impossible. Lana no longer believed in impossible.

Reaching the gleaming water's edge, she sat down and gazed out across the lake. Her thoughts returned to the Sherpa's absence, and then that strange chase in animal skin.

"I guess I lost you too," she muttered to herself, picking up a stone and rolling it between her fingers.

"Everyone who helps me gets lost."

"I'm sorry," she said, quietly at first. "I said I'm sorry!" she screamed, tossing the stone at silence.

The stone skipped across the surface of the water, leaving rippling trails of light. It then settled seven skips away, but did not sink. Resting atop the water, the stone began to vibrate and glow, shifting through every shade of a soap bubble on a summer's day. As the vibrations intensified, the rock turned into a pure orb of light. When the building engine of energy came to cumulation, the orb shot up into the sky.

Lana looked up in awe as it ascended into the heavens, leaving a luminous trail in its wake. Splashing into the cosmos, light rippled out across the sky. And then she saw it. The myriad stars had turned into infinitely complex six-dimensional constellations.

Every last one was the life of someone she had ever loved in superposition. And those constellations fit into a stellar tapestry of lives lived in every fractal iteration of the multiverse. Beholding something that both dwarfed her in its totality and yet resonated at the very frequency of her being, all Lana could think was:

'Life is heaven. Life is heaven. Life is heaven.'

And she searched out her mother, and father, and Tima, and the Sherpa, seeing them in those infinite movements of stars as she had never seen them before.

Nothing of suffering left its mark on the infinite. Death was simply the space between notes turning the cacophony into melody. And then all those dancing constellations vibrated like a symphony. And the old man's words made perfect sense.

And in a corner of the sky, she returned to a creaky parquet floor, where a tear in Mama's eye fell as Rachmaninoff's Piano Concerto No.2 crackled in old vinyl spin beneath a spotless dust cover. Mama turned to Lana and said you can still hear Heaven through all of that static. And Mama was right. The static was just the aftermath of the cataclysm that turned one speck of light into all. In its own way that crackle was just another part of the song. And Lana cried too. And in her tear that moment of Mama shedding her soul twinkled brighter than all of everything together.

And Lana and her mother were that music forever. And after forever, or a flash, Lana came back down to her perch on the bird bath, knowing she'd still have to find her little bird lest the dark were to reclaim all that light.

And after searching out forever for forever more, in another tiny corner of it all, Lana saw a lighthouse blinking on a shore. And the beacon was her little bird. And she knew exactly where she had to go to find him.

But how? How?

Lana stepped back from the infinity sea and surveyed the amphitheater until spotting the notch in Veles' Spine. It was the only incongruity in the perfectly rock-ribbed colosseum.

So, she made her way back toward the break. Despite the distance, the unresisting world allowed her to stay lost in the stars above until she finally reached the pass. And driving at the break in the perfect circle, she stared up as the towering pillars of stone fanned out into the forever.

But as she tried to step across the threshold between a god's observatory and the other end of the telescope in scale, the world began to push back. Each labored step was brought from feet to inches in seconds. And then the first licks of the algid air blowing with a solar wind's ferocity. Then came the first glimpse of the drop from God's head to his toes.

The terror put Lana on her back foot, and quickly over the threshold of omniscience — the land of silence and soft edges.

Lana slid down against the bowl of rock and hugged her knees. It didn't matter if a wingless bird could fly — an eagle would die if it dared to brave that frigid free fall.

Lana looked up into the infinite again and picked out the glint in Tima's eye amid the infinite stars. She lowered her lids as a droplet of love wrapped that gold in a bowl and fell to the ground. And that goldfish bowl sailed down to the bird bath, hitting the water with a splash. The pinprick of light chased that sparkling comet through the ever.

And in her little rabbit heart snare tapping a military cadence allegro, crescendo fell to diminuendo — ritardando, rallentando and then adagio — but without the painful strings of attachment. A voice cried out from the heavens — 'he is free!'

The earth behind her began to rumble. That rumbling ended in a ding. A red door swung open. A scissored-gate folded in on itself. A blue light buzzed in a bowl of silence. A shadow fell into a gibbous basin.

"Miss, are you ready to go?" a familiar voice asked from above.

That voice pulled Lana back into herself. She looked up. Above her was Gönpo, standing right beside his magic elevator.

"Gönpo!" Lana squealed.

"At your service, ma'am."

Beside herself, she ran up and hugged him. He tucked her into the strangely familiar with a gentle hand.

"But wait," Lana said, pulling away and taking him in with bright eyes. "I thought you said the elevator couldn't go up to the 84,000th floor?"

"Indeed, you are correct, ma'am, it cannot. However, it can go down from the 84,000th floor."

"But how can it come down from here, if it cannot come up here?"

"Why, miss, it makes perfect sense if you really think about it."

Lana looked back up at all of those stars and understood him without thinking about anything at all. She stepped away and offered a resolute gaze.

"I know where I have to go now. Please take me back to my world, to the lighthouse where me and my daddy watched the dolphins."

Gönpo cleared his throat and adjusted his collar.

"I'm afraid that's the one other place I cannot take you."

"Why not?"

"Well, that is not so easy to understand. Let's just say it's a very special place."

"What makes my world so special?"

"It's special because it's yours," he said with an uncharacteristically warm smile.

"But have no fear. I know exactly who can take you there. If you'll please follow me," he said, stepping into the cab.

"Let's go!" Lana said with new-found confidence. And so he took her back to the world-scaling shrine of Egyptian lotus light. And this time when the door closed, the gate snapped shut, and the pinwheel galaxy rose on high, Lana saw herself spinning in that starry, starry night.

Chapter 40

AFTER BASKING UNDER INFINITY'S CONSTELLATIONS, Lana was brought back down to the atrium without a sky above it, where ghosts drank their cognac to old Soviet songs, watching spectral snow fall through phantasmagorical panes of glass in one of Stalin's Seven Sisters.

Exiting the elevator, Gönpo tipped his cap to her, wished her well and then took his place by the red padded door. Lana gazed at the galaxy man who had become a veritable statue. And then that statue began to look like its own sense of eternity viewed from beyond. She tried so hard to wrap her head around how momentary still and infinite stirring could look like exactly the same thing. When an answer came, though not exactly in words, she raised a hand to the spineless pinwheel and waved goodbye.

Moving down the corridor, the muted echoes from her rubber soles traced the tempo of Mihalkov's whimsical stroll around Moscow.

The chandelier above sparkled like a hangnail sticking out of the vault of Heaven. The Yablochkov candles twinkled like stars.

Plumes of smoke from cellophane cigars rose as mist. Laughter from the dead — living as if they would never die — echoed out in muted tones.

But, in the center of the great hall, she heard a steady drip drop. She approached a growing black puddle. She did not wait to watch it expand.

With a shudder, she headed back into the catacombs, where oil lamps hung between skulls, bones and the icons forming fences between them.

The chill still carried a musty mummy's breath of dust and death. Then, after so many twists and turns, the clacking of typewriters was finally heard. Lana made haste down the dimly-lit and winding spaces, doubling back when turns took the clicks out of the clacks, and pushing on when the hundreds of dancing fingers crescendoed in the coinciding chaos of Cyril's accidental song.

One final bend and she made her way back into that baroque expression of underground (and afterlife) bureaucracy.

All those souls glowing in varying tones of death continued forming lines that looked like strings of Christmas lights from above.

She scanned the room until the booming voice of the matron broke through the din. She was with a large group of workers trying to fill a gaping hole in the ceiling. On each side of her, enormous oafs in zip-up blue jackets and trousers with heads shaped like loaves of bread peaked by askew side caps stood guard.

Lana ran over, stopping in the shadow of the matriarch's bosom.

"No, no!" she screamed. "It's positively getting worse!"

"Miss!"

The matron looked down in surprise as the little girl came carrying the sky in blue eyes beneath all that rock and earth.

"Why, young lady, I didn't fancy I'd be seeing you any time soon! And I have to say, you could not have come at a worse time. Just look at it. The pressure is too great to bear. Even our engineers cannot keep that water from coming! I'm afraid we're going to flood any minute now. You must get out!"

Lana looked around and saw the air of agitation squeezed into faces of every heart-shaped and diamond-cast design. Panic was clearly beginning to spread among the dead but not yet dead.

"Ma'am, I know where to go, but I don't know how to get there!"

The matron thought for a second.

"I think I know who can help. Follow me. And hurry! Time is of the essence."

As the matron led Lana across the room, leaks began springing across the ceiling, showering the supplicants who were somewhere between half-crazed or fully deranged. The cries of frustration, desperation, and outright lunacy created quite a tumult. Lana gulped as the matron pushed a path through the rowdy crowd.

Suddenly, a green-hued goblin grabbed Lana by the arm. She looked in horror at spinning eyes keeping time to an overwrought overture.

Lana, who thought by then she could face all things, screamed at the sight of a face who could not endure one more second. The matron bore down on the mad grabber.

"Now you release her this instant!"

It became immediately clear, however, there was not a lick of space to talk an ounce of sense into. And for the first time, real panic set in the matron's previously unflappable eyes. The temporarily damned could sense it. The madness began to spread like contagion. Countless hands closed in. The high priestess' command crumbled.

"Slava! Seva! Help!" the matron cried.

The two oafs began beating back the masses, without a care to who got trampled underfoot. The resistance was less a matter of people pushing back rather than riffraff tripping over each other and getting twisted in makeshift barricades of writhing bodies.

Their screams only ramped up the frenzy as the matron struggled with the green-hued bedlamite trying to drag Lana away.

Feeling the matron's grip slip, Lana sank rabbit teeth into a meaty purlicue with an iridescent green sheen, prompting her would-be captor to howl at an unseen moon. The matron managed to wrestle Lana free as Lazarus in limbo screamed bloody murder.

And then an enormous rumble followed by flying rock and a rush of water.

"Oh no! It's too late!"

The oafs grabbed Lana and the matron post haste. Barreling through the throng, they knocked aside bodies like bowling pens, leaving a befuddled 7-10 split in their wake. The matron squirmed and screamed, both incensed by her loss of authority and embarrassed by her endowments being smushed and squeezed between burly forearms.

But with a near riot set to be drowned in dark water flood, the mindless men's lack of decorum was a godsend. They battled their way through the tumult until reaching a dimly blinking emergency exit on the other side of the cavern.

They took one look back. The damned were scattering every which way as water overturned desks and sent typewriters away on waves.

The matron pushed open the creaking door and pulled Lana through, leading her down a series of winding passages. After a few twists and turns, they approached yet another alcove with a statue of an opened-mouth Anubis. She grabbed the black dog by the tongue and pulled down. The walls began to rumble, and dust fell as a secret passage opened in the wall. Back down the corridor, a crowd of mad voices escaping the swell came charging.

"Quickly!" yelled the matron.

Grabbing Lana by the hand, the foursome retreated into the secret chamber. The matron grabbed a lever on the wall and yanked it up. With a slow, grinding scrape of stone, the black dog had barely swung back into place as the zombified mass stormed past. Pressing her ear to the cold rock, Lana could hear the rumble, grumble and tumble of bodies on the other side. And then the water came.

"Hurry!" the matron urged, grabbing Lana by the hand and leading her down the passage. Huffing and puffing on the way down, Lana could tell this was the first time in a long time anything in any world had compelled the imposing lady to break her perennially self-possessed stride. Even fear could make mice of matrons.

They reached the end of the passage, where heavy doors led to an abandoned subway station. The oafs held them open, letting Lana and the matron through. After passing to the other side, the heavy slabs of glass swung back like hammers.

Further on through the dark vestibule, Lana was led to a poorly-lit entrance hall with a vaulted tile ceiling. A fluorescent light buzzed above one ticket window to the right of the unturned turnstiles. Lana and the matron approached the buzz and flicker. Behind the glass, a woman in a dark blue waistcoat with her face covered by a veil read a cheap romance novel. She only looked up from her tale after the matron cleared her throat.

"Oh, hello, madam. What brings you down our way?"

"Oh, nothing, Ingrid, our offices are merely being flooded by the forces of destruction and the dead are somehow drowning for a second time."

"Oh my. That sounds serious."

"I need your help. Somehow, this little girl finding her little bird seems to be the secret to stopping the end of everything."

"I'll do what I can. Tell me, little girl, where do you need to go?"

"I need to go to the lighthouse …"

"What lighthouse would that be?"

"The one by the sea."

"The sea of counted sorrows?"

"No"

"The sea of uncounted sorrows?"

"No, not that one either."

"Well, young lady, without a station name, it's going to be hard to send you on your way."

Lana searched her memory, trying to retrace a path from up on moonlit brides with Mom and Dad down to the belly of a whale; from Ukrainian countryside to a bustling Kyiv station; and further down to a lowland sea that forever emptied into the basin of black. And high up above that shallow sea, where dolphins danced and waves lapped, a lighthouse kept watch over the world. And Lana could see and feel every moment of that trip like it was itself a living being right before her — its own constellation shining in the infinite sky. And the station where they arrived to meet Uncle Andrei had a name. But what was that name?

Lana looked up and tried to turn those memories into words.

"I, I…"

"I might know where she needs to go," a gruff, adolescent voice boomed from behind.

The matron and Lana turned around, scanning the dimly lit hall. The figure of a young man emerged from the shadows of a marble column. At first Lana couldn't see his hooded face cast in shadow. But the spark reached her heart more quickly than the photons en route to her eye.

"Tima!" Lana screamed, running to embrace her long-lost friend.

Wrapping her arms around his waist, Lana pressed her head to his side and began to sob.

"I thought I'd never see you again," she sputtered.

Tima groaned, half-heartedly trying to peel her off of him. But then his heart softened, and he drew her in.

"No need to cry now. Good ol' Tima ain't goin' nowhere."

Lana pulled away and looked up, love-lit waters pouring from her eyes.

"But how, how did you get here? I thought I had lost you forever!" she implored, hugging him more tightly.

Tima scanned all the dark space above seeking out an answer to all those hows, whens and whys.

"You know, it's the damnedest thing. I remember falling into that water and then 'whoosh'! I was carried right over that fall. And there was nothing but bubbles and darkness and all my kickin' and screamin' to get myself away from something that was just too damn strong to get away from.

"And then I started goin' down and down until there wasn't no light no more, 'cept all that fire in my lungs. And I thought — this is it — I'm a gonner. And breathing all that fire I wanted to be a gonner, if I'm gonna' be honest. There I was waiting to die, just to get the pain over with. And then all that darkness just didn't seem so scary anymore. And that's when this glowin' blue hand snatched me up, just like that glove the elevator man gave you."

"I, I lost my glove," Lana exclaimed. "I dropped it right in the water before you fell. I was so sad. Gönpo had given it to me to protect me, then I lost it!"

"Well, you might have lost it, but it sure found me in the nick of time! I swear, as it pulled me up through that water everything burned blue like electricity. And I started burping up fire like I was one of those barrels the bums burn trash in at night. Then all those lil' bits of fire just sort of hovered 'round me. And all the sudden they started forming these shapes, you know, like the stars make shapes and people call them different things, like big bears and birds up there in the sky and all that.

"And then more and more stars came right outta' me. They all started becoming their own shapes too, until all I could see was everything. I got no words to describe it, but everything was what it was, Lana, it was all everything all at once. It was young and old and night and day and tomorrow and yesterday all just there — right there. And I was a great blue comet shootin' from one end of it to the other. I know it sounds crazy!"

"You don't sound crazy! Up on the bird bath I saw everyone and everything, and I saw you too, and I knew you would never leave me!"

And they looked at each other and saw all those constellations in each other's eyes.

"You know," Tima said, with an uncharacteristic air of solemnity, "when I was down there and watching all those lights, they all started to look like little birds circling 'round me. And I started to think, seein' them little birds flyin' and shinin': 'That's what Lana's looking for. She's looking for the light that saves you from all that dark.' And when I knew that I was free. And all them lil' birds started flappin' 'til all I could see was the light. And then there was no more me. Just all of this love and light. And…"

"And…"

"I don't remember nothin' after that. Just woke up down here, runnin' up and down the tubes in that there metro tunnel. But that metro ain't like none I ever saw before. The train that runs comes from some other world. You can kinda' see right through it. It's like a ghost wagon or something."

"You think it can take me back to my lighthouse by the sea?"

"I reckon that train can take ya just about anywhere. Question is, are you ready to go?"

"I am!"

"Well then. Let's go!"

Full of light in that dark, dark place, Lana and Tima walked back over to the ticket counter, where the matron was waiting.

"Well, young man, fancy seeing you here again."

"Ain't nothin' fancy 'bout it. I'm here, you're here — we're here."

"That's assuming you understand what here means."

"Oh, I know where here is. It's the place I'm trying to get the hell out of. But first we gotta get Lana sorted out."

"On that count we agree."

"Well good. No Lana's tryin' to get back to our world. Maybe she don't know the station name, but something tells me that train goes to a whole buncha' places Lana ain't got no business goin'. Now, Lana, tell us 'bout that lighthouse you was talkin' 'bout."

"It's where my aunt and uncle live with my cousins, in a little town by the sea. It wasn't the Black Sea. It was just above it!"

"Was it in Russia?"

"No. I remember late at night on the train they woke up Mom and Dad to look at their little books because they said we were leaving Russia. It's the only time we ever left Russia!"

"And where did you go?"

"Ukraine!"

"Well there you go!"

Tima looked up at the matron. "I figure if we can get Lana as far as Kyiv, it's gotta be a start."

"It is a start," the matron said. "But Ukraine has its share of coastal towns. Why, there must be hundreds of lighthouses!"

"That's true!" Lana exclaimed. "Why, the town we visited had not one, but two lighthouses!"

"Two lighthouses?" the veiled woman in the ticket counter chimed in. "Why didn't you say so? We've got a train that calls on Two Light House Station. My sister works there! Why, it should be coming any minute now!

"There's just one thing. I haven't seen my sister in a long, long time. Could you give this to her?" she said, pushing a book-shaped parcel through the slot in the window.

The matron took the parcel, who handed it to Lana.

"How will I know who your sister is?" Lana asked.

"You'll find her working at a ticket counter just like this. Chances are, she'll be reading a romance novel. She's the only person who loves them as much as I do! Tell her Ingrid sent you."

"Okay!"

"Oh, and don't forget these!" she said, handing over a sky-blue, faience-glazed scarab with separate wings.

"Now you press that beetle belly to the turnstile, and it will let you through. And once you're on the train, press the wings in, and it will take you where you need to go."

Lana's eyes grew wide.

"What's the matter, little girl?"

"It's just that, my little bird lost his wings too."

"Is that so? Well, I hope he finds them. Then maybe we'll get going where we need to. Now I'd hurry along, little girl, that train is coming any second."

But just as Tima and Lana were prepared to bid their farewells, the veiled woman in the ticket counter shouted at Tima,

"Don't you forget your ticket too!"

"I don't need no ticket," Tima huffed.

Unseen eyes shown beneath the veil.

"Oh, I think you do."

Tima begrudgingly turned back and put his hand to the tray.

And through the slot in the window, the veiled woman strongly gripped his hand and pressed his ticket firmly into his palm. Beneath the veil, there was no facial expression to be read.

"Now don't you go losing that ticket, young man. God knows what you went through to get it."

And Tima stared hard into the grille and fell completely silent. His rough hand slowly slipped away as she gave him a slow nod.

"Now, I have to go up there and see if me and my engineers cannot find a way to pump out that water," the matron said. "We'll be waiting for news from you. Heaven knows we'll be able to use your beacon with all the darkness coming our way. Good luck!"

"Thank you!" Lana shouted, before her and Tima ran over to the faregate.

Lana pressed the scarab's underside to the beetle-shaped indention on the turnstile, which opened up to let her through. Tima pressed his token to his palm, but rather than place it to the gate, he vaulted over the stile as he had done 10,000 times before, setting off a chiming echo in the cavernous hall.

Perfunctory cries came from the veiled woman, but there were neither guards nor police to take chase.

In the vaulted ceiling above, 10,000,000 pieces of tessera fell into place to form a mosaic of 88 constellations. And in the dark all the tiled stars shone.

The two took to the 10,000-step escalator and kept their eyes sky-high as they descended the endless depths. And somehow in descent a night sky seen only from Earth's greatest heights became clearer as they went.

They finally reached the platform of the pylon station. Down the central hall they saw 32 stain glass panels back-lit and bronze-bordered. The pylons and arches between them were cut from black marble and edged in brass.

The 32 mosaics of mandalas depicted 32 deities in the tradition of Guhyasamāja Tantra.

As Lana and Tima made their way down the platform, they turned right midway down and walked beneath an arch.

They both craned their necks to see down the endless black tunnel ahead. They looked back at each other bathed in the blue lights of the back-lit mosaics.

Then came the sound of a steam whistle. Down the tunnel, the light of a train was shown. Slowly, a spectral locomotive began pulling in. Lana grabbed Tima by the hand.

She squeezed his callouses as hard as she could, and he squeezed back with a grip softer than her rabbit pads.

"I'm scared, Tima."

Tima got down on his knees and looked her in the eyes.

"I am too," he said, with a glint in his eyes reflecting the light of all that shattered stone behind him. "I am too."

And he held her tightly as the train steamed and rolled in.

It lurched to a slow stop, two doors opening before two beings bound in embrace. Emerald fog poured from the doors. A conductor stood at attention.

Tima and Lana slowly let go, standing up and heading to the carriage before them.

"Ticket please."

Lana released her grip, showing him the scarab and wings in her hand.

"Very good. After you take your seat, and the doors close, please lock the wings in place and you will promptly be sent on your way."

"Okay," Lana said.

Tima stepped up next.

"Ticket please."

Tima likewise opened up his fist and showed the conductor the token in hand. And the conductor's eyes grew wide.

"I'm sorry, young man, but this train isn't for you."

"What do you mean it ain't for me?"

Your ticket is taking you somewhere else altogether. I, I haven't seen such a ticket in a long, long time. I cannot begin to imagine what you've done to get it."

"What's that supposed to mean?" Tima bawled. "You sittin' there accusin' me of something?" he barked.

"Not at all. My, oh my, even in becoming God, you've still got the bark of a dog. Didn't you look at it, and I mean really look? You've got a piece of God's heart in your hand, young man. Congratulations. You're moving on!"

"Moving on where?"

"Beyond this life and the millions before it that left you with that red hue. No more. You shall never be taken by another's hands again. You are delivered into his hands now. The rocky road ends here."

Rather than defense, like magic it all clicked. For the first time in life after life after life, every last ounce of anger and fight was gone. Tima raised his shaking hands to his hoodie and pulled it back. And for the first time Lana saw his face in full, awash in a red glow.

The levy, finally broke. Lifetimes of pain poured from his eyes. And Lana ran back onto the platform and held on for dear life.

"I'll never let you go, Tima, I'll never let you go!"

"How can ya say that when we're 'bout to leave each other?"

"Because she's taking you with her, and you are taking her with you," the conductor interrupted, pressing his hand to his heart.

And Lana let Tima cry out all the pain of never having gotten to be a child and dying young all the same. And she let that strong boy shake until she saw the little bird in him — something beautiful and light and eternal burning with all of the love in the world.

Chapter 41

LANA AWOKE ON A MOVING train. The other three berths in the second-class compartment were empty. She felt wide awake; wide awake in a dream called life. She no longer felt the difference between falling asleep and waking up, or whether there had ever been a difference between the two.

The early dawn light pouring in between blue curtains was the color of a pearl that had lost its luster.

Not knowing where she was, not knowing where she was going, Lana couldn't shake the sensation, that somehow, she was homeward bound.

She laid back in the rock-a-bye motion, breaking away from the tick of time. The pearl picked up a hint of a glimmer as an unseen sun sailed by.

After a few seconds, or perhaps it was hours, the train slowed against the flow. And there it was again, filing in the window, the mint green and white train station in that little city by the sea.

Faint memories flashed in her mind. Floating in her dad's arms. Chords strummed and melodies hummed by the fire. Meat grilled at dusk. Birds chirping at dawn. The bumblebee buzz of mid-day. The cicada crescendo sympathy at day fade. A dandelion blowball carried by a breeze. And torn bird wings in the shadow of a monster.

Then there was Tima, Tima who was finally free. And her soul longing for the greater whole from which that spark in her heart came.

Then came the faint hustle and bustle of passengers in the corridor as the train came to a halt. She slid open her door and slid between legs too tall, a few dull eyes looking down and then ahead, too travel-weary or otherwise preoccupied to pay much mind to a pint-sized stowaway.

She followed the flow of people out onto the platform. Cold air carrying a cigarette cloud hit her face. Turns out the land of summer and sea was just as much at the mercy of the Earth's axial tilt as her northern bog-land home.

Still bundled up in a blue jacket and capped in hat, the chill hit her glove-less hand, which she shoved into her pocket. The throbbing in her fingers reminded her of that blue lotus ferrying Tima to salvation. And then the sting didn't hurt so bad at all.

She wandered down the platform past the benches where train spotters planted themselves on warmer days. Following the crowd into the arrivals' hall, she shuffled her feet to a row of orange seats by the window under the timetable. People streamed under the chandelier pinned to the domed ceiling. Something about the pale blue walls made it feel more like a hospital than a train station.

Eventually, everyone filed out, leaving Lana alone. Alone that is, except for the middle-aged woman in a blue uniform seated crossways in the ticket window. She looked askance at the small, solo sojourner, before returning her eyes to a cheap paperback.

And despite having only seen her sister through the veil, Lana knew she was the one.

She got up and walked over to the counter.

"Excuse me, ma'am," Lana said, trying to shove her words into the box above.

"What is it, young lady?" the woman replied, peering above a dog-eared page.

"I have something for you. It's from your sister. She asked me to bring it to you."

At that awkward angle, Lana could not see the flash of lightning in the woman's eyes above.

"Sister? I don't know who you think you are, young lady, but your little joke is a cruel one indeed. My sister passed a long, long time ago."

"Wait! It was your sister, I swear!"

"Didn't you hear me, my sister is dead!"

Lana started to panic.

"Ingrid!" she blurted out. "She told me to tell you it was from Ingrid!"

The name struck a chord.

"Wait. How did you know? Who told you her name? Who sent you?"

"Ingrid sent me," Lana said, getting up on her tiptoes and sliding the parcel toward the slot. "Please, she asked me to give this to you."

With shaking hands, the woman behind the window gripped the package and pulled it through.

She slowly untied the rough, twine bow and pulled the folded sections of rough, brown paper apart. And then her eyes grew wide.

She raised the book to her face and breathed in the faint, musky smell. Hints of vanilla took her back in time. Delicately opening it up, an old, faded picture of two beautiful teens fell out, sending her back further still.

"I, I haven't seen this in 40 years," the woman said, gripping the picture in her hands. "Crimea. We were only 16. We were so beautiful then. This is the last picture we ever took before … before she was taken from us. How, how did you get this?"

"I told you, ma'am, she gave it to me."

"But that simply is not possible."

"Ma'am, I think everything is possible."

The woman returned to an inscription written on the flyleaf — words that rang out beyond time.

"My sister used to love these trashy romance novels. I got her this one for her birthday. No doubt about it, my words are right here: 'Dear Ingrid, may you find the love you seek this summer. Love, Ira.' Who knew that would be her last summer? Who knows anything about where life will take you? Who knew life would take me to a place where everyone is leaving, and I never go anywhere?"

"Ma'am, you can go anywhere you want. Just get on one of these trains!"

The woman let out a laugh.

"It's not that simple, little girl."

"Why not?"

But as she opened her mouth to lecture Lana about life, the cat got her tongue. It was the kind of question people dismissed to placate their fears rather than kindle their hopes.

"Maybe you are right … Maybe you are right. I haven't been to Crimea in 40 years. I sure would love to see it again before I…"

"Before you what?"

"Nothing, nothing. I still don't understand any of this. What do you want from me?"

"I don't want anything, but I would be very happy if you could tell me how to get to the lighthouse."

"The lighthouse?"

"Yes."

"Well, we've got more than one lighthouse in this city."

"I know. You have two! I want to go to the lighthouse where you can watch the dolphins. The one by the water."

"Dolphins? You aren't going to see any dolphins this time of year. The sea is just starting to thaw out. But if it's right by the water, you must mean the old one. But what about your parents? Family? How exactly did you get here anyways? Don't tell me you arrived on the train all by yourself, did you?"

Lana drew out the silence.

"Well…?"

"My father, he's at the lighthouse," Lana said, immediately feeling guilty for telling a lie, but also, in some strange way, not so sure that she had.

"Your father works at the lighthouse?"

She once again hid in silence.

"Okay, so you want to go to the little lighthouse down by the sea?"

Lana nodded her head.

At that instant, a taxi driver awkwardly ambled into the hall and sat down with a deep sigh. He placed his hands on his round belly, filling out his puffy blue vest. Bushy white hair formed cotton cloud cover around his head.

He twiddled his thumbs and fought the urge to whistle, lest he lose his last kopek, having failed to secure a fare.

"Hey, Oleg!"

"Yeah?"

"Looks like no one was looking for a taxi into the city."

"Yeah."

"Well, can you do me a favor?"

"What?"

"This little girl, she needs to go to the lighthouse."

"The lighthouse? We got more than one lighthouse, Irina, you know that!"

"Of course I know that. She wants to go to the old one!"

"The old one?"

"Yes!"

"That old lighthouse is a good 10 miles away! Who's gonna' pay me to go all the way down there?"

"Oh, come on now. What else are you going to do?"

"Sitting here and not wasting gas sounds like a start!"

"Pff. No need to be selfish. There's a little girl here who needs your help. Think of it as your good deed for the day."

"Good deeds don't pay as well as they used to!"

"That's what makes them good deeds! Are you really going to leave this poor little girl stranded here?"

"All right, all right," he grumbled, slowly getting up and ambling over to the ticket counter.

He gave the woman behind the counter a look of mild irritation before looking down at Lana.

"So, what's your name?"

"My name's Lana."

"Lana, as in Svetlana?"

"No, just Lana like Lana."

"Well, Lana like Lana, my name's Oleg. Time's a wasting. Let's go!"

"Okay!"

Lana matched the old man's pace as they ambled out of the hall.

Irina sat in her little box, gripping the photo of her and her sister. She still couldn't believe it. Had that little girl been some sort of angel? She felt as if she were dreaming it all.

She glanced over at the timetable. There was no direct route to Simferopol — it was closer by water than by land. But there was a train leaving in an hour to Melitopol that would get her just about halfway. She could always find her way from there.

She nervously tapped her fingers on the photograph for several seconds. And with a flash of inspiration, she filled herself out a ticket, put a closed sign over the ticket counter and headed out to the platform to wait.

After decades in the box, the cold air didn't feel so cold anymore. She sat down and opened the old book to page one.

Irina had spent years working at the station secretly thinking her life was over. And then one day a small visitor arrived to show her she was wrong.

Chapter 42

THE RIDE PASSED MOSTLY IN silence.

The few times Oleg tried to make small talk, his questions were mostly met with single word answers, if any words at all. From time to time he'd glance over to see Lana's face pressed against the cold glass, thoughts adrift in another world.

What he didn't know was that she was trying to catch a hint of days gone by, to no avail. Her one-time land of warmth was itself stuck in that awkward transition to spring. Droplets of water formed on the window. The dull pearl above sunk deeper into the sea. Long gone was her land of dreams.

But he took his failed efforts at conversation in stride, for it didn't compare to the wall of silence between him and his wife.

For while a few extra bucks in a world of pensioner paucity provided a pretext to get out of the house, Oleg, more than anything, sought escape from the panoramic view of the relational sinkhole into which his home had plunged.

Ever since their son had died in the war, all that Oleg and his wife had ever known of love had slowly died on the vine.

And yet they lived, through 10 long, arduous years of emotional and physical atrophy, they lived.

More than a decade before that decade of loss, Oleg's leg had been mangled in a plane crash. But a lifetime of limping could never compare with the pain of living with a crippled heart.

That was the greatest blow of all, he and his wife learned year by year, to go on as half a person, with everyone around you normalizing the absence of your very own reason for being.

From the outside, once the tears stopped and the small talk continued, everyone thought everything was more or less okay. But Oleg and his wife silently shared the darkness together. And they resented each other for knowing what no one else knew — they had become the living dead.

So, he gave his wife the only thing he could give her — distance from himself. And watching the droplets form on his window, allowing his mind to drift to the strange journey of this strange little girl, Oleg in that brief reprieve could cast his attention upon the sea and forget about sinking down into the trench.

— — —

They eventually reached the winding road to the lighthouse, which cut between sea arms hugging the gulf. A few shabby buildings surrounded by scrubby bush dotted the otherwise desolate landscape.

The car pulled up to the high, rusty gate fencing in the orange-and-white-beacon.

Power poles rose above the leafless trees. Transmission lines free of birds were held taut between the beams.

"Well, we're here. So, what now?"

Lana struggled to pull the door handle open. She finally succeeded and got out of the car.

She shuffled along the fence, staring down into the brown grass. Everything about her seemed so odd. She was as cute as a button, but unsettlingly distant. He felt as if they were only inhabiting the smallest slice of shared reality in a Venn diagram dominated by difference. He was already starting to regret his decision to take her. If they can't find her father, what then?

"The road to hell…" he mumbled under his breath.

He got out of the car, flung the door shut and followed Lana over to the gate in his awkward gait. He rubbed his hands in the early spring chill looking to kickstart his congested circulation.

As he approached, her tiny figure was eclipsed by his shadow.

"What are you looking for?" he asked from on high.

"My little bird," she replied sheepishly, crouching down and crab walking along the perimeter. "He, he ran away. I've come a long way to find him. He must be here!"

"Your little bird," Oleg said, slightly confused. "Our town's got more water fowl than you can shake a stick at."

But Lana ignored him, continuing her sideways scamper along the fence in hopes of finding the dandelion clock in the perennial weeds.

Oleg stayed close behind, feet slightly sticking against the damp ground.

"Look, I haven't got all day. If you want to go catching birds, you can do that on your own time," he said, although his gruff tone failed to break the spell.

"Do you see that?" Lana said, pointing up at the blanket of clouds. Shadow animals danced on the mist. A wingless bird cut a hole perfect blue, sailing over the unlit beacon. And then dark clouds slowly crept in, blotting out all of the colors and shapes.

"He's getting closer."

"Who's getting closer?"

"The nightmare man. We need to hurry, mister and find my little bird."

"Now listen here, little girl, I don't know what all of this crazy talk is about! But I don't have time to be messing around!"

"I understand," she said phlegmatically. "I'm sorry for troubling you. Thank you for helping me, mister," she said, walking away and entering the lighthouse grounds.

"Now hold on a second!" he cried out, chasing after her in his awkward gait.

Trailing her, he walked to the back of the two-story, blocky white annex which extended halfway up the tower.

Following her inside, his feet echoed on brown tiles.

They moved from the anteroom into the small hall, painted blue as high as a man's neck and white above that to keep his head in the clouds. The white French doors were already opened into the corridor. Across the threshold past a row of green doors, the head rest of a cross intersection led up the tower to the beacon. Lana headed straight for the door.

Oleg managed to overtake her, placing his hands on the frame and blocking her passage.

"Stop!" he implored. "We cannot just go walkin' round someone's property without permission. Especially a place like this! Now let me see if I can find the lighthouse keeper. I'll be back in a minute. And do not leave this room! The last thing I need is you wandering off somewhere you don't belong!"

Lana nodded as he awkwardly walked down the corridor. She listened to his retreating footsteps, the pain nearly audible in his permanently offbeat gait. Oleg called out for the lighthouse keeper several times, to no avail. He headed down to the stairwell and stuck his head around the corner, peering up the orange spiral twisting up 99 steps to the top.

Lana shuffled in place when suddenly, the faint sound of chirping provided counterpoint to her tiny-toed echo.

She didn't believe her ears at first. Walking back into the anteroom, with the front door leading outside still open, it seemed to get louder.

But when she stuck her head outside, it stopped.

She stood there and listened, but nothing. She gazed ahead into the row of trees several yards behind the building.

She stared up as the remains of pearl-cloud cover were slowly being blotted out by a spray of squid ink coming in from the gulf. Thunder rumbled in the kraken's belly.

Fine blonde hairs rose on the back of her neck. The eerie sky shook her electric. Fear of the blackening blue pushed her to step back inside. Just then, the tweeting started again, even louder than before. Lana took two timid steps across the threshold. The wind howled; the grass swayed. Spindly tree fingers shivered.

Suddenly, a dandelion head on dinosaur legs ran out from the brush.

Lana's heart beat a motivated rabbit run. Could it be? She ran several steps forward. It was, it was!

Legs small and smaller still converged in the center of the yard as storm clouds stomped out the light.

Lana dove into a limber-limbed crouch and extended a hand on which dinosaur feet were happy to land.

A girlish giggle followed the familiar tickle.

Two fingers gently grazed white velvet as shimmering black eyes stared at two shining circles of sky-blue sky.

"I'll never let you go," Lana whimpered in retreating grief and gaining joy.

But on the edge of the wood, in the diffuse light being gobbled up by darkness, a spectral shadow stepped outside of itself. Lana looked up at the black-on-blackening backdrop. In that void, she saw something horrifying and familiar — the melting face of the nightmare man taking form in deformity. In the tenebrious terror, color seeped into the dark figure at a slow contrast knob shift on the TV, turning, turning, from nine o'clock to three. All the while, his volume swelled a birthday-blown balloon.

Lana was frozen in horror. Her tiny partner sought shelter in a palm enclave and tiny finger palisades.

Fully manifest, the nightmare stepped out from trees, brushing dirt and crust from his dusty shoulders.

"Oh, it's you again," he snidely remarked. "The little girl who likes to take things that don't belong to her. I do believe you have something of mine. Looks like you're here all alone this time. No rotten little boys to help you cause mischief, I see."

Lana was dumbstruck.

He took a step forward.

"Don't you think for one second I'm leaving here before I get it back," he said, turning his head at an aberrant angle until his sickly smile was nearly vertical.

Eyes locked on her, his upturned face rattled with the shakes of an alcoholic's hands.

Lana stepped back toward the doorway, shaking her head in a broken record feed-back loop of fear.

"I see it right there, wrapped in your sweet, sweet little fingers! You know what they do to thieves in lands scorched by white desert suns? I think I just might take my little bird, along with the hands that took it!"

Stuck in the doorway, Lana's eyes grew big enough for the world to fall into them.

The nightmare man's head straightened with a cracked-knuckle cacophony.

"Yes, that's right!" he roared. "You took my little bird, and you're going to pay for it!"

Thunder rumbled in the kraken's belly again as lightning cracked blue against the black ink sky. In the surge, the leviathan charged at her like a bolt of lightning.

Lana let out a scream, darting through the door. She slipped and fell on the smooth brown tile, ignoring the pain in her knees and scrambled to her feet.

Back in the stairwell, the little girl's squeal sent shivers down Oleg's spine. He doubled back down the corridor as fast as his uneven legs would allow, blocking the path of the rabbit run.

"He's here, he's here!"

Oleg crouched down and grabbed her by the shoulders, staring into spinning blue parasols of terror.

"Who's here?"

"The nightmare man! I've seen him before, but I wasn't dreaming. My cousin, he, he saved me! But he's found me again. And now he wants my little bird, and he wants me too!"

"Your little bird?"

"Look! Look! I found him."

Lana uncupped her hands and extended them toward Oleg. In her open shell display crouched a small white sphere the size of an albino apricot, staring at him with shining black eyes.

"Wha … what is that?" Oleg stuttered, feeling himself slip into the spell of what he'd thought was solely a child's dream.

"It's my little bird! The kind old man told me I'd find him where he'd have no choice but to fly. We must go up! He'll show us the way out!"

Every ounce of his grey matter resisted the world of fantasy Lana's words were conjuring. But all that resistance was met with the reality of a cotton-ball creature pleading with black, sparkling eyes.

"Okay, okay," he muttered dumbstruck.

"Ninety-nine steps," Lana squeaked. "We have to go up ninety-nine steps!"

Oleg winced.

"You're really not helping," he said, planting his palms on his thighs to push himself up.

As Oleg slowly rose, a dark shadow stretched across the section of the main room visible from the corridor's end. Then blackness seeped into the white spaces until the shadow was either swallowed, or itself did the swallowing. Rolling thunder boomed through the walls and caused the lights to flicker.

Oleg was confused. Thundersnow just didn't happen in these parts. And yet some dark storm was brewing indeed.

A cold wind blew down the corridor as the lights began to flicker like candles. The hair on the back of his neck rose like antennae looking to catch signals in the air.

He beckoned to Lana to stay still as he stepped down the strobe-lit corridor. Thunder rattled the green double doors shut tight to his right. His pounding heart rattled the ribcage around it.

Oleg peered around the corner to the darkened chamber, blue-white walls barely visible amid the last remnants of spectral white light shining weakly from the anteroom.

Snow squall blew a banshee scream and arctic air from outside. The temperature had plummeted in the space of minutes. Oleg shivered in the shadows. He searched out a light switch with unadjusted eyes. Just minutes before the room had been aglow in diaphanous daylight filtered through clouds.

"This isn't right," he repeated in disaffirmation. "This isn't right at all."

The squall outside reached such a fever pitch, the shut doors in the corridor began to clatter at the speed of a spinning propeller. The sound was all too familiar. It was the sound of a million bad dreams and one nightmare day.

Then one heavy gust and the front door letting in light from the anteroom locked up the lighthouse like a tomb. The French doors leading to the corridor simultaneously slammed shut behind him.

The corridor door clatter built to the roar of an engine. And then with eyes opened and closed alike, Oleg returned to the most terrifying day of his life.

During the Angolan Civil War, he had been a flight mechanic in a Soviet crew flying an An-26 transport aircraft near Menongue one fateful night in November.

The world below was a semi-arid stretch of chaos, but logistics by air was an A to B affair. One could pretend, of mice and men, to be a double-headed eagle, sailing above the fray of politics and human consequence.

That was, until one of Savimbi's Stingers sent their spark spitting plane on a collision course with the thicket below.

In the dive bomb toward what he believed would be certain death, Oleg had seen his life flash before his eyes. In the dark shadow of demise, without God, without belief in the mission that had sent him to a faraway land to participate in a conflict he hadn't even bothered to understand, Oleg had felt a void open up from within that was even bleaker than the fiery end he was sure awaited him.

The adrenaline surge took his body through the darkness of an in-flowing siphon current, sucking his soul through an underworld sepulcher. The instrument panel faded out into deep sea phosphorescence; the pilot's frantic motions and the crew's mumbled prayers lost form and melded into one diving motion.

Drowning in midair, his flippant thoughts found focus on the faded faces of icon paintings in his mother's red corner. He pleaded to saints whose names he didn't know, promising if spared, he would return to his own quiet shore to live a peaceful life of friends and family.

And while the plane did crash, the deft maneuvering of the pilot allowed for a swan dive smash that broke bones and branches, but not lives. Oleg's lopsided legs were one such consequence of the fall.

But an expertly executed rescue mission saw four of the crew scooped up, although two more were left to the devices of UNITA forces. And despite being dragged across savannah, jungle and the length of the Bie Plateau as alleged bombers of civilians and proof of Soviet expansion, the two would one day be swapped in a prisoner exchange.

And Oleg did return home to his wife and boy, who in a sick twist of fate, would find himself years later burning to death in a Soviet tank crematorium. The zinc casket returning his remains would never be opened. From that day on, Oleg was plagued by a reoccurring dream where he was the one burning to death in a fireball shot down over an African sky, only to sacrifice his son's future to a devil-eyed joker born in Rublev's hand.

And Oleg would awaken in fire, extinguishing his burning heart with the most bitter of tears. And though he never admitted it to himself, he realized the most bitter truth of all. He had prayed to live in a falling plane just so he could die 10,000 more nights. He sometimes thought he would give anything to have died that day, just so his last memories would be those of a world free of the imagined screams of his dear Alyosha burning up back-to-back with his commander above a fuel-seat throne.

And there, in that darkened room, Oleg once again felt himself diving toward the bottom of a tree-covered trench, his son engulfed in flames and screaming a maniac's laughter atop the spark shooting propeller. Thumbnails dug into his temples as he wailed to block out the kettle scream rising on the Stygian marsh.

Blood trickled from his brow beneath fingertip roots breaking ground. He collapsed in the depths of hell, letting out a resounding wail.

From beyond the double doors, Lana heard his tortured screams. Lest she be dragged down into the nightmare man's torturous depths, she and her little bird sought higher ground in 99 steps.

Way up above, the beacon burned blood red.

Chapter 43

GALYA BOLTED OUT THE DOOR. Fresh powder glowed orange under the blinking street lights. She ran around the backside of the building.

A gathering wind hurried along straggling clouds across the sky, revealing a silver moon in slivers.

Shards of sheen fell on the un-iced water rippling along the pavement.

A rainbow nimbus shone around the cloud edges. Laughter erupted. Dark clouds enveloped the light. Galya looked back in terror. The shadow followed. The water rose above the pavement.

Reaching the end of the building in splashing retreat, Galya turned right and noticed a faint red glow emanating from the basement door. She ran down the stairs and took shelter inside.

As the door slammed shut she slid to the floor, back braced against the cold metal, gasping for air. Galya waited a minute, but no one came. The faint red light had died down to the red tint of blood on black in freshly shut eyes in a now dark room. Moments later, a pulse of red light returned.

Galya made her way across the room on hands and knees, looking to examine the odd glow. A large pop resounded through the room. She froze in her tracks, listening to the sound of her heart in the darkness. It was just the door sighing. Steadying her labored breaths, she waited. The sound of muffled wind rising was faintly perceptible. The glow intensified, revealing an array of splashes on the floor.

Galya crawled to the edge of the large, carmine circle. In what appeared to be a partially ionized ring of red fire, a man with a knife stood before the tower planted between four and five o'clock. A prostrate body lay before him in flames. The killer held a blue-eyed rabbit by the ears.

The wind built to a howl outside. Red sparks galloped from every direction, falling on a big blob of a beast running down the radius to dusk. Three smaller sparks were already on his trail. One got in his way. Then there were two as the third faded out.

The basement door flung open. The towering shadow stood in sharp relief to the lavender-lit night sky. Snow began falling as baby's breath.

A trickle of blood fell from Galya's finger and dripped into the perfect circle. A bird hanging at the 360th degree dive-bombed to intercept the drop. She felt a whooshing sound build in her ears. The circle began to rise and rise as a red wave, cresting at the ceiling and crashed over her.

At first the fear was total; a single cell shot through the artery of existence. But the feeling of drowning shifted to something akin to free fall. Red faded to black. The crushing force of the rush took on the feeling of zero gravity weightlessness.

Opening clinched eyes, she saw the silhouette of the hooded man retreat into the distance, lavender light trailers and snowfall constellations gazed at through a telescope lens. And for the first time in her entire life, Galya let go of everything.

Floating through deep space, inner space or even interspace, if there was a difference, for the first time ever, she was free. Free of the burden of self, the burden of selfish and selflessness, free of the fear of death, as well as the fear of life. What had felt like a body now seemed like a trap, a way to sequester a spark of being from the infinite fire, a storm forever brewing on the horizon, looking to snuff out the shine and inundate a being with infinite darkness.

Oh, what a thing to become a part of the storm, to not be hammered by waves until going under, but to rise and fall with the whole.

But somewhere, in the myriad mandala of multiverse, an image of Lana in peril buzzed like a yellow jacket. Then there was Viktor in disarray; then the wasp whir was a side-by-side duo. And in the whir begot worry of buzzing thoughts, a hand that was not there reached to pluck out a hair not to be found. The swarm-yellow storm grew to fury.

And the more she strained against dissolution, the more the electrified pestilence roared.

And in her mind, the fluid state of things was made ceramic in the fires of control. She opened up her mouth to scream. Plague and pestilence made in foundries poured in. And then there was a hand, and there was hair to be torn.

And each strand fell to the earth. And Galya fell with them.

Chapter 44

VIKTOR CAME TO HIS SENSES snow-covered in the slack of a sand dune, shivering and staring at black clouds above. He'd fallen through infinity only to wake freezing and fetal-positioned, thunderheads shaking off frost like a wet dog.

He slowly rose to his knees, trying to snap the cold and confusion alike. A crack of lightning sent him back down, leaving Viktor to belly crawl up the dune on bent arms at a snail's pace.

Cutting a channel through three inches of powder, he reached the top on stiff elbows.

Scouting beyond the slip face, a series of waves appeared frozen in free fall. Past the unbreaking breakers, a 17th century brigantine under partial sail was suspended in Viktor's disbelief. A squall screamed something ancient and hateful. He buried his head in arms to shield his aching ears.

As the gale blew and blew, the ice waves choppily moved — painted theater flats on tracks from a Georges Méliès' dream. Spectral sails sent wind horse couriers to appease Sagarmatha's rage. Red lightning cracked the black eye of heaven bloodshot.

Down the gulf and further inland, a beacon burned a red star. In this mad, mad world, Viktor somehow knew he had been here before.

He waited for a lull in the wind and descended the dune down onto the shore. Hugging himself with the cold settling into labored movements, he stumbled past the moving row of upturned ice blades. As the sky grew darker, the beacon burned brighter.

The wind picked up and the sting of snow abraded his face. He thought about the cop chase, the trip through space and then Lana. Always Lana. Standing before a fall-down world, a cold gust rocked him again.

It was going to be a long walk to the lighthouse.

Chapter 45

BOOMS OF THUNDER RESOUNDED IN the stairwell as Lana made the laborious ascent nearly on hands and knees. The steps were just too big, her legs too small. The ledge running the length of the stairwell was likewise too high; the top of the twisting grey rail was well out of reach.

The last time she had ascended all 99 steps in her father's big, sturdy arms, sunlight pouring down, laughter sailing up. Now in the darkened lighthouse, she headed up in a near sideways crawl.

Twenty steps below, down the corridor and through the French doors now so tightly closed, Oleg's tortured screams cut through the thunderclaps. Then, somewhere closer still, a crazed cackle ran along her skin with a static electricity pop.

Lana's heart beat so hard the little bird panicked in her pocket, kicking its tiny legs against the lining.

She braced herself against the wall, staring down at her now trembling friend. The little bird stared up shivering in fright.

"Don't worry," she whispered plaintively. "We're going to be okay. We're both going to fly away."

Time and again, the tenebrous tower was punctuated with bursts of red lightning. After each flash through the windows above, the walls pulsed in a pink rhodonite hue, manifesting shadow hands reaching every which way.

Lana pushed on up the steps — 21, 22, 23.

Another flash and spindly shadow fingers stretched inches from her back — 24, 25.

After the next flash pincer fingers flew off the wall and dove to pick the little bird from her pocket. From the corner of her eye, Lana glimpsed the dark hand darting like a raptor.

She almost fell face first on the cold concrete step before catching herself on her palms. The prayer-less mantis foreleg barely missed its prey and retreated back into the post-lightning dark. Lana was left sobbing against the cold stone with a bruised cheek, scuffed hands and spared teeth. Maniacal laughter once again erupted from down below.

She pushed herself up slightly, fearing she'd smushed her tiny companion on the way down. She rolled onto her back and let out a deep breath.

Her tiny fingers probed the little bird in her pocket, doing its best to hide from the monsters that lay beyond. It nuzzled against her.

Lana once again dreamed of a world where they could switch places. But she knew if her little bird was ever going to fly, she would have to rise first. So, she got back up with a wary eye on the wall, waiting for the next flash of lightning to come.

Chapter 46

WALKING ALONG THE SERRATED SEA, Viktor watched metallic dolphins jump through the ice blades and hang suspended in the air — silver crescent moons.

When the wind abated he began to think about the bite in the frost. When it blew anew the pain gave no quarter to the luxury of thought.

The ghost ship beyond the unbroken breakers glowed with an iridescent hue. White flakes fell from the coal black clouds. The thundering and lightning in red gave the feel of a devil-night disco.

Reaching the road, Viktor clambered up the dunes on numbing hands, slipping several times with knees digging into snow, then sand. Rising on legs half-locked in frost, his tired eyes surveyed the road, twisting along the sea arm and then further inland to the lighthouse.

He walked down the well-worn asphalt with weighted steps, tumbledown shacks and abandoned buildings dotting the unlit path. As he passed each structure, specters on four legs scurried from one shelter to the next. Viktor whipped his neck around to catch a glimpse of his stalkers, but there was nothing behind him expect a plastic bag flapping against the asphalt.

He stared through two sets of windows in the skeleton of a half-built concrete cabin. As the wind howled, three sets of tiny red dots lit up like carbon-burned embers. Dying down, six eyes dissolved into the darkness.

Viktor knew he was being hunted but had no choice but to press on.

After three steps, the scurrying continued. He pushed on down the path being pursued in parallel by the unseen pack. His nerves were beyond shot. The stress of the unrealized ambush began to ache beyond the pain of whatever savagery would follow.

A few hundred yards down the road, murder content to track him from the shadows, the silhouette of something not quite human formed. As the two marched down the middlemost point between them, a towering figure in a black-hooded cloak was cast upright against the snow.

Viktor fought against himself in every step forward.

On the approach, their snow crunching feet fell into synch. The wind was still. Thick flakes fell.

They stopped several feet from each other beneath a burnt-out street light. The hooded figure had half a head on Viktor, whether it had a head of its own remained to be seen. It gave off the putrefied stench of rotting flesh.

Arms fell akimbo in suppurated salvation pose. Black ink dripped from slackened sleeve and hem. The drops hit the ground with a hiss.

Viktor reached for his gun. There were three, maybe four rounds left in the clip.

Adrenal flow turned the world a tunnel without a light at the end. Viktor raised the gun.

"Back off!"

Whatever was standing before him spumed in the space where a mouth should have been.

Squared up in snowfall, the wraith took flight.

Viktor unloaded on him. The bullets hit with a hiss but didn't stop the charge.

"Dammit!" Viktor cursed, clinching his stiff, thick fingers into a fist as the creature reached striking range.

Viktor threw a shot down the pipe, but the wraith dipped, smashing behemoth bones into his ribs.

Pain pealed through his body; paralysis settled in his legs. Viktor fought not to double over as an inverted cross cracked his face. Viktor stumbled forward into an uppercut. Through the spray of sparks, he fell face first into a snowdrift.

A vice grip snatched the back of his neck, ramming his maw into the snow. No air was to be found in the iced earth and blood-bubble nose. The cold crush burned hot in his lungs and eyes. White turned black to red.

Viktor dug into the snow trying to find a grip with frozen fingertips. The squeeze around his neck pushed his face deeper into the cold. Viktor raged to wrench his neck free, desperately in search of a single breath. But the squeeze was too strong. He sucked iron and ice into asphyxiation. He was half-drowning in himself. Panic sucked the oxygen from his blood. And then, as the black seeped in, calm.

Apnea sang an aria telling him to let go; an ode to limbs singing flail no more. Ice crystals shimmered like stars. Fingers began to slacken. The pain of burning lungs gave way to numb. Sleep the voice from the deep said. Sleep.

But just as his body began to jerk a final fish flail out of water, a deep thunk followed by a pierced lung pop and blood drop erupted on top.

The sound of a pipe burst hiss plangently blew a pungent kiss in the night.

Viktor's face was lifted from the snow and dropped as his would-be assassin's grip was snapped.

Viktor gasped and rolled onto his back.

Up above, a cloaked-killer shrieked on the forklift tusks of a massive walrus.

"What the…?"

Vapor steamed from puncture holes. And with a snap of the head, that black sack cloth of death was slammed to the ground.

The wraith erupted like a hot spring, shooting black water seven feet high. The walrus turned its head away from the stench. And after a noxious spurt of sixty seconds, give or take, the geyser died down to a gurgle, until nothing was left but a black-cloak heap.

Viktor laid on his back sucking air. As his lungs reacquainted his body with breath, the behemoth looked down at the heaving sack of life.

"Viktor!" the walrus barked.

Even after nearly being murdered by what appeared to be a seven-foot sack of sewage and bone in the seventh circle of hell, Viktor wasn't ready for a pronouncing pinniped.

He slowly surveyed the lumbering beast from the corner of his eyes.

"Viktor, it's me!"

"Jesus Christ."

"Not quite. It's Irakly!" the walrus said with a rattle of clicks.

"Irakly!" Viktor exclaimed, somehow finding the tenor of a familiar friend filtered through the fantastic. "But…"

"I'm a walrus," he bellowed, letting off another volley of clicks without clacks. "Don't I know it!"

"But how?"

"It's the damnedest thing," the walrus chortled.

"There I was, drinking away with Tigran. Just as we had gotten into the swing of things, that buxom broad behind the counter put the kibosh on the festivities without the courtesy of a last call.

"So I went back to the bathroom to relieve myself. And standing there, all these strange figures started glowing on the stall. I made the mistake of putting a wet finger to 'em. Big mistake," brother! Before I knew it, I was shot right through the crapper and took a mad trip through the sewers and outer space. And when I came to, I was a walrus! Someone must have spiked my drink. I have to be dreaming this! And here you are, sharing my dream!"

Viktor chuckled until pain pushed blood bubbles up his nose. Then he groaned.

"You look worse than the last time I saw you."

"You're one to talk."

"Where the hell are we anyways?"

"I, I don't know."

The two looked and surveyed the world of black fire in silence. Overhead, a bumblebee woke in the ballast. A steady electric buzz filled the awe-filled silence.

An infrared halo formed, melting a circle. Viktor felt the warmth on his face as the itch of circulation returned to his hands.

A hooded crow sat atop the burning pillar of light. The harbinger had a body of ash, with head, wings feet and eyes of black.

"Hello," Viktor called out to the bird, which failed to even turn its head in his direction.

"Viktor, are you trying to talk to a bird?"

"Irakly, am I talking to a walrus?"

"Good point."

"Hello," Viktor called out again.

The walrus smacked the street light to a wobble in a bid to dislodge the bird from its silence. The bird crapped on his head in response.

"You little son of a bitch!" Irakly bristled, flipping snow onto his head to wash off the bird droppings.

Viktor burst out laughing.

Irakly chucked a not-entirely snowball his way. Viktor ducked just in time.

"Don't get that on me!"

"When I get my hands on that little…"

"Flippers?"

"Same difference," Irakly barked, smacking the street light to an earthquake shake.

"He did this!" the crow suddenly cawed with an overhead flap, talons marking runes with a swaying street lamp tap.

"Aha! So, you can talk!" Viktor shouted.

The hooded crow danced as the wobble in the pole slowed.

"He did this!" the crow cawed again.

"Explain yourself, bird," the walrus said.

"He collapsed the cake! The layers between the icing before did not touch! But he smashed the red velvet and turned all of everything to mush!"

"Did he say something about cake?" the walrus asked.

"The hell if I know. Would you mind repeating that? You aren't making a damned bit of sense."

"You reached into shivering terror and pulled Apep from the void. You cut a hole in the seventh world of the seventh plane and let him slither in. He punched his fangs into the pablum feeding the threefold soul, poisoning God in man and man in God. His venom is now coursing through Pisces, whom you cast into dark waters, straight into the belly of Typhon!

"Look up! The stars are falling down a 30-degree span of the celestial sphere. All the starry regions shall fall! Seven planes of all are permeating poison. The lines are dissolving in a sea of venom. Cosmological cataclysm is upon us!"

Basking in the warmth and pain of the thaw, Viktor's words were at a loss.

Viktor gave Irakly a bemused look.

"I think he just said you messed up!" Irakly finally chimed in.

Viktor sighed.

"That's what I thought."

Irakly spit on a flipper and gave his soiled dome one last rub down.

Twisting his head with eyes scrunched tight, he shot a question the bird's way:

"Where the hell are we anyways?"

"Oh, that's an easy case to crack," the crow clicked. "You're in a place you once were, a place you've never been, a place that never was, a place that always is; a place where the membranes between outside and inside have broken down. You are in you, outside of you and beyond being you bounds."

"That clears things up," Viktor moaned. "I'm telling you, Irakly, part of me thinks I fell and cracked my noggin back there and am hallucinating all of this."

"Fall, fall you did," the crow squawked.

"Cracked, cracked cracked your head. And now you're leaking nightmare black all over the world of worlds of worlds!"

Viktor's cracked head began to spin. His through-the-looking-glass view defocused in double vision. Thoughts previously put on ice rose to the surface of consciousness like condensation. He found himself fighting the gravity of yet another fall. His thighs itched furiously from the thaw.

"Who are you? Why are you telling me all of this?"

"Me? I'm a high-flying courier between the worlds when lines defining lines are otherwise intact."

"So, you're saying they're not intact now?"

"Do they look intact? The entire world is now living under a shadow-shadow black."

"A shadow?"

"Caw!"

"How can that be?"

"Gateways open, gateways close. Beings from without, within, and beyond do go. Portals formed, but the barriers stayed. Sometimes those portals were purely chemical gateways, but then all the time, all paths are chemical paved.

"Endogenously and exogenously, in meditation and peregrination, gateways, pathways, highways and byways open and close up and down slippery-slip-slip roads of infinite abound. Sometimes when a frame gets warped runners have to set them straight. You ran into one such runner below who set you prostrate.

"That running runner was too late anyways. The rabbit had already bounded through the crack in the door you blew open in wolves' din rage. The darkness stepped through the barrier that you shattered. He will not stop until he has dined upon the last speck of light and matter."

"Devil take me," Viktor said, fighting off the spin in the world again.

"I have to be dreaming."

"You are dreaming this just as much as this is dreaming you. The dreamer and dream have gotten all mixed up it's true. Chaos, chaos, chaos on cue!"

Viktor began to nervously pace along a crescent section of the red light.

"This is madness!"

"Madder than talking pieces of matter who think what they think matters!"

Viktor's back and forth cadence crescendoed to a double time clip, as if his feet were somehow trying to keep up with his frantic thoughts.

"So, reality is on the verge of collapsing because I … somehow opened some portal to other worlds?"

"In a word, caw!"

"How can I stop this?"

"There are two blue jewels set in a rabbit woven-section of Indra's net, where all the other jewels remain reflected without Set seeping in cracks turning universal glimmer dimmer. Carry those blue jewels to axis mundi shine. Turn the beacon doubly bright, let the lighthouse burn on seven planes bright! Only then can you beat back the darkness creep!"

"Irakly, did you catch any of that?"

"You've got me, Viktor."

"Go to the lighthouse, stupid!" the crow snapped. "And take the blue jewels with you!"

"Blue jewels? Where the hell am I supposed to find blue jewels?"

"Why are you asking me where to find them?" the black-and-grey bird jeered. "You're the one who made them!"

Viktor punched a hole in the coal clouds and star sailed to a memory back on Earth.

Clear waters. Girlish giggles in summer light. Two blue eyes shimmering asterism sapphire bright.

"Lana!"

"Caw!"

"She's here?"

"Oh, she's here, and trouble is near. And for all of your trouble, this trouble didn't spring from your broken weir. This darkness stumbled upon your little Lana like a black bolt out of blue. And gobble her up, that's just what he'll do!"

Viktor nearly doubled over with the bends. Vertigo came with the whirlpool whir of the world.

"Viktor, are you okay?" Irakly asked.

"No," Viktor pleaded, palms planted on knees about to give in to gravity. "This darkness, what is it? Where does it come from?"

The hooded bird let out a rattle.

"Who? What? No one really knows. He comes, he goes, mostly back to whatever dark hole of the universe he sowed.

"Some time back, a portal opened on the Sea of Black. For eons he stuck to dark water dreams. But for all of that murk to lurk down below, the moonlight dance on the surface made his incandescent anger grow.

"So every night he'd emerge from those depths to dine on the sun's water shine. But one day, a sliver of light not looking to fall into that blight grew wings and flew away.

"That little ray made its way up the Azovian arm and found a nest of birds

~ 234 ~

in which to hide. And somehow the blue jewel carrier stumbled upon that nested ground, just as the nightmare was on the prowl. Boy oh boy, did he take a hating to her. Felt like he stumbled upon two rays of light to shadows' lure — rabbit pair down with a single shot sure.

"Luckily for you, that nephew of yours has fire in his heart. Took the nasty sucker by surprise, gave him a start. But not before the kraken ripped off the little bird's wings. Turning bird song to screams and screams. But still that little bird wrested its way free. Set off on sojourn with your little girl to be. And up in Moscow is where she was found. And now back here she's sailed down. Before passing through many a plane straight through. A teardrop traveler through heavenly dew. And the shadow knows the luminous pair is here. Look at the sky the end is near! The kraken seeks to gobble up the last of the light for good. To turn the vessel of life into drowning driftwood.

"Can you set the beacon bright? Bringing rabbit star eyes to wingless flight? Can you raise the levy you razed, plunging the world in dark water days? Can you hold one inch of solid ground, and keep the lighthouse from falling down?"

Frenzied thoughts filled Viktor's mind. The squall beyond the nimbus reached a hurricane pitch. Thousands of eyes illuminated the night in terrestrial constellation. The heavens rumbled. Shooting stars crashed into the sea.

"Oh, no. You're doing it all wrong. That, that is not the way you need to go. That is not the way at all. Otherwise, we're all doomed."

"I'm sorry, I'm so sorry."

The discharges of lightning seemed to intensify, rolling thunder shaking the fault lines. Beneath red light, tears streamed down Viktor's face.

"Viktor," the walrus whispered.

Viktor wept and wept, waiting for it all to be over.

"So, is this it?" the hooded bird asked.

Viktor peered at the crow through blurry eyes, cerise shine refracting off of his tears, turning the crumbling world the color of murder.

"Lana, no … no … I, I did this," he sputtered through sobs. "I will die … I'll do anything," Viktor pleaded, falling to the ground and prostrating himself before a bird on a wire.

"If all the darkness came into the world, then end me. End me!" he pleaded, shaking without and within, face pressed against salt stains on steel-toed boots.

A Neptune squall opened up above. The darkness below prepared to abscond with the young maiden. Viktor continued to shake, a bear reduced to a sack of black goat hair quivering in the ashes of the world he set aflame.

"Please," the crow cawed. "There is no more time. The center will not hold. Before the blood-dimmed tide is loosed, the rabbit drowns, the hawk deaf to the call of hope hits ground, you must stand up. Only you can keep the sky from falling down."

From his prayer position, Viktor stared up at the heavens, pulsing like a plasma globe on the fritz. He closed his eyes, breathing in and out, air filling the deepest recesses of his lungs. His mind returned to a calm sea, Lana in his arms, Galya by his side.

Her laughter filled the air and their hearts. Viktor and Galya locked eyes as Lana cast light on the shore.

Tears sweet like honey from the comb trickled down his face. Opening his eyes, snowflakes fell from the still sky. Each one met the red cone of light with a tiny sizzle.

The crow was gone. Irakly the walrus was nowhere to be found. Viktor offered a palmless prayer to the illusive vista. Free of thought, he rose from his knees, exiting the halo with the snow-crunch under his soles. He felt nothing as the cold air hit his face.

Viktor surveyed the path ahead, where thousands of twinkling ovals dotted the horizon. It was time to astral project through a constellation of killers.

The burning red beacon showed the way. Somehow Lana would be lifted on high to turn sky blue that murder red light. Somehow…

Chapter 47

48 ... 49 ...

Lana had done her best to keep the shadow hands at bay, pushing her belly to the ground after each thunderclap to avoid the phalanges freed by flashing light.

The fiftieth step twisted around to a window looking out onto the world. But it wasn't the same world she had arrived on by train earlier that day. Heavy snow was falling in the darkest of nights. And yet it wasn't even dusk? Or was it? Just how much time had gone by?

The flurries started to spin like a whirlpool in a snow globe. Bursts of lightning — orange, red, blue, then violet — formed nets between clouds and threw spears at the Earth. The tower seemed to shake under the force of thunder.

Black silhouettes of trees bent toward the point of breaking under the force of the squall. The window rattled so hard in the frame Lana feared it would shatter.

She closed her eyes, wishing she could somehow dream herself into a better world. But the nightmare man felt at home behind closed eyes. She felt him watching her. Another mad cackle sounded out, but she was unsure whether it was from without or within. Lana opened her eyes and saw nothing short of a hellfire storm unleashed upon the world.

She was scared, more scared than she had ever been in her life.

How could she release the little bird into this? How could it find wings to fly in a sky turned to fire?

Down below, she heard feet pounding against metal stairs. He's coming!

51 ... 52 ...

Lana tried to pick up her pace as the nightmare man's steps hit a tap-dancing clip of terror.

But then she was stopped by the faint sound of grinding. Louder now. What sounded like an army of cockroaches clicking grew and grew. That swelling cacophony was not coming from below. Pouring down like lava from above, the sea of pestilence was surging down the steps.

67 ... 66 ... 65...

"Oh no," Lana shrieked, bracing against the wall for the oncoming swarm.

63 ... 62 ... 61...

Chapter 48

VIKTOR FELT LIKE AN EGG that had been cracked, scrambled and then shoved back into its shell. The mad world was still mad but had briefly fallen into slumber after a bout of blind, suicidal rage.

The catharsis of confession eluded him. The glow of the warm water embrace had washed out to sea. Everything simply felt gone. Thoughts and feelings had been sucked up into the blot of sky. All that was left was a conscious recorder of the fluid moment and muscle memory driving the machine in man.

If Viktor had thought to think whether this was what he needed to be to go wherever it was he needed to go, and do whatever it was he needed to do, he might have thought — maybe. But he thought and felt nothing. Instead, he simply moved like the snow fell.

Several hundred yards down the road, which wound around frozen salt pounds and ribbon-cut tidal channels, stood the lighthouse.

A dilapidated two-story white building with a blue gabled roof cut from aluminum was just beyond the intersection ahead. The building's view was partially obstructed by a small copse.

When Viktor moved parallel to the trees, the rustling began again. A green tractor was parked outside. Several inches of snow had accumulated on the glass-enclosed cab. It was attached to an old disk harrow with a cross section of carbon steel blades.

A light switched on the second floor. Viktor looked up but saw no one watching from the sole rectangle of fluorescent light.

He heard the scurrying again and cut across the lawn to take shelter beside the pulling machine. Set against the rear tire was an old shovel with a rusted blade.

A low, guttural growl broke the silence. Ten yards away, a large wolf had appeared.

Viktor grabbed the shovel, slowly pulling it away from the tractor with a metal scrape. He took it in both hands like a baseball bat, turned his body to the side and looked down, doing his best to avert eye contact.

The bristling beast took several steps forward. Viktor's grip tightened around the warped wooden handle. Averted eyes met. The wolf snarled in murder mien with fur standing on end in tawny tones — black gums, white teeth and grey eyes seeing nothing but red.

Viktor took up a batter's stance.

Behind him four legs of fury were running at a breakneck clip.

Viktor turned around just in time to catch another wolf flying through the air with snapping jowls. He instinctually swung the shovel from his hips, smashing the broadside of the blade into the beast's ribs. Its anguished yelp cut through the night.

The canine fell to the ground with a shattered side and a punctured lung, scampering away with a pathetic whimper. Another forward charge and Viktor swung around ready to swing again. The grey-eyed wolf stopped several feet from him, the pain of his broken brother's howl still stinging his ears.

Hateful eyes locked on Viktor, smoldering in the snow. All around, a constellation of killers lit up the landscape. Tens, hundreds, then thousands of eyes twinkling in the night.

These eyes were getting closer. And as if the gates of Hell themselves had been opened, a stampede of mottled murder machines zeroed in on him. The vengeful beast before him seemed to grimace before retreating to rejoin the surging pack. There was nowhere to run.

The grey storm of death was upon him.

Chapter 49

77 … 76 …

As the swarm descended, the clamor increasingly took on a metallic tinge. Whatever unearthly force that had touched this sclerotized swarm had turned their exoskeletons into steel-squeaking suits of gothic plate armor. Green eyes glowed by the thousands. Their ocellated wings cast evil in auriferous eyes.

Lana was caught between terrors both high and low. Whatever was coming, she couldn't allow herself to descend into the hands of the nightmare man. Quaking in her boots, she ducked down on the steps and pulled her jacket over her head. Chomping metal mandibles and thousands of squeaking legs verged upon her. Any second now, the metal machine avalanche would swallow her whole.

She squeezed her eyes and shook. The little bird from its presidio was infused with the trembling of her heart. First it glimmered and then glowed. Lana's jacket canopy pulsed.

Just as the crest of the wretched wave was set to crash, as if by some force of magnetic repulsion, the sea of pestilence parted, pouring past her in a clicking, creaking, squeaking clamor. The flow of munching mandibles and metal legs scurrying down the stairwell blended into the din of thousands of iron bones being ground down to filings.

An island of life in the metal swell, the spaces between the sounds were swallowed. Lana felt herself sailing away in a static sea. White noise filled the darkness.

One by tens by hundreds, blatta burned by the beacon fell down the spiral to avoid the light. Then the surge abated. Tiny specks of silence pushed holes in the wall of sound. And just like that, they were gone.

The little bird's light dimmed to nothing. The jacket lost its electric shine. Lana opened her eyes and pushed herself up. She peered down into her pocket. The little bird looked up with half-closed eyes that slowly shut out of exhaustion.

"Thank you. Thank you…"

Chapter 50

VIKTOR CLIMBED UP THE METAL steps to the tractor cabin and yanked on the door. But try as he might, it had frozen shut.

He looked down toward the lighthouse to see the super pack pounding paws across the snow, countless canines on the hunt, howling and barking in the charge.

Viktor wedged the heel of his boot on the upper step, pushing a palm against the slanting tire cover. Finding his balance, he drove his shoulder into the glass door, fearful one slip would spell the end. Time was running out.

He strained with so much might the glass seemed poised to pop. But before it gave, the ice shattered around the seal and the door flung open.

10 ... 9 ... 8 ...

Viktor fell backwards, driving a snow angel into the ground. The fastest wolf was pounding at a gallop.

7 ... 6 ... 5 ...

He scrambled to his feet without checking to see if his breath had returned to him clambering up the steps to the chest-high cab.

4 ... 3 ... 2 ... 1...

The spearhead of the charge lunged as Viktor threw his body inside. The wolf snapped the sole of his boot in midair before hitting the ground.

Viktor pushed himself up and spun around, diving for the door. He grabbed the metal handle and tried to pull it shut. A yelp rang out. Viktor grabbed the handle with both hands and kept slamming until the cries ceased and the latch caught.

He panted heavily, steam breath rising in the cabin.

The throng surrounding him swelled to horrifying dimensions. An army of killers were all training their sights on one man. Nothing but a bit of height, glass and metal kept Viktor from being torn limb from limb. But for how long?

To his side, the light on the second floor of the house flickered.

Viktor looked up, seeing a large man in a plague mask surveying the tumult. The neck of the mask branched out into tentacles that writhed around his neck. Tears of blood dripped from black glass eyes to beak.

The masked man bent down and pulled up a rabbit by the scruff, dangling it above the fray.

He turned his head, black eyes locking on Viktor. Even from a distance, through the foggy glass of the cabin, the rabbit's entire body shook with its pounding heart.

The masked man dropped it into the grinder. The rabbit was eviscerated with such haste it seemed to explode midair. The wolves snapped at fur, meat, bones and then each other, vicious fights breaking out in the pit for morsels already devoured. More wolves packed in beneath the window, internecine agitation growing in the crush.

The executioner picked up another rabbit and dropped it into the swelling frenzy.

Then came another, and another, and another.

But with each sacrifice to the swarm, the bloodlust only grew.

Viktor was transfixed by the cruelty. The sound of nails scratching against every inch of the tractor's metal frame was relentless, rocking it to and fro. It was bound to tip over. The blood, guts and fur continued flying through the air in the outdoor abattoir.

Viktor's breath clouded his view on the savagery beyond.

A terrible scraping sound tore at the counterweight before the beast clambered up onto the engine compartment. Viktor turned to meet its smoldering grey eyes.

The wolf took several steps forward, hot breath fogging up the glass. They were inches away from each other, but Viktor's eyes lay a thousand yards away.

He glanced over to see one rabbit after another being thrown into the blender. His hands began to shake. The wolf began bashing its own head against the glass. The vault of Heaven shattered in a fibrous crack of cloud-to-cloud lightning. A roil of thunder followed.

Smack, smack, smack! Soon it would break through. Snapping teeth of predation ripped innocent things to shreds. The collapsed face of murder. Love. Hate. Passion. Exhaustion. Sweet surrender at the end of the line.

Viktor returned his gaze once more. Black eyes met him. The masked man picked up another rabbit, much smaller this time. Even from afar, the tiny eyes twinkled as little blue stars.

Viktor's soul stirred under a bathtub-shaped body filled with murky water. A drowning spirit within a man swam to the surface. He cried out in the cab, banging his fist against the steering wheel.

The masked man raised his other hand and wagged a finger at Viktor. Then he dropped the blue-eyed baby into the blender. Viktor pressed palms and face against the glass, painting a fleeting message of desperation in condensation and smudges, with a trail of tears running between the two. The wolf on the engine stopped bashing its head, channeling its inner hyena to laugh.

The moonstones fell in sharp relief against a bejeweled backdrop of ruby-red eyes and dagger teeth. All time slowed to a crawl.

Viktor had lived and loved and killed a million things in his own life before he finally killed another man. And that man, from the beyond, came along the road to perdition and stared right through him without eyes.

Another smack and micro fissures formed on the glass. Galya's touch. Lana's laughter. Viktor had often thought the world was going to Hell and felt himself the victim. Now he could only think — how amazing to have ever been loved despite it all.

And the words of the poet swam in his head. How does one find calm amidst the storm?

Light filled the broken man. Rise, Viktor prayed to the moonstone eyes ... rise.

As the rabbit fell and fell, a raptor suddenly swooped down from black sackcloth sky, snatching blue-eyed innocence from a million jaws of death.

A sea of wolves howled in anguish. A mask cracked, tentacles squirmed, the black-eyed murderer raged.

The wind howled and the hawk relaxed its wings, rising above the darkness without a single flap to counteract the fury.

Another broad headed smack snapped Viktor out of his stupor as a hairline fracture formed in the glass. A crack of lightning traced the fissure.

Viktor turned his head to the steering wheel, seeing the keys had been left in the ignition. He slid over into the driver's seat and pushed in the clutch.

The engine cranked but wouldn't turn over. In a world beset by electric storm, Viktor almost laughed at the plugs without ample spark.

He stared into the wolf's eyes, rivulets of blood flowing down the triangular taper from head to snout. It seemed to offer him a twisted smile in return.

Viktor's hand vibrated on the key before he gave it a hard turn. The unseen plug released a beautiful flash of light and the tractor roared to life.

The numb man let out a laugh. He threw the transmission into first gear as the grey sea of murder parted. But in the crush and the feeding frenzy, wolves with nowhere to run howled in the wake of the harrow, sliced to bits by the slow-motion threshing machine. Fire raged behind grey eyes.

Chapter 51

AS LANA MOVED UP THE spiral, an ermine-trimmed mantle spilled down the stairs. She tried to step over the slippery fur runner, whose silver threads scintillated when lightning struck outside.

In the circular landing above, behind the birdcage shaped handrail, a woman was perched beneath the cascading cloak, face buried in flowing fabric.

Lana approached in trepidation.

With each step, the temperature dropped a degree.

Lana's "hello" echoed a condensation cloud. She hugged herself and shivered. The figure bundled up in the mantle perked up.

Lana shuddered. As the fabric sea parted, she saw what was, what wasn't, her mother's face.

Eyes dilated to the size of saucers opened cavernously beneath black brows and lashes.

Her black hair was swallowed up in a silver headdress that crested a crashing crescent moon. Her face was as white as a ghost's. Cheeks dabbed in rouge and red lips parted. Her jaw dropped in a black tooth smile. She slowly wrapped her slim white fingers around the bars, pressing her face to the baluster. Enormous black eyes locked on Lana.

"Oh dear, where have you been? We've been so worried. I've been waiting for you. It's oh, so cold up here. Can't we go down?"

The opposing gravities of Lana's greatest love marred by monstrosity tore at her tiny heart.

"Mama," she croaked. "Please, we have to go up."

"Go up, why would we go up, my dear? There's a terrible storm. No, no, no! We must go down. We'll be safe there," she said, final syllables tinged with a sibilant hiss.

A knot welled up in Lana's throat.

"Please, Mama, please."

"Now, Lana, you listen to your mother," she said, kneading the bars with her hands.

"Mama, the nightmare man, he, he is down there," she stammered. "We have to go up. We have to save my little bird!"

"Litte bird!" Galya hissed, releasing the bars and craning her head around the baluster.

"You caused all of this trouble by taking his little bird? You have to give it back!"

"But..."

"Now look! I'm your mother. You will do as I say!"

Lana was frozen in fright. A tiny voice inside said: 'you can't go down, you can't, can't ever go down. No matter what.'

Behind Lana, the mantle began to undulate a weasel-body's wiggle, rising and slowly wrapping her up. Lightning flashed Galya's face to overexposure. A roil of thunder rumbled under the spiraling steps.

"All you have to do is give him his little bird back and this nightmare will be over — just like that!"

Galya began to hum a haunting melody, raising her voice to a singsong lullaby.

Cradled in the mantle that drew itself to the black saucer eyes and red lips, Lana fell under the soporific spell of the charming snake. Galya's dead-eyed gaze was unflinching. Lana's eyelids became heavy. Snowflakes formed and fell in her icy breath. Entirely drained of her will, Lana slowly began floating up the stairs, until finally being deposited into her mother's arms.

Tears fell in the fur.

"There, there now," Galya said, cradling the frozen rabbit.

"We will go down now and ask the darkness for forgiveness. Forgiveness for all we have taken."

The woman in the mantle rose to begin her descent.

65 ... 64 ... 63 ...

Somewhere down below, a good man cried, and a madman laughed.

Chapter 52

CUTTING THROUGH THE SEA OF wolves on the approach to the lighthouse, Viktor couldn't shake the killer surfing the engine. A sharp enough turn to send it flying likewise might tip the tractor over.

He searched the cabin for a weapon. A sickle was laying on the floor.

He strained his arm to reach it, keeping his eye on the approaching gate. Fingertips grazed the handle before he managed to reel it in.

Amidst the howling chaos, Viktor headed for the chain link fence surrounding the lighthouse.

The gate directly facing the road was open.

Viktor lined up with the entrance, releasing the gas yards from the fence. He swung a tight arc, almost flipping over. The wolf hurtled through the air, crashing into the snow.

Viktor parked the cabin door parallel to the gate and hopped out. Looking back, there was no sign of the grey-eyed wolf, though countless more were visible down the road, swarming beneath the balcony, swallowing unseen innocence tossed down by the masked executioner.

While the entrance was blocked by the tractor, there was still enough space between the driving wheel and the cabin for a hungry wolf to squeeze through.

They would come — they had to come. Time was running out.

He tried to open the door, but it was blocked by the post. Viktor hastily lay on his back, lifted his legs and slammed his boots into the glass. It cracked, and then shattered under piston-pounding feet. He grabbed the reaping hook and beat out the glass teeth looking to take a bite out of him before squeezing his way out.

Hot-footing a trail through the cold, Viktor reached the lighthouse, swinging around the two-story annex. Out back, snow stood in for the unbloomed blossoms of apricot trees, covering up the hunchback grass.

He ran up the stairs and entered the anteroom, pulling the door shut behind him. It was pitch black. Viktor heard weeping inside.

He entered the main hall. Down the corridor on the opposite side of the room, the lights flickered the low burn of dying embers. Waiting for his eyes to adjust, he saw a man hunched over in the corner. Viktor's hand tightened on sickle.

"Hello," he called out, cautiously approaching the figure.

The sobbing continued.

Viktor slowly walked over, kneeling down before the mourning.

"Hey, buddy. Is everything okay?"

It felt like a stupid thing to say … he couldn't think of anything else.

"Hey, buddy," he said, placing a hand on the man's shoulder and gently shaking him.

The man flinched at first touch.

Viktor thought to tell him to relax, before realizing there was nothing to relax about. The whole damned world appeared to be ending. If there was a time to lose it, that time was now.

"Is, is he still there?"

"Is who still here?"

"My, my son. He, he was in the corner — burning."

Viktor scanned the room.

"Take a look for yourself, there's no one here but us."

"I'm afraid I can't do that," Oleg said. He lifted his head, blooding streaming from sockets.

Viktor stumbled back in shock.

"I, I couldn't take it anymore, you see. I couldn't stand to see my son burn. Now all I see is darkness. And darkness is where I belong."

"I, I will get you help," Viktor stammered. "I will get you out of here."

"Oh, you don't understand, you don't understand anything at all. Get me out of here? I am here. There is no getting out."

Viktor felt like the man had gone mad. But the world had gone mad with him.

Suddenly, the sound of ferocious scratching erupted at the door.

"You must go! He is coming for you. Please, help the little girl."

"Little girl?"

"The girl with the strange little bird — Lana."

His daughter's name hit him like a shot of adrenaline. Viktor nearly dove onto Oleg, gripping him around the shoulders.

"Lana, you've seen her here?"

"Yes, yes," Oleg coughed, brushing his face against the cold wall. "I brought her here."

"Where is she?"

"Up," he muttered, raising a stiff finger in the air.

Scratches overlaid scratches as the door rattled in the frame.

'There's not much time. Go help her before it's too late. I let my son burn. Save her! Save her from the fire!"

Viktor shot to his feet.

"Hold tight. I, I will come back for you," Viktor stammered as he turned and sprinted down the hall, not waiting for a reply that never came.

Chapter 53

24 ... 25 ... 26 ...

The pain no longer mattered, not in his knees, not in his lungs. Charging up the spiral stair case, his steps were syncopated with lightning claps and thunder rolls.

Before him, in the black-red strobe of the lighthouse walls, all he could see was the man who had collapsed his own eyes.

And in that quivering man quailing in the extinguished red corner, Viktor saw himself.

He felt like he had been blind for all of this time, running through life like some feral beast, lashing out from a sewn-up sack in rage, donning a wolfskin cap and wrestling with demons, waiting to be dropped into the sea — vainly fighting the fate of Poena Cullei.

Funny how his anger had blotted out one simple truth. The world could take everything from you, but not your love. Viktor was the one who had killed the love in himself. He was the one who had extinguished his own light.

31 ...32 ...33...

He saw clearly how the fault was not in the stars, but in himself. He wanted nothing more than to take his family back home, wherever home might be.

Up and up, the shadow of a banner unfurled flashed on the wall with a flash of lightning. Something was coming. Viktor kept up his pace.

42 … 43 …44 …

An ermine-trimmed mantle was twisting down the stairs. Viktor's grip tightened on the sickle. But when he saw the descending Venus in furs, his grip loosened, and his jaw dropped with the curved blade.

Black brow, black lashes and bottomless eyes, Galya looked like a 17th century merchant's wife risen from the dead. And there, wrapped in the fur runner, was Lana.

"Galya, my God!" he said in shock. "What happened to you?"

Running up the runner, he slipped on the covered steps, grabbing the rail so as not to tumble down.

"You happened to me, Viktor. You happened to all of us."

What was before him was — wasn't — his wife.

"I, I'm so sorry, Galya, I'm sorry for everything that I've done, to you, to Lana, to our family. I want to, I will make this right."

"It's too late, Viktor. Can't you see? It's over."

Her breath buzzed electric like a power line.

Lana stirred under the fur. Viktor felt an instinct to lunge for her, and felt guilt, guilt from being afraid to see his daughter in his own wife's arms.

"You're right. There's no taking anything back. What I've done, I've done. And I'll pay for it. But not Lana. This isn't on her."

With the sound of her daughter's name, the buzzing grew louder. The blue hue of her breath intensified. A yellow glint of light glimmered in dead pool eyes.

"No, Viktor, Lana's going back. She's going to return what she's taken."

"No!" Viktor cried, pulling himself up by the rail, hand-over-hand, as the fur beneath him seemed to squirm. "I don't give half a damn what's gotten into you. Lana isn't going back down there!"

The buzzing in Galya's breath intensified with a surging squall beyond the lighthouse walls. Each ionized breath a prayer to St. Elmos. Condensation clouds glowed in corona discharge blue.

Viktor stepped forward. A bolt of blue knocked him down. Viktor fell back several steps, smacking his head into a wall before grabbing onto the rail.

Dazed, he began pulling himself up, slipping on the squeaking scrum beneath. Another bolt of blue sent him tumbling.

The howl of the wind, like a million wolves in flight, raged outside. Lana's eyes pried their way out of slumber.

"Mama!" she cried.

Smoke rose around Viktor as his body lay still.

Lana stirred in her cold, taut arms.

"Mama!" she cried again.

Lightning flashed bright enough to burn shadows onto the wall. Lana wrenched her body around. Blue sky fell into dead pool eyes.

"What did you do to Daddy? We love you, Mama, we love you!"

The little bird scrambled out of Lana's pocket, twinkling like Sirius on a cloudless night.

Moonlight from a Moscow bridge shone in Galya's black sea eyes. Silver tears slid down her cheeks. The tired little creature scampered back down, having given enough of itself to break darkness' spell.

In aurora shine, the black hold on Galya faltered. And Galya's grip broke with it. Lana slipped out of her arms and ran down to Viktor.

Galya fell back, coughing violently. Her mantle erupted into a thousand ermines, squeaking and scampering down the steps. Galya's silver crest turned into a Cheshire moon. Black hair cascaded down her shoulders, as she writhed around on the floor violently coughing.

Her mouth opened up in a silent scream. A swarm of gilded yellow jackets poured forth. But as the cloud of pestilence rose, the gold plates turned to rust, dissipating as dust in air.

When the last buzz evaporated the night, Galya looked up with blue ocean eyes.

"Oh my God," she cried. "Oh my God."

Chapter 54

HE WAS LYING IN A dark room, face pressed to a cold floor. Cool air washed over him. Everything called pain had been left elsewhere.

It was the feeling of no past or future, no attachments, no appointments, no regrets, no needs. It was the feeling of waking up in the middle of the night from a pleasant dream with no thought to all the vagaries of life.

It was sitting down after a long day of labor at sunset, when suffering as prologue becomes its own kind of joy. My work is done, he thought. My work is done.

A door opened onto a vista. Bird song came in. White light. Warmth to fill the darkness. He rose and approached the door.

A voice called out to him.

He moved toward the light.

The voice rang out again.

In the echo he heard a familiar tone. Galya. It was the first string to pull on his heart. And then came Lana's voice too. The burden of attachment bearing on his will.

Then in the darkness, the screams of an eyeless man called out to him. And Viktor knew all he had to do was walk through that door and all that beckoned would evaporate in the light. All that pained him would be gone, forevermore. But he could feel it in the very core of his being. There was a still a debt to be paid.

'Not yet. Not yet.'

He turned his back on the light. On the joys of dream's retreat. And he followed voices crying in love and pain into the dark.

Chapter 5 5

GALYA'S FACED APPEARED BEFORE BLURRY eyes.

"Viktor."

He struggled to open them. His entire body felt like a wet thumb that had been stuck in a socket. There was too much ache to even think where it began or ended.

"Galya," he said weakly.

"Oh my God," she said with a faltering voice, wrapping her arms around him.

"Daddy," Lana squealed, wrapping her little arms around his thick neck.

Three leaves on the family tree formed a trinity symbol halfway up the lighthouse. Some sort of horror roared in the darkness below.

"Where are we?" Galya finally asked.

"We're in the lighthouse," Lana said.

"The lighthouse?"

"The one where we watched dolphins, back when we were happy."

Galya looked at Lana with pained eyes before scanning the thunderstruck walls of the tower.

"I, I remember this place. Why, why here?"

"We have to take up my little bird," Lana said, pulling open her pocket to let Galya see her little passenger inside.

"He's very tired now. He helped me, just like he helped you and Dad. Now we need to help him. The nightmare man, he wants to take him. We have to take him up so he can fly."

"The nightmare man?" Galya said, looking at Viktor. And they both saw the shadow in each other's eyes as the mad laughter roiled the world below.

And the words of the hooded crow returned to Viktor.

"We've got to return the light to the moon."

"What was that?"

"Lana's right. You have to take her up. I don't know anything, but I know that."

"What do you mean 'you'? *We* have to take her up."

"You go first. I have to go back down. There's a man down there. He's hurt bad. He needs my help."

"Please, Viktor, no. You have to stay with us," she pleaded, drawing Viktor back into her arms.

"Daddy's right," Lana said. "We cannot leave Mr. Oleg."

"Mr. Oleg?"

"He's the kind old man who brought me here. He said he was coming after me. But he never came. The nightmare man, I think he got him. But maybe we can still get him back. Tima showed me that. Sometimes you have to go down to go up. Sometimes when you think you have lost someone forever, that's when you see you can never lose them."

Galya was amazed by her daughter's cryptic, yet wise words. She had too many questions to ask but didn't think there were any answers to be put into words. All she could do was trust the light of her life once more.

And she looked at Viktor with more love than eyes could hold. And that love traveled down a faithful flume right into his soul.

"The last thing I want to do is leave you. Christ, I just found you again. But I have to do this. I've done some bad, bad things. Things I might never be forgiven for. Something tells me if I leave that man there, I'm going down, no matter where we go."

She cupped Viktor's face with her hands.

"Then go make things right," she said, trying to steady the quaver in her voice.

Viktor wrapped his arm around Galya. He felt himself once again in a Sunday-lit bed, leave-lattice canopies and mid-bloom breezes washing over the Kingdom of Blankets. He never wanted to leave. He gently kissed her on the lips. Long dormant butterflies stirred. Open eyes glistened.

"I will be back, I promise."

"I believe you, Viktor, I believe you," she said, warm tears streaming down her face.

Viktor kissed Lana on the cheek and handed her over to Galya.

"Whatever you do, don't stop. I love you, so, so much."

"I love you too."

Viktor looked at Lana, whose eyes glowed with the world.

"I love you, my little rabbit. Do you remember watching the dolphins jump along the waves?"

"I do, Daddy, I do!"

"You just wait, we will watch them again."

He wrapped his arms around them and squeezed.

Lightning flashed. A cater-cornered glare from the stairs caught his eye. The sickle was still there, propped up against the steps. Viktor picked it up and handed it to Galya.

"I pray you won't need this."

"I pray you're right."

Turning his light on all the light in his world, he headed down the spiral.

And in his heart of hearts, despite his fear, he knew it was the right thing to do. For once in his life, he had to move away from love to get closer to it.

And with each falling step, his heavy spirit rose.

Chapter 56

VIKTOR REACHED THE BOTTOM OF the stairwell and leaned his back against the wall, trying to slow his breath. An orange door opened into the hallway. The light beyond glowed like a jack-o-lantern's yawn. Then a draft blew through and the consumptive pumpkin coughed a fire-mouthed flicker.

The white French doors at the end of the corridor were drawn open like a wooden overcoat. Viktor stepped inside. Silence. Not a murmur from Oleg, not a wolf's howl. The green doors lining the righthand side of the hallway rested in their frames.

"Plop."

The sound of a solitary droplet echoed on impact. Then another, and another. Black water began to seep beneath the green doors. And out of the darkness ahead, a small white figure emerged. A white rabbit seemed suspended in midair, glowing will'o'-wisp.

The jack-o'-lantern then inhaled, sucking cold air down the corridor, extinguishing the light. Viktor walked over the wet floor toward the apparition.

Two glowing eyes emerged above the ghost light in fright. Then another rush of wind. Predator and prey were alike swallowed out of sight. There was just the darkness. Sticky steps. A maniacal laugh.

Viktor navigated his way down the corridor with an outstretched hand. Catching the end of a door, he stepped over the threshold into the main hall. The shoulder-high sky wall and the clouds above were all recast in brume.

Hand tethered to the wall, he stopped and listened. Oleg's previous cries had died down to a barely audible whimper.

Viktor moved around the room until finding the cast-down corner where Oleg had collapsed.

"Oleg," he whispered. There was no response.

"Oleg," he said again, slightly raising his voice. "I'm going to get you out of here."

He crouched down and put his hands on the old man. Hands searched out shoulders stained with blood.

"It's too late," Oleg said with a weepy voice. "I cannot see."

"Neither can I," Viktor replied, lifting Oleg's arm over his head and pulling him to his feet.

"Please," he said. "Go back to your little girl. There is no hope for me."

"If I return to my little girl without you, there really will be no hope for me."

And then Oleg saw him without eyes.

"Okay," he said. "Okay."

Viktor pressed his arm against the wall to guide them in the dark.

Howls erupted outside. The annex entrance was beset with furious scratching. A lunatic's laughter filled the hall.

On the threshold of the corridor stood a black-on-black silhouette.

"Hey, Grandpa, do you have a lighter, matches, anything?"

"I, I think I do."

Oleg dug around his pocket with a stiff, shaking hand as Viktor steadied him on his aching shoulder. He finally fished out a lighter, pressing it into Viktor's palm. Viktor squeezed that hand to steady before letting go.

He struck the flint wheel with a thumb, cutting a halo of light out of the darkness. Beyond the warm glow, the nightmare man stood with a knife.

The clamor at the door mounted. Snapping teeth and claws sent splinters flying. The crush was growing. The door would not hold. Viktor was stuck between two points of murder with a blind man on his arm and a fleeting flicker of light that would wilt under a breeze.

"What do you want?" he screamed at the silhouette.

The shadow convulsed in laughter.

"Who's there?" Oleg asked.

"My just desserts," Viktor replied. "Do me a favor," he said, pressing the lighter into Oleg's hands. "Shine a light for me. Keep the darkness out for as long as you can."

Oleg nodded, gripping the lighter with shaking hands.

"Christ," Viktor said, standing up as the din of snapping splinters and teeth grew to a fever pitch. The door would give any second. "Here we go."

Girding himself, he let out a guttural yell, charging the shadow on the threshold. A light shone in Oleg's red corner. A long forgotten prayer was murmured. The shadow lifted its blade. Viktor crashed into the darkness.

Once, then twice, a knife hit him between the ribs. The door cracked down the center, snapped and collapsed on the floor. The wave of wolves came. Blood poured from a punctured lung.

Viktor gripped his hands and with all his might slammed the shadow back into the hall. It scrambled to break free, stabbing haphazardly. Adrenaline ate most of the hornet stings. Viktor wrapped the nightmare in a bear hug, holding it down on the floor. Tentacles wrapped around his face, sucking the life out of him.

The grey wolf rode the crest of the wave, crashing into murder and man.

"Lord Jesus Christ, Son of God, have mercy on me, a sinner," Oleg chanted over and over and over, seeking strength in a long unspoken prayer.

Bravery could not stop his blood from curdling at the sound of the brave man's screams.

"Lord Jesus Christ, Son of God, have mercy on me, a sinner."

The sound of the feeding frenzy built to a crescendo. And without eyes, Oleg saw, the man and his shadow, piece by piece, torn apart.

"Lord Jesus Christ, Son of God, have mercy on me, a sinner."

The flame from the lighter burned his thumb. And then he saw his son again, burning in a tank, in a zinc coffin, in Oleg's heart.

"Lord Jesus Christ, Son of God, have mercy on me, a sinner."

Then Oleg saw himself in that very corner, wan face and pallid light, madly driving his thumbs into his own eyes.

"Lord Jesus Christ, Son of God, have mercy on me, a sinner."

He felt the pain of loss in his wife's heart, ten years of separation from her son — from her husband.

"Lord Jesus Christ, Son of God, have mercy on me, a sinner."

The savagery was so total, there were no longer screams or snaps or howls or growls. Just the sound of everything erasing everything. Sitting on the edge of that storm, Oleg awaited his own submission to the tempest.

"Lord Jesus Christ, Son of God, have mercy on me, a sinner."

And then he saw images of an old man by the road a common era ago, the Son of David in the midst of a throng by the walls of Jericho.

"Son of David, have mercy on me!"

And the rebukes of the crowd roar with ravages of wolf and man. But the one at the center of the storm subdued the babel to hear out the supplicant.

And he was brought to that man, who asked him what it is, of all the things that could be wanted, of all the things one could be, that he was seeking.

And without thinking about his eyes, Oleg replied, "All I wish is that I may see."

Chapter 57

SOMETHING LIKE HELL SEEMED TO be rising from below. Galya's left arm was shaking with Lana's weight. The other swayed with sickle in hand. Despite the strain, she remained steadfast in the throe, whole note breaths to eighth note steps in the crescendo. Galya had spent a childhood embracing pain to embody control. There was no entertaining thoughts of stopping now, not to catch her breath, not to ease her burden, if only for a deciduous diminuendo. She'd rather lose that arm than risk letting Lana go. Rest was in the coda, the cadence of another world — or this world made otherwise.

Thunderclaps from gods' hands sent dust storms down the spiral. Lana strongly gripped Galya's neck but didn't make a sound.

Galya bounded up the final curve of the spiral staircase ascent. She rose in the presence of the finish line, taking the final bend on feet of feathers and trembling wings.

But rounding the vertex, a monstrosity stinking to high hell stopped her in her tracks.

On the final circular landing, a dark-spotted frog puffing on a papirosa was blocking their precipiced path. Galya tightened her grip on both Lana and the bagging hook.

A steady draft sent shivers through disparate bodies. Steam rose from skin in the unexpected refrain. Rabbit paw flukes looked to moor deeper into

Galya. She winced, steadying Lana in aching arm and whispering words of calm.

Cold amphibian eyes steamed in the presence of warm blood anchored in ardor.

"The window," the frog said, belching out a billow of smoke. "I always said … close the window. Hear, the bear never did hear. Now cold. Cold now … forever …"

The voice was sad, distant and yet somehow familiar. A vertical pupil framed a rabbit in hand.

"Your daddy … He opened the window … and out came the wolves … and the wolves eat the bear … but who, who eats the rabbit? The kraken or Kek?"

The round ball of beast erupted into a gelatin jiggle of smoke billowing laughter. That laughter soon turned into a coughing fit, leading it to expectorate something greener and slimier than its warty skin.

Galya instinctively took a step back in revulsion. She felt her foot hover over an abyss before planting it back on the step. Down below an unbridled orgy of chaos raged. The hairs rose on the back of her neck.

'Where are you, Viktor?'

Amphibian eyes locked on a nesting doll of beating hearts.

"Please … let us pass."

"I … I can't do that … No, I can't do that at all … you see. If my nightmare doesn't get his little bird … I … I will never be free."

What might or might not have been a crocodile tear slid down slimy, crypis skin. The burning cigarette dangling on the lipless frown hit the floor in a shower of sparks.

A foothold trap mouth snapped open. A sticky tongue uncoiled a whip crack and wrapped around Lana, rending her from Galya's grip and throwing her down the pipe with a swallowed scream.

Galya shrieked and flew up the stairs. A sticky tongue shot out again to catch a bird in flight. It snared her around the ankle and tried to fling her into its gullet — a glotal stop to life. Galya hit the steps with a smack, twisting her body around to sink her talons into the stone before her. The reaping hook hit several steps below with a clang.

The beast tried its best to reel in the raptor. Galya fought tooth and nail as her leg strained at the knee-pop socket. She thought of Lana in the belly of that beast. In her pain she summoned a preternatural strength to pull herself down against the tether of death. She extended her hand as fingers brushed the sickle handle. But one arm could only fight the force for so long before splitting fingertips returned to hook the edge of cold concrete steps.

Sinew in her knee was strained to snap. Galya willed herself against lachrymal lacerations, driving against the shredding of her own ligaments. And in the pain she felt first agony and then release. Her body was the least she'd give for Lana. She saw two blue eyes sinking in murk. Galya became the pain propelling herself forward. Talons hooked the blade. Closer. Metal scraped against the floor. Collagen was cleft from bone. Onward. Fingers pull a handle to palm. Cinch. A body twist and slash. A severed tongue wildly danced an unhanded firehose spray of bloody black murder.

No time. A broken-legged raptor found wings to fly. A sickle plunged in slimy skin and cut a belly from end to end. A beautiful bird without mercy ignored gargled wails and round robin gasps. Galya desperately dug through blood and guts until her hands touched her daughter. She mustered every ounce of strength to rend Lana from the quivering dissection of death.

Lana wasn't breathing.

"No ... No ..."

Lips to lips and hands to heart but a hawk couldn't make a rabbit soul start. Blue eyes turned white and white cheeks blue.

God shuddered; mother screamed. Some sort of prolapsed perdition finally ceased, completely split from seam to seam.

Chapter 58

REACHING THE TOP OF THE metal nest, the large electric beacon shone a phantasmal red. Galya quaked at the sight of the soot-like sky. Black ash fell in acuminated diamond flakes. Lana's little body remained limp in her arms.

Then the gods clapped angry hands again, fracturing the vault of Heaven, opening a volcanic vent on high. Burning marmalade poured into the sea. Further down shore, the ghost ship, still trapped in ice, fell under a gauze of steam.

Heat hit mercurial dolphins stuck in the sky, melting quicksilver from the bottoms of broken thermometers.

The world, whichever world that may be, was ending.

"Viktor, where are you!" Galya wailed, falling to the floor, cradling her lifeless love.

"Lana please .. Lana please…" Galya wept, brushing her hair with a shaking hand. She sang Lana a lullaby in a quivering voice. She pressed dry warm lips to a cold cheek. The force of life filled her inner worlds with memories too beautiful to find anchor in outer decay. The heart of Lana beat beyond the narrow ken of death.

"I love you more than love, I love you more than love…"

The rumbling sky reverberated through the swaying tower. Cracks formed in the rattling window panes.

Then a flash of lightning turned the world blind. All at once the angry gods punched out the storm panes. Galya shielded Lana's body with her own from sundering spray.

She was doused in a shower of stings. Tiny trails of blood ran from the back of her neck and ears. Galya pushed herself up, glass fragments cascading down her back. Lana was lying on her belly. Gale pulled the lifeless little girl to her heaving chest.

Up above, the beacon spiraled down in Fibonacci steps like a crystal pinecone. Cables leading up from the ground turned to snakes, wrapping around the base of the red-burn light. The earth began to quake without thunder. Galya pushed herself up on broken glass, nestling all she knew of love in her arms.

The cold wind hit her face as the snakes swayed in the wind. Down below, she saw an eidolic duo walking away from the lighthouse on the road toward the sea.

Her eyes grew wide.

"Viktor," she screamed. He looked up and met baby blue with an uncanny calm. It was less dispassion than regard beyond the apogee of earthly concern. It made Galya feel smaller than a human heart holding the sum total of suffering in her arms. How could he forsake her now?

The hooded man lowered his cloak. Below was the face of a boy, two tiny grey dwarfs twinkling next to the Polaris-pair shine of Viktor's North Star eyes.

She repeated Viktor's name in a whimper, trembling lips and eyes glimmering from behind the nebula.

The stars in the specter of man pulsed love and leaving. The stitches in Galya's sides were rent as she fell apart. The pair turned away and continued down the road. A ghost ship now freed of its icy berth was ready to set sail. Two more passengers were making their way to the soon-to-be dearly departed.

Galya fell to her knees and cared nothing for the glass gouging bone. She let out a shrill shriek that seemed to split the sack cloth covering the dark. Two red rivers flowed between the shards.

She trembled. Something stirred in Lana's chest.

Galya opened eyes nearly blind with epiphora.

The little bird popped out of Lana's pocket.

Galya tearfully took in its tiny dimensions. The little bird took in the burning world with glowing eyes and hopped down onto the floor.

"It's over," Galya cried. "It's all over. She's gone … everything … is gone."

Galya pressed together stigmata hands in a Godless prayer. In the space of two black eyes, she saw the shine of 88 constellations. Heavenly drama unfolded.

Ursa Major nailed to crux beneath Eridanus in Aquarius arms. Corvus cawed, Lupus bayed, Lepus loped in stardust wake. Aquilla sailed across space and lifted Ursa Major on high. Apus found feet in the southern sky and serenaded a silver moon with Helios light.

One, two, three and then four tiny wings extended from the little bird. It began to grow and grow, until finally transforming into an upright man with a raptor's head. A tunic fell down to his ankles. A tasseled shaw was tied around his waist. Both were embroidered in Kármán vortex street fractals. The fabric flowed like sky.

A rabbit opened blue eyes to hawk cries. The ancient Assyrian expanded its wings in cloud vortices.

Wrapping arms around the beacon, the red light turned white and then shifted through the luminous range of an iridescent pinecone cut from pearl.

Letting out a sundering cry, he uprooted the beacon and shot up a star through the ceiling, leaving a rainbow trail in his wake.

The earth rumbled collapse. Ninety-nine stairs fell like teeth from a shark's mouth. And just with the final tremor, as the floor gave out, the hawk snatched up rabbit and rode a rainbow wave up on high, all the black washed in a watercolor sky. One more look down and she watched a bear embark with a grey-eyed wolf. Tears of love streamed and steamed a sky-written farewell.

Faster and faster, through the cloud-part they soared, ghost ship setting sail through vapor veil and Saint Peter's light sparking signal lamp spar. Up through the blue, then violent-black hue, high into the star light vault arched above day and night. The blackness of space was set afire in love and flight.

The raptor was the rabbit was the bear was the light. Two tiny blue stars turned electric the darkest night.

Chapter 59

"IT'S THE DAMNEDEST THING. HIS body is just … gone."

"What do you mean, gone?"

"I mean we went down to the morgue with next of kin to identify the corpse, at least the tattoos on it, there was no face left to identify, mind you. But when we got there — Poof! It had vanished into thin air."

"You're telling me someone … took it?"

"Either someone took it, or a dead man walked off on his own accord."

"Devil take me!"

"He sure took our victim," Major Kuzminov said, dragging on his cigarette, staring out onto the same light boulevard in the same dark cafe where they had met before.

But what a difference a few weeks could make. The snow was all gone, the puddles dry, the trees bearing green leaves, giving joy to passers-by.

"Bloody ghouls we've become. Someone must have sold his body for spare parts. Of course, no one's talking. That was the last piece of evidence in this nightmare of an investigation.

"Everything from the apartment — trashed. I don't need to tell you that our forensics department has gone to hell. Or that you couldn't find a glass in the whole joint that didn't have a hundred prints on it. Or that we did manage to pull a few decent prints and send them to the lab, only to discover that one is from a paramedic and the other from the same damned officer who dusted for the prints in the first place because he was drunk when the call came in and forgot to put his gloves on.

"Did I mention not a single neighbor saw a thing? Man smashed to bits with a wide-open door and the whole block mysteriously went blind. Oh, and the other victim is still in a coma. So, with no body, no evidence, no suspects, no witnesses, well, the worst murder I've seen in my entire career is going into the grand stack of the unsolved. Try smudging out that statistic. There's going to be hell to pay for this!"

Sergeant Novoselov became pensive. After a long pause of cigarette smoke and silence, Major Kuzminov's curiosity came to boil.

"You got awfully quiet. What is it?"

Sergeant Novoselov jabbed at the clove-studded slice of lemon at the bottom of his cup. He hadn't told anyone about the wild chase down the tracks. Being swallowed by darkness. Waking up the next morning on the cold basement floor as if nothing had happened.

In the weeks after, reality had become more and more slippery. He didn't feel so firmly footed in the only world he had ever known before then. All it took was a rustle of leaves, shadows moving down escalators at a certain speed or an old song seeping through a wall to pull part of him back to the other side.

"Nothing. The last few weeks have just been strange."

"You're telling me," Major Kuzminov said, lighting another cigarette.

Sunlight shone through wisps of smoke, diffusely reflecting off of the metal table.

Sergeant Novoselov looked down and caught a glimpse of himself, faintly visible on the warped metal. A smile twisted up in the reflection. People walked up and down a boulevard set to bloom. Shadows flitted across the sun-lit walls. The difference a few weeks could make. That dark world of March melt giving way to petrichor, pollen and warmth.

Sergeant Novoselov started to feel life was nothing more than such distorted reflections vacillating on the surface of time. He had spent all of his life resolved to the hardness of things. But the truth of the matter was quite sticky indeed.

"You know. Maybe that body of yours wasn't stolen. Maybe he rose from the dead."

Major Kuzminov let out a laugh.

"Is that so. Well could you do me a favor?"

"Anything."

"If you happen to run across our good Saint Lazarus, ask him to turn himself in."

Chapter 60

THWACK! THWACK! THWACK! A NUMBER of sharp jabs to the ribs pulled him from the darkness.

At first he was too befuddled to register the pain. That didn't last long. Better the toebox than the top piece he reckoned.

It was a woman's voice, a bitter-sweet lilt stepped in fifteen years of sherry and cigarettes.

"Ugggggggghhhhhhhh. That really smarts, lady, could you knock it off?"

"So, you're alive, fat man."

Thwack! Thwack! Thwack!

"Knock it off I told ya!"

Her heel gently echoed as she set it down after the final prod.

He rolled his face across the tile. Meaty jowls peeled off the sticky ceramic like bread rent from a grilled cheese sandwich. Filthy, absolutely filthy.

Blurry eyes opened to the bottom of grime-streaked ceramic. He laboriously rolled over onto his back. He felt like a beached whale. And then he remembered.

Fat fingers frantically started patting down familiar folds of flesh beneath a sweater. They were definitely the folds of a man and not some blubbery beast of the sea.

"I'm me!"

"That ain't much to be proud of," she quipped with a sherry-steeped sally.

Irakly slowly sat up as his blood pressure dropped. The smell of stale urine and cigarette smoke hit him.

He felt like passing out again.

"Are you gonna be okay, fatso?"

"You wouldn't believe the night I've had. I think someone spiked my drink! How long have I been out?"

"Well, I told you to get outta' here 20 minutes ago. But then you went and passed out in the toilet. I wasn't sure if I was gonna have to call the hospital or the funeral wagon."

"Twenty minutes, that's … that's impossible! The dreams I tell you, the dreams!"

"Speaking of dreams, I really dream of going home sometime tonight. You think I 'dream' of having to deal with drunk bums like you ever day? It's about time you went and died in your own bed. For the hundredth time: We're closed!"

Irakly rubbed meaty mitts to his sallow face.

"You're a cold lady, Red."

She burned a hole in him from above.

Irakly struggled to his feet with some effort. The bartender hovered over him with the well-worn wedge of a broom in hand, impatiently sighing as the rotund man struggled to get his feet beneath him.

His knees hated him more than the barkeep, popping a bubble wrap cadence on the slow ascent.

He hobbled over to the sink with legs half asleep and splashed water on his face. Even behind the buckshot spray of black spots in the mirror rot, what was the face of a man could still be seen in those shrinking stretches of silver. He touched his cheeks again.

'Me … it's really me.'

A heavy sigh was sounded to hurry him along.

Irakly slid his two still sleeping legs across the grimy tile, eventually shimmying out of the bathroom.

The buxom publican cursed him on his way out. It wasn't personal; it wasn't a matter of persons at all.

It was the system, the feedback loop of infinite return, the same series of actions, and then results, perpetually reincarnated in different forms.

Tomorrow. There would always be another one tomorrow.

With some circulation having returned to aching feet, Irakly staggered out onto the street. He perked up with the first cold air kiss of night.

The sky was clear. The moon was sterling. Irakly scratched his head. It had all felt so real, the trip down the crapper, the walrus corpus, and saving Viktor from the sack of stink down by the sea. Then there was that talking bird waxing poetic about the concertina door of reality collapsing in on itself. None of it had made a bit of sense. But still, all of that senselessness felt so, so real.

Irakly fished a crumpled pack of cigarettes from his pocket. To his dismay, all of them were alternately snapped, split or smushed.

He threw the packet to the ground with a grunt. But with both nostrils clogged from hours sunk in the dive, he figured a bit of fresh air wouldn't hurt him. His wife had been getting on him to quit for a while anyways. Irakly had always dismissed her. "I'm a man, I smoke!"

Even he knew, deep down, that really didn't make any sense. The thing was, he'd been smoking since he was a kid. No matter how much he seemed to wheeze these days, he didn't know another way. And then the thought hit him. He was simply scared. Scared to change anything. People never change. The Soviet man was all boilerplate. And yet, he had been a walrus. At least in a dream.

Still stuck between worlds, Irakly wobbled down the street, around the side of the brutalist building to his car. On a street light above, an ashy grey bird was perched. He looked up at the curious corvid, which met his gaze with piercing eyes.

"So tell me, bird, are you gonna talk too?"

The bird remained silent.

"Let me tell you, I ran into your brother. He was talking all sorts of nonsense. And I, well I was a walrus. A dream … it I was all just a dream."

Nothing.

"I've clearly lost my mind."

Irakly sighed and finished walking to his car, which was parked directly beneath the post. He was almost embarrassed.

'What an idiot I am, talking to a bird, as if that somehow, could make any of it real.'

"But really, bird," he called out, almost defiantly, "nothing is real, is it?"

Silence. Keys jingling in pocket. Keys jingling in hand. Silence again.

Irakly sighed one more time before unlocking his car door. But just after pulling it open and leaning in to sit down, bird droppings hit him smack dab on the top of the head.

"Why you little…!"

"CAW!"

Chapter 61

"HEY, COMRADE, ARE YOU OKAY?"

A strong hand shook his shoulder.

Face pressed against the cold floor, he opened his eyes. A gnarled old face shaped by sea, sun and suffering was staring back at him — tired blue eyes shimmering with concern.

"My God, I can see!"

"Well, ya' got two eyes. I reckon you should be able to. You wanna tell me what you're doing here?"

Oleg propped himself up against the wall. Early morning light filled the hall, turning each speck of suspended dust into a twinkling star. His mind was filled with fog, droplets falling as memories into his conscious world. Then fell Viktor and the shredding machine; then fell Lana waiting for his return.

"Have, have you seen a little girl?" he asked from a waking daydream.

The mangled old man straightened up with some difficulty. His shoulders were completely off kilter. He had the look of someone bending from the side to pick up a too-heavy bag with one hand.

A nose curved like a question mark. Heavy lids drooped over asymmetrical eyes. His face had Picasso proportions. But as battered as he looked, there seemed a kindness etched in the lines made by less than kind days. This man looked like he'd been through Hell and never lost himself. Nonetheless, Oleg's question did cause a bit of confusion.

"Hmmmm," he said. "Little girl, can't say that I've seen any little girl. I came here looking for my assistant. He's late. Little devil is always getting into trouble! I guess I got into a bit of trouble myself when I was young. But I need him.

"I can't climb up those stairs anymore, you see, the body doesn't allow it. But the beacon needs to be shut off. Shades need to be drawn. Don't want to damage the optics. But if he doesn't come soon, I'm going to have to drag myself up those steps and do it myself!"

Oleg still couldn't tell if he were dreaming, or if he'd dreamed all that came before.

He put his hands to his chest, feeling the coarse texture of his coat. He remembered, the circle of death and Viktor in the center, holding a light he couldn't see. Wolves. A prayer. The Lamb of God. And then … nothing. And now he had awoken from that nothing, something, someone who could see. But what fate had befallen that little girl? Where did all those little pieces of her father go?

"I am terribly sorry to have disturbed you," Oleg said, standing up against the wall with stiff legs.

"A little girl, Lana was her name, Lana and not Svetlana, she was sure to remind me, had told me her father was at the lighthouse."

"Why, there's more than one lighthouse in town."

"I told her that too. But she talked about watching dolphins, and I figured this had to be the one. So we stopped by yesterday, but no one was here. Then, there was that terrible storm, and I, I sat down in the corner waiting for it to pass. I must have fallen asleep."

"Storm?" the lighthouse keeper said with a quizzical look. "There wasn't any storm last night … Are you sure you're okay?"

Oleg's heart sunk. Had he dreamed it all? Had there even been a little girl? Was he going senile with old age? Reality began to feel slippery again, the floor beneath him ice. He pressed his hands against the wall, less for balancing his body, and more for giving his mind a sense of solid things.

"Frankly speaking," Oleg said, "I'm really not sure at all."

The lighthouse keeper looked at him and scratched his head, not with judgment or scorn, but concern, concern and confusion. His mind seemed to be calculating what was the best course of action to resolve this uncanny encounter. It wasn't every day your average citizen took up shelter in the annex, hiding from a storm that never was. Oleg saw himself in the lighthouse keeper's spinning wheel, waiting to land on insanity, dementia, public intoxication, larceny or a good old-fashioned knock on the noggin.

But whatever conclusion he came to, it was nothing that needed saying.

"Well then, are you going to be okay getting home?"

"Getting home will be the easy part. Explaining all of this to my wife, that, that won't be so easy," Oleg said, slowly making his way toward the door.

"I imagine not," the lighthouse keeper said with a gruff laugh. "I used to have a wife once, a son too. There was a time when I resented it all. The responsibility. Someone fretting about how many bottles you drank or how many minutes you spent out. But when you reach a point in your life when no one is keeping a light on for you, no matter how dark the night, well, you learn something."

"What's that?"

"Freedom is overrated."

Oleg thought about his wife, back home, and for the first time in years, genuinely considered the worry brewing within her. As much distance as there was between them, the final thread had not been broken. There was still time.

"I really had better get going," Oleg said.

"Of course."

But just as he got to the doorway, he stopped and turned to the wizened old man.

"You know," Oleg said, looking the lighthouse keeper in the eyes, "even if no one is keeping a light on for you, at least you are keeping a light on for the rest of us."

Gruff laughter filled the hall.

"I do my best, comrade, I do my best."

— — —

Oleg walked off into the brisk morning air. His car was still parked by the fence where he'd left it. The ground had the subtle squish of early spring, damp, but otherwise no sign of the squall that had raged as visions of fire drove him to push in his own eyes.

The sound of distant seagull caw ebbed and flowed with the tide. Cirrus strands wrapped around a periwinkle bouquet of sky, punctuated by lavender whorls and orange pincushion styles.

Oleg couldn't explain it, but he felt sanguine. Whatever had transpired almost felt like some sort of bloodletting to reduce the near breaking-point pressure in him and the world. He'd been walking around with a hypertension heart since his son's death, just waiting for it to explode. The pain was still there. He couldn't imagine a world where it wouldn't be. But the scream had quieted.

In some way, the pain had been so great for so long, he'd never ever been able to mourn his loss. It's hard to meditate on the tide while constantly under the waves.

For the first time in a decade, he felt like he could breathe. Perhaps he'd had to lose his mind to find some sort of peace.

He did, after all, feel … okay. He didn't trust the beauty of the sky, nor the brisk bite in the wind — they were nearly idyllic.

Then again, the squish in his step, the pain in his knees, the slight tingle in his spine and the cracks in his fingertips reminded him that suffering remained. The burden was just, finally, bearable.

And then it all came back to him. An ancient pain in an ancient land, when he was blind and brought before that man, asking that he might see. When his sight was restored, the man was in in fact his son. And his son said 'dad, loving me doesn't mean not living anymore. Saying goodbye doesn't mean forgetting. Go, take care of Mom. Go, take care of yourself'.

Tears formed reflecting pools that extinguished the coronal flame. He embraced his son. He embraced himself. He wept until the flow formed a sea.

Eyes on the horizon, Oleg fell into the slipstream of a waking dream. The blackness released its grip, kaleidoscopic light dispersing through his prism heart.

And knowing he could see, he was no longer afraid to close his eyes. And then the lighthouse keeper's hand pulling him back over to the other side.

Did it matter if it had all been a dream? Whatever he was, he was alive.

His fingers lingered on the cold metal of his car door before pulling it open to step inside. It felt so wonderful just to feel. His key was still in the ignition. He looked out at that morning sky framed within a pane of glass, cracked but intact. He was ready to go home.

He started his car.

And out of the corner of his eye, something caught his attention. A tiny blue glove was laid out next to him. He took it in his hand and sighed.

"May you and your little bird fly, Lana, may you and your little bird fly."

Chapter 62

EVERYTHING WAS COLOR, AND COLOR was everything. A million ceiling fans in the vaulting of a mansion flitted sun-bubble iridescence across every wall. The terrace view was all marbled mountains of opalescent stone and a shimmering sea of sunset sparkle.

When Lana looked beyond the balustrade, her sense of self began to dissolve, making it hard to tell where she stopped, and the wind and light began. And in that expanse of flow and motley glow, she felt nothing but bliss.

"So what do you think?"

Lana turned around and saw Tima walking toward her in a white tunic. His blue eyes shone beneath waves of golden tresses cresting on his ears.

Reaching her, Lana immediately embraced him. And in time she realized she could feel his warmth even after she let go. And she saw the warmth of Tima, the light of her mother and the fire of her father as the exact same everything sparkling beyond the vista.

"Tima, what is this place?"

"What do you think it is?"

"I don't know, but I want to feel this way forever."

"This place is forever, and this is how it feels."

"Is this where the train took you?"

"This is where the train takes everyone."

"Even the bad ones?"

"Everything bad gets dropped off along the way. This is all that's left by the time you arrive."

"But why does it have to be so hard to get here?"

"Because all of that hard teaches you what here really is. There's just one thing. This is the waiting room. You ain't seen nothin' yet. But there is one catch."

"What is that?"

"Once you enter, you can't go back."

"Go back?"

"Back to the place where gears grind in the imagined spaces between me and you."

"One day everyone will stop talking so funny!"

Tima laughed.

"I mean back to that world! Back to Moscow! Where people get angry, people get old, winter comes and winter goes. Back to life on a line."

Lana thought about his words for a long time.

"A little bird came to me," she finally replied. "I thought he was so small. But he was bigger than everything. There is no darkness here. I will simply be a bit of light in a lot of light. And that's a good thing. But back there, being a bit of light can be everything. I think I still need to go back there for a while. I need to give back what was given to me. Oh, I will miss you so much, Tima," she said, hugging him tightly.

"I will think about you every day until we meet again."

Tima smiled.

"Something tells me when you finally take the last train home, you're going to bring a lot of folks with you. I think you will show so, so many people the way."

"I hope so, Tima."

"I know so, Lana like Lana. I know so."

Chapter 63

THE FIRST SENSATION WAS WARMTH. A soul squeezed into a body, a body wrapped in a duvet stuffed in down. Three-quarters asleep, she shimmies off the blanket too hot for seaside sunrise.

A cool breeze carries in the smells of spring. A sparrow dirt bath song is underpinned by the brood of lovelorn cicada call.

Eyes were almost afraid to open lest this regress into amniotic amnesia wash away.

She raises her arms into fifth position. Her spine arches a venetian canal. An extended hand touches a man's chest.

A sense of self forms in the fog. Last night. Hell world. A god, a bird, a rabbit in flight. Lana! Heart skips a beat. Eyes wide open.

A half spinal twist in a familiar bed. He turns to her in turn, a cherubic expression on his handsome face. Viktor! And not the man from the night before, or the many lost nights before that. She breathes in as the floorboards exhale. Lace curtains flutter in the breeze. Shadows flit across the wall. She'd forgotten the feeling of a morning so bright you never thought you were going to die. And wasn't that always the secret of time?

Death hangs heavy on the pearl clutchers and river riders afraid of the day of ingress into sea. But it all goes away, except for the great big everything that is everything and more. If the hold on life does not dam the flow until the basin is cupped in quivering hands, tearfully taking the last taste until the desert's dominion is total, one can live in the ocean forever. But one will be one no more.

Galya and Viktor had reached a point where standing water in a basement was all that was left of the flow. But in the blessed morning air as the once drought-choked river was made right as rain in rising, they now floated as lilies on a water meadow.

And there he was, all signs of violence gone, untouched by the pungently sweet smell of soulless spirits on his breath.

He was sleeping deeply, chest rising and falling to the metronome of his heart. For the first time in a long time, whether asleep or awake, he finally appeared at rest. For the first time in a long time, she saw the man she had fallen in love with.

Galya had to swallow her shout, the one wanting to ring out from every rooftop: 'He's alive, my God, he's alive!'

And then, fluttering like butterfly wings, his blue eyes opened. Before thoughts could form banks around the river of self, he found himself floating in her tidal pool eyes. He didn't even think to think how or why he'd ended up here whole after being wholly devoured by the storm.

A hand touched her face to mirror the warmth in his heart. Her hand reached out in turn. They felt each other as they had once imagined they'd feel, when feeling was just a May day dream of another life that had once been their own. A falcon from a vista of sky surveyed 42 to the power of 42 pieces of man scattered across the universe. One by one, she put them all back together.

Back down below, Isis drank in Osiris reconstituted. Factory clocks and fears lost their hold on time.

Shakti stared at Shiva in Maithuna remarried. The morning blew more kisses through the bedroom window. The part of them that would never be apart recommitted themselves to eternity.

And then tiny feet pattered across the floor. A door flung open. Lana's eyes were already dripping oceans as she took her rightful place as the princess in the Kingdom of Blankets.

A little bird sat on the windowsill, parted a veil of cloth and soared.

Chapter 64

ANDREI WAS ALL HUGS WHEN he arrived.

He didn't ask too many questions when Galya called from the post office to tell him they were staying at his dacha. The romantic in him admired the bold gesture to simply abscond without telling a soul. If there was anyone in the world who might be open to whatever words could make out of the truth, it was him. But neither Viktor nor Galya had come close to finding those words.

Masha greeted them with a dour expression, not out of malice, but simple habit. It was the wall she had built up over years between her, her customers and herself. Old habits die hard. But even she managed a meager smile that was warmer than it might have appeared at first glance.

Pasha had grown a head since their last meeting. Sasha seemed to have expanded the other way, though his mirth was irrepressible. But their diverging bodies, and attendant social bounty as the vagaries of adolescence would soon kick in, had done nothing to drive a wedge between them.

Pasha was beaming when he saw Viktor again. There was something still ill-defined which he aspired to in the big man. Little did he know, the big man likewise aspired to something in him.

Blind, uncomplicated loyalty bound in family and love. Pasha had gotten it right from the jump.

When Viktor looked into Sasha's eyes, squinting in an ear-to-ear grin, he couldn't help but think what a different life would lay before that boy if not for the brother beside him. And he knew, with the utmost gratitude and relief, that as long as Pasha could help it, Sasha, through thick and thin, would never be alone. And Pasha had taken on his burden with grace. Viktor beamed with pride thinking of the man that boy would one day become.

— — —

Fingers picked out the mourning of Dolsky's rainy September day and cast them off into warm April ardor.

Shashlik on skewers grilled on the mangal, sunset dancing behind smoke in heat-shimmer haze.

The kids ran around the yard, sticky glass trampled in zigs, zags and circles. Masha smoked a cigarette, contented for once, far away from the daily grind, where the color of life was gradually rubbed out of the cotton against the rigid washing board.

She couldn't help but feel the glow of Viktor and Galya, cuddled up like long lost lovers under the arbor, where withered woody vines clung long after life.

Andrei, with a serenade in saudade, looked over at the woman he had loved for all of those years, and still saw something of her shine. In all of his optimism, he was simply incapable of not seeing her as he had first seen her in their best days. He was incapable of not believing that somehow, someway, their best days were yet to come. Whatever may come, that belief shone a light on today. And even without knowing a way back to a better expression of her, she was made better in his eyes.

And she loved him for that, even if she never had the words to say it. Two angry drunks had taken her words long before she'd met him. But something of the feeling that glowed eternal was hidden away like a firefly in a mason jar. And at night, when she and Andrei were all alone, she sometimes opened that jar and let her little light shine.

And now, looking at Viktor and Galya, sweet, sorrowful words floating through the air, she felt content to sip her drink rather than chase the great big nothing at the bottom.

These were the days that made it all worth it. She heard the kids' laughter and smiled. This was why they called it home.

Chapter 65

VIKTOR WAS ALMOST AFRAID TO fall asleep. Lana nestled in the cove formed between them, the night was the perfect combination of warm bodies and cool breeze.

It wasn't that he was fearful of dreaming. Rather, he feared the instant he closed his eyes, he'd actually be waking up. Waking up in a world where all was lost.

He put his hand on Lana, feeling her tiny chest rise and fall. His hand gently glided to Galya's face, who instinctively wrapped feather-light fingers around his wrist. To fall asleep seemed to risk losing this, something he never thought he'd have again; something perhaps he'd never had before. Love revealing itself after the fall. Love found in the return from such a dark, loveless place. He felt guilty for every second he'd ever tried to kill. What was a moment was all moments. Kill one and you kill them all.

He meditated on their breathing. His chest synched up with the rise and fall. His heart stilled. The knot that had been building in his throat unraveled. This is real. Even if it isn't real, it is realer than anything real has ever been before.

The cool weather continued to blow kisses through the window. The sheer white curtain danced a spectral waltz on a moonlit stage. Somnus sat in the corner singing a lullaby. 'It's okay,' she sang, 'it's okay. Just drift away, just drift away.'

And in that song he felt: This is a place I can never leave … unless I choose to.

Lana jerked. Galya gave his wrist an unconscious squeeze. Viktor let the curtains drop to face what was on the other side of closed eyes. And through himself he fell.

— — —

The sea was calm. The air free of bird song. Light from the beacon had long since faded.

He stood on the starboard bow of a spectral ship, coal clouds parting to reveal stars glittering metallic in a dome of blue goldstone.

By his side was the man he had killed, standing still, watching electric platypuses leave comet trails under dark water.

"I, I thought this ride was over."

Losh laughed without taking his unseen eyes off of the water. A shooting star in play shot under water.

"This ride never ends."

Viktor looked away to survey the endless sea. He resigned himself to not asking just which ride he was on.

Firework flashes of bioluminescence formed mandalas on the water's surface. The lapping waves lulled Viktor into a place beyond time. In silence they moved across black water under star-shimmering sky.

And then seconds, days, eternities later, a white sun rose over the horizon. Land was ahead.

Along a rocky cove, cormorants were perched in wing-drying pose.

"This is our stop," Losh said.

The ship anchored at mooring. They hit the calm sea in a rowboat and skied an oar to strand.

On approach, the flock ascended into Heaven.

The pair stepped onto a beach of tiny shells crunching underfoot. There was nothing but a flat white forever laying ahead. Viktor asked Losh which way they should go.

"The only way we can go," Losh replied, "forward."

So they walked and walked, without a bite to eat or a drop to drink, until all that was blue was far behind them. Hardly a word was shared on the way.

And then, in the middle of the deserted island, a pyramid took shape in the distance. On approach, a 21-foot-high pile of skulls seemingly gathered by Vereschagin's hands took form.

Standing at the pinnacle was a crow.

Viktor slowly approached the black bird, which gazed at him with blacker eyes.

"Did they make it?"

Rather than reply, the crow kicked off the pile to take flight, sending the uppermost skull tumbling to the ground.

Losh lowered his hood and turned to Viktor. His pewter eyes shone above a soft smile. All signs of violence were gone. At least in this world, he had been made whole.

"I'm sorry," Viktor said.

"I'm sorry too. I didn't quite get a handle on being a being that time around."

"I don't know if anyone ever really does. So what do we do now?"

"Me, I'm going to stick around here for a while. Something about this heat and sun feels so good after all of that darkness. I've got some wandering and wondering to do. What about you?"

Viktor looked around the vast expanse, free from the touch of humankind. Thoughts seemed to evaporate before forming in the desert sun. And for the first time Viktor realized that despite the bright white light burning bones and swallowing clouds, not a drop of sweat trickled down his face.

"I think I'll be heading back, whatever way back is."

"Whatever way you go is forward. Pick any path. It will get you where you're going all the same."

Viktor smiled.

The two shook hands, blue sky eyes meeting grey rise on the upswell of sea one last time.

Then Losh donned his hood and walked off until he was washed away in the waves of heat.

Viktor lingered in the valediction before setting off.

He kept on walking, as a bird of prey soared up high, until all he knew of color and shape dissolved into the light. And then, just as he had forgotten himself, forgotten all things, that bird swooped down, pulling him up into the sky. And he sailed on high, enraptured, alive. He thought and thought and thought: 'I just want this to last forever.' But then the directionless spin slowed to a halt. And in the fulcrum of that motion, he slowly began to take form.

First sounds poured in. Bird song wafting on a gentle breeze. An unhurried exhalation. Something called him, squeezed behind the blackness of shut eyes. So he opened them and let the formless fuzz flow in.

Then the blurred lines slowly came to the foreground. At first the outline of an angel appeared. Then all of the depth and dimension poured in. He blinked. On the other side of an instant of blackness, there it was, life in full focus. Lying across from him was Galya. Between them was Lana. Everything, everywhere was home.

Chapter 66

WHILE ANDREI AND KIN SLEPT in, Galya, Viktor and Lana took a trip down to the sea.

They returned to that same comma-like curl of gulf where Viktor had first taught Lana how to swim. But on this brisk April morning the water was too cold to wade in, though the lapping of small waves gave way to a meditative calm.

The sky appeared cut from blue lace agate, white bands of ribbon wrapped around the morning welkin. The sun was hidden behind the blue-striped stone.

The sand shone with the solid gloss of scratched concrete. Lana ran ahead on tiny legs, chasing something even smaller.

Viktor returned to that crossroads in the stairwell, meditating on fight or flight, remembering himself in the water with Galya and Lana. For a time, it had been all he knew of Heaven. It had all come full-circle. And yet, this world was nothing like that one at all, nor the one from which the memory was borne.

A gentle breeze blew, and Viktor looked Galya in the eyes. His heart swelled in the flow.

They had not found a language to discuss what had transpired however many nights, however many lifetimes ago.

All they could do was look at each other and know, know everything that could and could not be known. Pieces of tesserae were lifted up to see the mosaic into which they had fallen. Turning back within, they saw the same tessellated motif repeating itself in endless iteration. There was something in it of love, if only because that was the only feeling in this life that had opened a door onto that boundless beyond. And yet, it was so much more than love. Or perhaps, love was so much more than they had dared to believe.

Over the course of 4,000 footprints set to be washed away when the tide came in, they tried to tell each other the story of so many lost years lived side by side. And they looked out at the waves and realized there was no point in excavating the ebb and flow. And they let go of all that was lost, and all that would be lost, finding boundless grace in the fleeting reprieve of interlocking hands.

Up ahead, Lana's laughter danced atop the waves. Golden strands of hair fluttered in the breeze. She turned back and saw Mom and Dad, hand in hand.

She returned her eyes on high, seeking out Tima in a sliver of the cloud-covered sky. And through a crack in the grey, a ray of light stretched across eternity.

And there he was; there he had always been. And there they would forever be.

In the heavens, the bells of the perebor rang from smallest to largest and then no more. And after the last wave of the peal descended into silence, the unseen ringer reversed course. And with the last stroke in unison bridging the sevenths between them, self was emptied of form.

The obscure night gave way to light; the bear finally slept; the rabbit ran; the falcon soared.

A little girl smiled as a little bird found its wings and then flight. The once-hungry wolves howled no more.

What had come to pass had passed. And what was past was present no more.

Blue eyes shimmered.

Forgotten lovers remembered.

Lana walked on the shore.

The End